THE SCOURGE

JENNIFER A. NIELSEN

Scholastic Press · New York

Library of Congress Cataloging-in-Publication Data

Names: Nielsen, Jennifer A., author.
Title: The scourge / by Jennifer A. Nielsen.
Description: First edition. | New York : Scholastic Press, 2016. | Summary: When the lethal plague known as the Scourge returns to Keldan the victims are sent to Attic Island, and Ani Mells of the River People is among them—but Ani does not feel sick, and with the help of her best friend, Weevil, she sets out to uncover the truth of what is happening, and expose the lies the people of Keldan have been told.
Identifiers: LCCN 2015048825 | ISBN 9780545682459
Subjects: LCSH: Epidemics—Juvenile fiction. | Communicable diseases—Juvenile fiction. | Conspiracies—Juvenile fiction. | Government, Resistance to—Juvenile fiction. | Best friends—Juvenile fiction. | Adventure stories. | CYAC: Epidemics—Fiction. | Diseases—Fiction. | Conspiracies—Fiction. | Government, Resistance to—Fiction. | Best friends—Fiction. | Friendship—Fiction. | Adventure and adventurers—Fiction. | GSAFD: Adventure fiction.
Classification: LCC PZ7.N5673 Sc 2016 | DDC 813.6—dc23 LC record available at http://lccn.loc.gov/2015048825

10 9 8 7 6 5 4 3 2 1   16 17 18 19 20

Printed in the U.S.A.   23
First edition, September 2016

Book design by Christopher Stengel

To all those who battle great odds and win.
In my life, you know who you are.

To each reader with a courageous heart,
Ani is for you.

THE
SCOURGE

CHAPTER
ONE

Few things were worth the risk to my life, but the juicy vinefruit was one of them. Even more so today because I was long past hungry. If I didn't eat something soon, my life was in danger anyway.

Not immediate danger. Mama had poor man's bread at home and, indeed, was expecting me back soon for supper. But I couldn't stand the thought of gnawing on those thick crusts for yet another meal. Especially not now, not after spotting a vinefruit this close, in perfect ripeness.

Getting it would be simple.

Well, not *simple* in the traditional definition of the word. But simple, meaning that I intended to get that fruit if it was the last thing I ever did.

It required a climb up a tall tree with thorns that tore at the only good dress I still owned. I also had to avoid the sticky vines that loved to tangle my arms and legs, leaving behind a terrible rash wherever they touched skin. So far, so good. All I had left was to shinny across a thin branch, avoiding the hecklebird that nested there. Hecklebirds were mean, with long narrow beaks that pecked mercilessly at whoever disturbed their eggs. Well, I didn't want the eggs; they were disgusting anyway. I only wanted the vinefruit next to the nest.

So out onto the limb I went, patiently inching my way forward, listening for the hecklebird's ugly caw. I got about halfway out and then heard a crack.

The limb snapped in half, and I clawed for anything that could keep me from falling. My hand found the vinefruit, which actually might've helped save me if it had not been so perfectly ripe. Instead, it came with me as I fell.

I went down headfirst, crashing into another hecklebird nest, which sent a particularly foul-smelling bird fluttering into the air in anger. It'd be back. Then a vine caught my leg in a tangle, leaving me suspended in midair about twelve feet above the ground.

I caught a yelp in my throat, reminding myself I was not the type of girl who panicked over ordinary near-death experiences. I was, however, a girl whose heart was racing far too quickly. I needed to breathe, to think. But mostly, I needed to not fall any farther.

Granted, this had not turned out as well as I'd hoped. But my best friend, Weevil, had said he'd meet me here today. If necessary, he could help. It wouldn't be his first time saving me from my own stupidity. This wasn't even the worst mess he'd have caught me in.

Blood rushed into my head, and everything around me turned upside down. My skirts threatened to tumble over my head as well until I bunched them between my knees. At least I still had the vinefruit. I had originally intended to bring it home whole to my parents, but it had crushed in my hand and would never last. Thick red juice ran in lines up my arm. Better that I eat the vinefruit alone than let it go to waste.

That's what I told myself to pretend I wasn't being selfish. I knew my parents were every bit as hungry as I was. But I'd have to drop the vinefruit before unwrapping my leg from the vine, and that'd ruin it.

The longer the vine stayed on my skin, the worse the rash would be, but I didn't care. My hunger now was worse than a little itching later. Despite the awkward angle, I ate the fruit, trying not to let the red juice stain my mouth the way it had stained my arm.

I finished the fruit, letting the pit fall somewhere into the underbrush, when I heard the crunch of leaves beneath me. I swung my body around, expecting my friend. Then I immediately went still.

"It figures we have to come get the grubs," one man said. "There're men younger than us who should be doing this work."

These were wardens. Their cocked woolen hats gave them away. I prayed they wouldn't look up and see me. The wardens and my people weren't exactly friends.

"Grubs" was a reference to those of us who lived up in the river country of Keldan. The term wasn't much worse than our description of the townsfolk below as "pinchworms," but they started the name-calling first, so we felt justified. Besides, pinchworms were known to eat grubs, so the nickname was accurate.

"Governor Felling is punishing us for what happened last week," his companion said. "Punishing *you* and made me come along for protection."

Protection? My people were peaceful. Well, we had been peaceful so far. If the wardens were here, then that might change. It all depended on what they wanted.

Governor Nerysa Felling wasn't a popular leader. Compared to our neighboring country, Dulan, most of Keldan was poor, and everything the governor tried only increased the burdens already weighing heavily upon the people. Whispers of overthrowing her power grew louder, and increasing numbers of challengers stepped forward each year. Everyone knew Dulan looked at our borders with hungry eyes. It was only a matter of time before they attacked.

Governor Felling was even more disliked by the River People, whom she loved to blame for the troubles in Keldan. Each year, she pushed us back, farther from the towns and higher into the hills, where food was more scarce. About a year and a half ago, she forcibly recruited several men, many of them River People, for an exploration north to find new resources. Weevil's father was taken amongst them. But the Scuttle Sea is famed for its terrible storms, something Governor Felling certainly should have known. The ship was lost. There were no survivors.

There was only one reason Governor Felling still remained in power and perhaps only one reason why Dulan had not yet brought us a war.

The Scourge.

The disease first appeared three hundred years ago. It swept through our country and cut our population by a third. Fear of its spread shattered our economy, isolated us from neighboring countries, and created outcasts of my people, who were accused of originating the disease. The scars it caused within Keldan were still apparent today.

After four long years, the terrible sickness went away, and the people of Keldan were free to breathe again in peace. The worst tragedy in our history was over.

Or so we thought.

Last year, the Scourge returned.

This time, it started in the prisons on Attic Island, cleaning them out entirely before it moved into the general population. It was a disease without mercy. Highly contagious, but with no clear sign of how it was transmitted. Symptoms were nearly impossible to detect until it was too late, and there was no treatment. The Scourge always ended in death. Always.

The one good thing Governor Felling had done was hire physicians who determined that if the disease was caught in its earliest stages, even before symptoms appeared, then it was less contagious. They used the old records to develop an early test to identify and isolate Scourge victims, which seemed to keep the disease from spreading as quickly. But for those who did test positive, Attic Island was transformed into a Scourge Colony, where victims were sent to live out the rest of their short lives. It was the governor's way of hoping to contain the disease. Fear of the disease spreading over its own borders had also kept Dulan at bay. For as long as the sickness reigned, Dulan would not cross Attic Island's waters.

The disease wasn't Governor Felling's fault, obviously. Inheriting that problem was just her bad luck. But she was the River People's bad luck. Proof of that was in the wardens' presence below me.

I craned my head enough to see the two men. The first warden, the stockier one, had requested a break to remove a rock from his boot and was taking his time about it. "Governor Felling ordered us to take five grubs for testing." The shaking of his voice betrayed his worry about being here. "If she only sent two of us to get them, how does she think that'll go?"

Five of us, to test for the Scourge? Since we were isolated from the towns, so far the Scourge had not touched my people. We never mixed with the pinchworms except on the rare occasions when we needed supplies, and in those cases, we never went to towns where the Scourge had appeared.

So why was the governor sending wardens to test us for the Scourge?

"It may sound like a hefty punishment, but it's deserved," the second warden said. "Grubs always cause the worst uprisings."

What was he talking about? There was no uprising. The last trouble we'd caused happened when those men were taken for the exploration, and even that was minor. There'd been nothing close to an uprising since then.

A caw sounded off to my right. An angry, nasty caw that only could have come from the hecklebird. The hateful thing was back, but why now?

No doubt it smelled the vinefruit juice that had dried on my arm. It knew I'd disturbed its nest. It wanted revenge and would get it now, better than the bird could've ever expected.

That bird would expose me to the wardens below.

CHAPTER
TWO

The wardens looked in the direction of the bird's warning cry. They instinctively ducked because such a foul sound would make even the stupidest people—such as the wardens, for example—crouch to protect themselves.

I used the moment to pluck a stick off a nearby branch, ready to take a swing at the bird. All I could hope was that the wardens would crawl away, like any pinchworm would, and then I could fend the thing off until I got free. It had been foolish of me to hang here while eating the fruit. Even if I got down now and even if I escaped the attention of the wardens, the rash that would soon appear on my leg from the vine would cause me a fair amount of itching.

Except the stocky warden heard the stick crack and looked up. He called to his companion and then shouted up at me, "You, girl, my name is Warden Brogg, in the service of Governor Nerysa Felling. I order you to come down."

"If you want me, come get me!" I shouted back. I could take a swing at the warden just the same as the hecklebird. They were equally ugly.

"I might," Brogg replied.

No, he wouldn't. Even the lowest branch wouldn't hold his weight, and I doubted he could climb to the top of an anthill without pausing to rest. Climbing required a special set of muscles that most pinchworms didn't have.

However, they did have axes, and the second warden, a tall man with legs too long for his body, pulled out his ax now, which he began using to chop at the tree.

"Stop that!" I yelled. "When this tree falls, it'll land on you. I don't care about that, but it'll crush me too."

"Then come down!" Brogg called.

"Can't you see I'm stuck?"

Even the hecklebird knew that. He dove directly at me, sharp beak open. I swung for it and missed, but it forced the bird out of my way. It came around again and pecked at my arm, leaving a small nick there. I swung a second time, and a few feathers fell before it flew away. I hoped I had injured it as much as it had just hurt me. Maybe the vinefruit hadn't been worth it.

The wardens below seemed to have traced the vine holding my leg to its root in the ground. Now they were chopping at it. I knew they had the right vine, because it shook every time the ax hit.

"Leave me alone!" I raised up my body and took hold of the vine, which would now leave a rash on my palms. Then I began working my leg free. Otherwise, I'd fall on my head, which from this height would leave me with the kind of headache that made people permanently stare off into empty space.

They kept chopping, cutting through the vine, which dropped me almost a third of the way to the ground before it tangled on something else. I cursed at the wardens, then pulled my leg free. At least I was right side up when the vine finally gave way and I fell the rest of the way to the ground.

I landed hardest on my right ankle, but I didn't think it was broken. It stung, though, preventing me from running away. One warden grabbed me, the taller man, who, it turned out, had an iron grip.

He pulled me to my feet and then said, "What's your name, girl?"

"What's yours?"

"Warden Gossel, in the service of Governor Ner—"

"Yeah, I already heard the rest." I grunted. "My name is Ani Mells. I've done nothing wrong, and I'm an honest citizen of Keldan. Let me go."

He sent a mocking look to his companion and held out one of my arms, the one with the vinefruit stain on it. "Look at this, Brogg—reddened skin. That's one symptom of the Scourge."

"It's fruit juice, you fool," I said, struggling against him. "The pit is somewhere beneath your feet, and the approximate size of your brain, I'd guess. Let me go and I'll find it."

"And look at that open wound on her other arm," Gossel said. "That's probably how she got the disease in the first place."

With my good foot, I tried to kick at Gossel, but only collapsed on my sore ankle. "The bird just did that to me," I said. "You saw it."

Brogg knelt in front of me. He ran a finger along my lower leg where the vine had already irritated the skin. "Rash here, and the skin is warm. Fever."

"I don't have the Scourge," I said. "I'm not sick."

When I squirmed, Gossel tightened his grip on me and said, "We're taking you in to be tested, but just from looking at you, it's obvious how that test will come out."

"You can't take me away!" I wiggled free, but he got me again. "Don't do this!"

"Get her quieted down," Gossel ordered. Then my arms were pulled behind me, and Gossel began tying them with rope while Brogg stuffed a rag into my mouth and tied it in place with another rag. I fought them, but at that point, it wasn't hard for them to carry me out of the clearing to where I saw an isolation wagon parked.

My panic rose. They really were taking me, without reason, without explanation, without even telling my parents. As far as they'd ever know, I'd have just disappeared.

The back of the wagon was already open, and they tossed me inside. Then Brogg hefted himself in to tie me to one wood-paneled wall. I struggled against it, but with every passing moment, their hold on me was increasing.

I had done nothing wrong, and nothing was wrong with me. They couldn't possibly believe that the signs they were seeing on my body were symptoms of the Scourge. It was only because of the vinefruit—surely they knew that! This couldn't be happening.

"Untie her," a voice ordered.

I sat up while Brogg turned around and slowly raised his hands. Beneath my gag, a smile widened on my face. It was my best friend in the world, holding a hunting knife. Late to meet me, as always, but at least he was here now. Weevil had come to help.

Admittedly, Weevil's parents had given him a name that hardly helped with the fact that my people were known as grubs. But Weevil didn't seem to mind, so neither did I. He was strong, and friendlier than he looked at the present moment, and most important, he would never let the wardens take me away.

"This poor girl has got the Scourge." Brogg's sympathy was as fake as a painted coin. "We're taking her to be tested. If it turns out she's healthy, she comes home."

"She's plenty healthy," Weevil said. "The Scourge hasn't come to the river country."

"What if it has?" Brogg was slowly oozing his way out of the wagon. "It'd wipe out you grubs within a month. Only way you can be safe is if your people let us test you."

"We'll take care of ourselves," Weevil said. "And we'll take care of Ani. Let her go or I will throw this knife. I never miss."

Privately, I rolled my eyes. Weevil often missed. Hopefully, Brogg wouldn't test his aim, especially if he was standing anywhere near me.

Weevil was so intent on Brogg that he failed to notice the other warden who was sneaking up behind him. I squealed and gestured with my head for him to look back. Weevil turned, and Brogg dove from the cart and pounced on him. Weevil rose up for the fight, but Gossel took the butt of his ax and crashed it down on his head.

I screamed, muted by my gag. Weevil had stopped moving, but they grabbed his body and threw him into the back of the wagon with me. Blood seeped from a wound on the side of his head. I tried not to panic. Head wounds bled a lot; that didn't always mean they were serious.

Sometimes they were very serious, though. Weevil wasn't moving.

"These are only children," Brogg said. "If this is how the grubs are going to be, we'll need more than just you and me."

Gossel nodded. "Let's take these two. If the governor wants five, she can come get the rest herself."

And the door slammed shut behind us, leaving us in almost total darkness. Minutes later, the wagon began driving away, taking us from our home.

CHAPTER
THREE

A knife was in my boot. I had expected it to fall out while I was hanging upside down in the tree, but by the angels' mercy, it had somehow stayed in place.

I kicked that boot off now and then contorted my body in any way necessary to slide the knife closer to my hands, which were tied near the floor of the wagon. It wasn't easy, and the lack of grace I showed in managing that trick would've made my mother's hair curl. She had given up on me acting like a respectable young lady years ago.

Once the knife was in my hands, I twisted it around to saw at the ropes. In the process, I jabbed myself more than I would've liked, but when the last piece of rope snapped apart, I immediately forgot about the sting from the cuts. I pulled the gag off my mouth, then used the fabric to press at the wound on the side of Weevil's head.

Weevil had too much hair—that was the problem with stopping the bleeding. He only got around to cutting his hair when I teased him, although, secretly, I liked it longer. His was lighter in color than most of our people's and stubbornly straight, making it stick out sideways after a haircut. But I liked that too. It fit his mischievous grin and the sparkle that always danced in his brown eyes.

Except for now. Nothing about him was dancing right now, and that worried me.

"Weevil?" I whispered. "Weevil, wake up."

He stirred, thankfully, but his eyes weren't open, and soon he went quiet again.

A couple of years ago, the farmer who lived nearest to my family was kicked in the head by his mule while plowing his fields. He'd walked into his home with a wound just like Weevil's. The man's wife put him to bed and even brought a pinchworm physician up to see him, which we only did at the most serious times. The farmer woke up a week later, perfectly well. Or almost. He remembered his kids, his mule, even remembered where he'd left off plowing before he was kicked. The only thing he couldn't remember was his wife. People said he was fine, that the forgetting was his way of getting back at his wife for all the times she'd yelled at him over the years. I had laughed at that, thinking maybe it was just one big joke.

But I wasn't laughing anymore. Maybe what happened to our neighbor was real, and a hard blow to the head really could change your memories of people. What if Weevil didn't remember me?

He had to. He had to remember me because, right now, he was the only person I had left in the world. I was scared, accused of having a disease that might get me sent to a place filled with actual sick people who would end up getting me actually sick. Sick enough to die. And now, whether he still had a memory or not, Weevil was headed there too.

I shook his shoulder, gently, but hard enough to wake him up. "Weevil? Are you all right?"

"No," he mumbled. "I can't remember . . ."

His voice faded, and tears came to my eyes. So this truly was the same condition our neighbor had. How damaged would Weevil's memories be? Would he remember me at least?

"You can't remember what?" I asked. "Do you remember the rivers? We were supposed to dive for fish this afternoon, do you remember that? How we got here in this wagon? Weevil . . . do you remember me?"

Weevil rolled to his side, facing me. Blood had pooled beneath one of his cheeks, and a bump had formed on the top of his forehead. He opened one eye first, as if testing to be sure whether he wanted to wake up, then the second eye.

"I can't remember why I ever decided to be friends with you," he mumbled.

I almost punched his arm, but thought better of it and decided to save it for later. I did help him get to a sitting position, which was the least he deserved for trying to save me.

He leaned against the wall of the wagon and asked, "How long was I out?"

"Not long, maybe only fifteen minutes. You had me worried."

"Good. It shows you care."

I sat across from him and picked up my knife again, clutching it in my grip. "We're in a lot of trouble."

"You're always in some sort of trouble, Ani. Why should this be any different?"

"Look where we are!"

"I'm looking at you, and even without much light in here, I can see you're a complete mess. Luckily for you, I've seen worse."

For that comment, he received one of my special glares. "I only look this way because I ate a vinefruit, and I fell out of a tree, and I got in a fight with the wardens."

Weevil smiled. "So it's been a slower morning than usual for you." Then his grin faded. "Tell me honestly, is there any chance you might have the Scourge? Have you been exposed to it?"

"No!" Perhaps I said it too forcefully, or too confidently. We both knew nobody in the country was entirely safe. Then I added, "I don't have the Scourge, and neither do you. But I overheard the wardens. The governor wants to start testing the River People for the disease."

Weevil checked the fabric I'd given him to see if his head was still bleeding. With such little light in this isolation wagon, it'd be hard for him to know for sure. He needed to keep the fabric in place.

After he'd checked, he said, "The Scourge is a terrible disease. You know as well as I do what it's done to other areas of the country once it set in. If the governor wants to test the River People, then it means she's trying to protect us the same as everyone else."

"When has Governor Felling ever cared about River People? We're only useful when it's time to collect either taxes or explorers." Weevil flinched at that last part, and I instantly regretted the reference to his father. "I know how awful the Scourge is, but protecting the River People is not the reason we're here."

"Well, then she wants to be sure that we don't spread the Scourge to any of the pinchworms. Listen, Ani, I don't want someone making my family sick or yours. These are hard times, and hard decisions must be made."

I'd made plenty of those hard decisions already, and so far had avoided any serious consequences. Until now.

"We're not sick," I said, even less sure of myself than before.

"Then she'll test us and find out the only thing wrong with you is that you're foolish enough to challenge a hecklebird for a vinefruit. And the only thing wrong with me is that I decided to be your friend. We'll be home by nightfall."

I knew how important it was for him to get back home. When they came to take his father for the exploration north, Weevil offered himself up instead, claiming that his father was far more valuable to the family. But Weevil was rejected; he was a finger width too short. That same summer, he grew three finger widths in height—I think it was a matter of pride for him. Unfortunately, his father never returned.

Weevil had five younger siblings, all of them with far less interesting names. Once his father left, Weevil became responsible for providing for them. Although he did the best he could, it was never enough. That bothered him, more than he'd ever admit, even to me. Or maybe, especially to me.

I was my parents' only child and, as such, the center of their world. When it was time for that exploration, the wardens never came for my father, possibly because they knew the north would be entirely explored, pillaged, and settled before they ever got his cooperation. Unfortunately for my sweet mother, I was far more like my father.

I had her long dark hair, lean frame, and round eyes, but that was where our similarities ended. The fire constantly beneath my skin belonged entirely to my father. Whenever trouble happened with the River People, everyone's first question seemed to be, "Where's Ani?"

We had ridden for some time in silence. The sun gradually shifted overhead, letting in less light from this angle. Because of that, I couldn't tell if Weevil had fallen asleep again. Finally, he said, "What is that sound you're making?"

"When I fell from the tree, my leg got tangled in the vines. It's starting to itch."

"Don't scratch it."

"Why not?"

"Because scratching is the second-worst sound in the world."

"Live with it, or I'll show you the worst."

He smiled, then came over to sit beside me. He took my hands and gripped them in his. "Now you can't scratch."

I pulled away and scooted to another part of the wagon. "You should stay back from me."

"You'll give yourself scars." He reached for me, and when I sat farther back, his brows pressed together. "What's wrong with you?"

"I just think you should stay back."

He was silent a moment. "Are the wardens right? Tell me again, could you have the Scourge?"

"Of course not."

He didn't believe me this time. The change in his expression was subtle, but even with such little light, I saw the tilt of his brow. The problem was that he knew me too well, enough to sense when to doubt my words.

Still watching me, he said, "It probably takes more to get the Scourge than just sitting beside a victim."

"How sure of that are you?" I asked. Neither of us really knew the answer.

Finally, he leaned his head against the wagon. "I'll stay away, then . . . unless you scratch."

I lowered my hands and clasped them together, forcing myself not to think about the pestering itch. "How's your head?" I asked.

"Every time this wagon drives into a pothole, I feel like that warden is hitting me with his ax again."

"If I had some thrushweed, that would help." The River People knew every plant and its uses. Pinchworms thought we were less educated than them because we didn't have their expensive medicines or tests like the governor would probably try to administer on us. I figured we were just differently educated. They knew the world that came out of books, but we knew the world that went into them. I'd have loved to see a hungry pinchworm challenge a water cobra for its fish. Mostly because no River Person I knew would ever try such a foolish thing. In river country, we all learned early to respect things that could swallow us whole.

"I hear you scratching again," Weevil said.

"The itch is so bad it stings," I said, but I stopped.

He raised his head and stared at me. "What will the governor think if you show up with a rash all over your leg? Rashes are a sign of sickness."

"They're also a sign of someone whose leg was caught in a sticky vine."

"Pinchworms don't know about sticky vines. All the wardens know is you refused an order to come down and talk to them."

"Well, in the first place, I couldn't obey his order because I was stuck in the tree. And in the second place—"

"In the second place, you wouldn't have obeyed it because you never do as you're told," Weevil finished for me. "Listen, the wardens are angry, and you probably will get some sort of punishment for refusing to obey them. Maybe it'll be a fine or work hours in the towns. But they won't send you to the Colony because neither of us is sick. We'll be home soon."

"I hope you're right," I said, though maybe he was wrong. There were things he didn't know, couldn't know.

"I hope I am too," he said. This time, the doubt in his voice was unmistakable. That worried me more than anything else. Even Weevil wasn't sure he was right this time.

CHAPTER
FOUR

Both Weevil and I were asleep when the wagon stopped sometime later. It was completely dark outside now, meaning we had traveled much farther than I had expected. Scourge testing was available in Windywood, the nearest town to my home, but that was only an hour away by wagon. We were nowhere near Windywood anymore. Nowhere near home.

One of the wardens seemed to be tending to the horses while the other had gone off, probably to notify a doctor of our arrival.

"Be ready," I said to Weevil, drawing the knife from my boot.

But Weevil shook his head. "This isn't the time to fight, Ani. Not yet."

So I replaced the knife, but made sure it was in the boot with my uninjured ankle. Then I stood in the wagon, partially to test my other ankle—which hurt and had started to swell—and partially so Weevil would not offer to help me up. I was pretty sure he understood that too, because although he stared at me with concern, once he saw that I could walk, he didn't offer any help.

Warden Brogg opened the door and had his ax raised against us, which made me smile. Was he expecting us to charge at him, yelling some crazy battle cry? Then the knife shifted in my boot, and I remembered that until Weevil had advised otherwise, charging at him had been my exact plan. The crazy battle cry was optional.

Brogg's eyes shifted to the ropes that had been on me before. "You were supposed to keep those on."

I smirked at him. "You were supposed to tie them with real knots."

Weevil nudged me with his arm, a warning not to start any arguments now. But then he smiled too, as if he wished he had thought to say it first.

"If you hadn't fought us, we'd never have tied you in the first place," Brogg said. "For your own sakes, take my advice and cooperate."

My eyes narrowed. "If I had obeyed your orders before, would I still be here right now?" When he failed to answer, I nodded. "Just as I thought. Cooperating would only make your life easier, not ours."

"We are cooperating." Weevil's voice was low, and he spoke slowly. "We'll come out together, without fighting. In exchange for that, wherever we're going next, you must keep us together."

He took my hand. I started to pull away, but he mouthed the word "together" and redoubled his grip.

I nodded back at him, and when Brogg gave us permission, we jumped out of the wagon. My swollen ankle landed badly and Weevil started to help me straighten up, but I pulled my hand away and balanced myself.

"That's better." Brogg cocked his head forward. "Now walk."

It hurt to walk evenly, but I forced myself to do it. I couldn't stand the thought of Weevil reaching out to help me again. I felt his eyes on me, and if I looked, I'd have seen the worry in them. He knew I was hurting, but I gritted my teeth and refused to look back at him.

Or maybe his worry wasn't about my ankle. Maybe his thoughts were the same as mine. *What if I do have the Scourge? What if they're right?* Because if I was being honest with myself, I knew it wasn't impossible.

I hated having to be honest with myself.

We had driven into a large courtyard with an even larger building straight ahead. It was square and plain with an enormous green cross flag of Keldan hanging from the roof. A government building, then. The closest one of this size I knew of was in Marisbane, very far from my home.

Considering that we were near government offices, the building didn't seem particularly well guarded. This struck me as odd. Surely, others suspected of having the Scourge had been dragged here in the last year. Didn't they resist the test? Maybe not. Maybe pinchworms always did as they were told, like fence-trained sheep. Well, let them bring in a few River People, and they'd think differently about the need for more guards. If they had brought five of us in, as the governor had ordered, we'd be in a full battle by now.

"We want to speak to whoever's in charge," Weevil said. "Is that you, or the man who played batball with my head?"

"Warden Gossel is my superior," Brogg said, "but until you're tested for the Scourge, no one can set you free." He led us to his left toward a series of much smaller, empty-seeming buildings, including a narrow one that was undoubtedly meant for us. It was a lone prison cell, with a thick log roof and metal bars along one wall.

I dug in my feet and shook my head. "This is a place for criminals."

Either Brogg didn't hear me, or he didn't care. He unlocked the door and held it open for us. "You'll stay here until morning, when the physician will test you. There's only one blanket. I suppose you two can fight over who gets it."

"We don't fight," Weevil said.

We didn't used to, I thought. But we will. That seemed inevitable now.

I went into the cell first. It had a small bed, ideally sized for anyone who was the approximate height of the average rabbit. A chamber pot was in the corner along with a bucket of water that probably hadn't been changed in several days. I wouldn't touch either of those. This cell was clearly designed for only one person. For that reason, I was grateful to Weevil for making the deal he had with the warden. We'd have been split up otherwise, and I couldn't bear the thought of finishing this night without him.

Once we were locked in, the warden stood on the opposite side of the bars and stared at me. I stared back, determined not to be the first to look away.

"What were you really doing up in that tree?" he asked. "Spying on us?"

"If I were spying on you, I wouldn't have been caught that easily. As I told you before, I was eating a vinefruit. I would've shared some if you'd asked." Or dropped it on his head.

"If you weren't spying, why didn't you announce your presence?"

"Why didn't you announce yours? You were on our lands, not the other way around." I shrugged. "The warden who dragged Weevil's father off to die at sea looked a lot like you. For all we know, it was you."

"That wasn't me." Brogg scuffed his boot on the ground. "You should've announced yourself," he mumbled. "I'll come back for you in the morning."

As soon as he had gone, I sat on the bed to take the weight off my ankle.

Weevil immediately turned to me. "Whatever secret you've been keeping from me, it's time to say it. Do you have the Scourge?"

I ignored the fierce itch on my leg so he wouldn't bother me about that too. "I told you already, I don't have a single symptom!"

"That's not what I asked. You're hiding something, Ani, and obviously worried about how this Scourge test will come out."

"No, I'm not."

Yes, I was, and he knew it.

"Who exposed you to it? If any of the River People are sick, you can't keep that a secret, for everyone's sake. Once the symptoms appear, you're contagious. As soon as we get back, we have to warn the others."

"It's none of them!"

"Then who?"

I turned away and began massaging my foot. To do a proper job, I should've removed the boot first, but I didn't dare. I worried that with the swelling, I'd never get the boot back on.

"Let me check it." Weevil's tone turned sympathetic now.

"It isn't that bad," I said. "You saw that I can walk on it."

"You were limping."

"I can walk."

"Fine. Now tell me again, do you have the Scourge?"

I sighed, wishing these questions would end. Or better yet, that there was no need to ask them. "If I thought I did, do you really think I'd expose my family, or any of the River People? Or you? I'm not sick, Weevil. I only want to go home."

He hesitated a moment and looked around, making sure we were alone. "Then that's what we'll do." Weevil reached into his own boot and pulled out a long quilting needle. "For this, I need your knife."

CHAPTER
FIVE

Most people considered Weevil's and my friendship as unlikely as a deer voluntarily spending time with a wild boar. He and I had fixed reputations—everyone knew which of us was the deer and which was the boar.

Weevil was often asked how we could be friends, as if he was only nice to me out of the goodness of his heart, or maybe because my mother paid him on the side. Nobody ever asked why I was friends with Weevil. I was considered to be on the receiving end of his charity.

However, they didn't know Weevil like I did. He was every bit as stubborn as me, if not worse. He loved the jokes we played on people, though he was more clever about getting away with them. He had plenty of other flaws that only I knew about, such as his pride, which he clung to like it was life itself. And . . . well, he probably had even more faults that I could think of if given enough time. But above all, Weevil had a talent that neither of his parents knew about. Nobody knew, because if anyone suspected him of anything, the blame was laid at my feet instead and I never disputed it.

Weevil could pick a lock faster than a scalded cat runs.

He carried two long quilting needles everywhere with him, just for those times when he encountered a lock that needed opening. He never stole from anyone—Weevil was too good a person for that. But he used to borrow blankets or firewood from the pinchworms in town, just over the winter, then return whatever was left in the springtime. Of course, he didn't borrow things anymore, not since the Scourge. But the lack of practice hadn't dulled his skills with those needles. He would've already used them in the isolation wagon except that lock was on the outside of the doors.

This cell had a fat lock on the door, though, one just begging for him to open.

"It's a long way back home," I said to Weevil. "As soon as they notice we're gone, they'll start searching for us."

"Every town has a river," Weevil said. "We'll find it and move upstream. Once we get home, there are plenty of places to disappear until the wardens forget about us."

He jammed the tip of my knife into the lock to hold the tumblers steady while he inserted the needle for the more delicate work inside. I was never sure how he did it. Every time he tried to teach me, I ended up breaking the needle.

Sure enough, only seconds later, the lock snapped apart, and he handed my knife back, then slowly pushed our cell door open. The metal hinges creaked louder than I would've liked, but we paused for several tense seconds and nobody came.

We tiptoed out of the cell and back into the wide court-yard, which was surrounded with a few useless lamps that barely gave any light. Our wagon was still parked where we'd last seen it, though the horses were already unhitched and had been moved elsewhere. I motioned to Weevil that we should look for their stables. I was good on a horse. I could get us away. But Weevil shook his head, which probably was the right decision. A locked-up cell wasn't worth guarding. Nobody wanted to be within miles of anyone suspected of having the Scourge. But horses in Keldan were extremely valuable.

Beyond the courtyard were a few small shops on the road, all closed for the night. Past the road was a wooded area, one that seemed dense enough to give us shelter until we found a river.

We had only just gotten to the worn dirt road when our absence was discovered. An alarm bell sounded, and then men began shouting.

"Run!" Weevil and I yelled to each other.

We darted across the road toward the field, but quickly found ourselves in thick underbrush that tangled at our legs, slowing our escape. Frightened as I was in this unfamiliar darkness, I reminded myself to focus and get through this. I was often out at night and had run through dense under-brush before, though never with an injured ankle, or so much at stake if I were caught. I heard horses galloping toward us—how had the wardens collected that quickly? I turned back, checking whether I could see them, but the brush was already too thick to see much of anything.

"This way!" Weevil hissed, but when I turned to find him, his voice became lost in the darkness. I followed as best I could in the way I thought he'd gone, but didn't dare call out to him and give away our position. Beyond that, my ankle was throbbing and slowing my run. Where was he? Did he realize we had become separated? If so, was he panicked too?

Finally, I pushed through the underbrush and came out on another road. I had no idea where I was now, but at least I'd escaped the wardens. This road was lined with rows of houses, set back behind long yards that were lit with bright lanterns the government courtyard should have had. These weren't like the log shacks where my people lived, with gaps between the logs wide enough for mice to crawl through, or to leak in winter rains.

No, these homes were made of stone and cut lumber, put together for style and beauty rather than our inexpensive, practical methods. I checked behind me again for any sound of the approaching wardens. Hearing nothing, I stopped for a moment and stared at the homes, wondering what it must be like to live in such a fine place. Were they just as beautiful on the inside?

"Help me!" a voice called from up the road.

I headed that way before I could think better of it, before I realized it wasn't Weevil calling for me, or anyone who sounded even remotely like him. This was a girl's voice, with the accent of the pinchworms. With their fine breeding and manners, why was one of their daughters out so late?

"Help!" the girl called again.

The voice came from below a bridge. This was surely the same river where Weevil was headed. If I went upstream, maybe I could find him again.

I slid down the slope, expecting to see someone in danger. Instead, I was greeted by the funniest of sights, illuminated by the moonlight. A girl with auburn hair and a dress made of silk, lace, and snobbery was standing in a small wooden boat under the bridge. Not only was she standing, but she was *holding* the bottom of the bridge with both hands, trying not to let the boat drift any farther downstream. She was probably two or three years older than me, but clearly didn't have the good sense of a River Person half my age.

"Thank you," she said as she saw my approach. "You have no idea how long—"

I couldn't help but laugh. "What are you doing?" I asked.

"Oh!" Her tone was immediately condescending. "What is a grub doing in Marisbane?"

"I can go away if you'd like." In fact, I'd be happy to do that. The only thing keeping me here was the likelihood of finding Weevil near this river.

"No! You're just the person to help me. Grubs are used to getting dirty, aren't you?"

"Not really," I answered. Though of course we were, almost as a rule. If there was another way to live, I didn't know it.

"Can you help me get this boat to shore? I missed the ramp, and the next exit is quite a ways down."

My eyes narrowed. "What are you doing out here so late?"

"None of your business. Can you help me?"

The Scourge hadn't come to the river country, but it was in the towns and probably was an infestation here. Whether I endangered her, or she endangered me, I started back up the shore. "I'm sorry, I can't."

"Please! I can't hold on much longer, and if I let go, I'll be in so much trouble!"

I sighed. "Okay, but slide back in the boat as far as you can." As far away from me as possible. Then I hiked my skirt and waded in the water toward her boat. I knew full well that the wardens were still somewhere on the road searching for me, but I had just gotten an idea. It involved this girl's boat after she got out of it. River country was upstream, but the wardens knew that, so they would search that way as well. Once I found Weevil, he and I could get away very quickly if we went downstream for a few miles, then went home another way tomorrow.

I said to the girl, "For your future escapes or whatever pretend reason you're out here, you don't need a ramp to dock your boat. Steer it into any thick patch of weeds, and it's just a short splash of water and you're out."

"Look at my dress," the girl said, holding out her skirts. "Silk ribbons are worth a fortune! Tomorrow morning, my father would surely notice even a short splash of water."

I nearly splashed her, just for saying that. But instead, I asked, "Why *did* you sneak out?" This girl was more interesting than I had expected. Not a typical pinchworm.

"My family has money and power you can't even dream about," she said. "I don't need to sneak."

No, she was a typical pinchworm after all. And a liar too. Perhaps more than anyone, I had experience in sneaking. By now, I could recognize it anywhere.

I steadied the girl's boat and then dragged it toward the shore, making myself plenty wet in the process. That wasn't all bad, though. The water cooled the itch on my leg and washed the vinefruit juice from my arm.

"Can you help me to shore?" the girl asked. "I mean, without getting me wet?"

"Sorry," I said. "You're on your own for that." Aside from the fact that I had been accused of having the Scourge, if I was halfway in the water and surviving, then this girl could surely dip a toe in it too.

"Stop right there!" a voice shouted, followed by the sharp cock of a pistol's hammer. Warden Brogg. My heart sank. If I had put aside my pride and just helped this girl get out, I'd have her boat by now.

The girl immediately reached out and slapped me hard

across my cheek. "How dare you steal this boat?" she said. "Filthy grub!"

Stealing? Well, sure, I had planned to steal it, but not while she was still inside. I was so stunned by her accusation that I didn't know how to react. I even opened my mouth to speak, but nothing came out.

Brogg edged down the shore and wrestled me out of the water. "So, Ani, you're a thief too?" he snarled. "I should've expected this from a grub."

"I didn't—" I started to say, then let it go. Trying to fight this would be like taking a swing at a snake. I might hit its mouth, but it'd swallow my arm. There was no way to win.

"How many more crimes will you commit today?" he asked.

Hot tears stung my eyes, but I pushed them away. The answer was, as many crimes as it took to get away from this place. I just wanted to go home.

CHAPTER
SIX

Brogg held me while Warden Gossel came down to help the girl out of the boat.

"My name is Della Willoughby," she said, and then pointed. "My home is right there. This grub—Ani?—dragged my family's boat over here to the water. I heard it and came outside to stop her. She forced me into the boat and who knows what she'd have done once we got away!"

Gossel turned to me. "Is this true?"

I was too furious to speak. Of course I could deny the charges, but what would be the point? There was no way these wardens would take my word over hers, especially since I had just escaped from their cell. Obviously I had been trying to escape, making Della's story more plausible than mine.

"Where's your friend?" Gossel asked. "The boy who was with you?"

I kept my eyes straight forward, refusing to look either up or down the river. Weevil would be somewhere nearby—

I knew it. But the last time he revealed himself, he ended up with a bump on his head and a long ride in an isolation wagon. I prayed he would not reveal himself now, not even for me. Especially not for me.

"We'll find him," Brogg said. "We always find the escapees."

"So a lot of people escape that cell?" I asked. "Does the governor know how bad you are at your job?"

Ignoring my questions, he pulled me with him up the steep riverbank, and then Gossel took Della's arm as well, to help her along. Once we reached the road, Brogg led me toward his horse, but Gossel said, "She walks."

"Her ankle is injured," Brogg said. "She's limping."

"If she could limp away from the cell, she can limp back to it."

Brogg frowned at me, as if the injured ankle was somehow my fault. Then he tied my hands in front of me and climbed onto his horse, tying the other end of the rope to the back of his saddle. I barely looked at him. He could ride as fast as he wanted. I'd keep up with the worst he could do. Or at least, I hoped I could. My ankle was throbbing worse than ever.

"This other girl should ride," Gossel said.

It took Della a moment before she realized they were talking about her. Then she stepped back. "No, my home is over there. I can walk."

"The grub is suspected of having the Scourge," Gossel said. "You came in contact with her, so I'm afraid we'll have to test you too."

"What?" Della turned to me with a look that could have started fire. "You have the Scourge?"

"I'm half-dead already," I said, and coughed, just to make it sound worse. "You probably caught it when you accused me of stealing your boat." If she could lie about me, then I'd feel no guilt for lying to her.

"Knowing that, you came down to the river?" she yelled. "How dare you?"

"Maybe you shouldn't have slapped me," I said. "I told you to stay back."

But I was the one who should've stayed back. I should have ignored her and any foolish ideas about taking her boat. I didn't have the Scourge—I was almost sure of that— but I still should've walked on. Obviously.

"We'll notify your father of your whereabouts," Gossel told Della. "I'm sure we'll have you back home first thing in the morning."

Two offers that had not been extended to me. My parents were probably still awake, desperate for any news about me. My father would've gone to Weevil's home, hoping to find me there. Weevil's family wouldn't know what had happened to him either. Then my father would check the road to the towns, or the towns themselves. He'd expose himself to the Scourge that way.

I wasn't sure how far away we were from river country, or how late at night it was, but a full day of wagon travel could put us fifteen or sixteen miles away, maybe more. Once he got safely out of this town, if he found a good road, Weevil could be home by tomorrow night. I hoped our families could last that long without going out of their minds with worry.

I didn't look for Weevil as I was led back to the courtyard. If I had seen him, I might've reacted and given him away. So instead of looking, I kept focused on moving forward. My limp was quickly getting worse, and each step begged me to stop. Nor did it help that my boots were wet now, making my feet heavier than before. However, every time I tried to slow down, the rope yanked me forward. My only choice was to keep going or be dragged back to the courtyard.

Luckily, we weren't that far away. The first thing I did once I was back inside the cell was to collapse onto the bed and give my foot a rest. It had swollen so much that it pressed on the leather of the boot. I probably wouldn't be able to take the boot off now even if I wanted to. Or if I did, I'd never get it back on again. So although it hurt to leave it the way it was, that was how it'd have to stay.

"In you go, miss," Gossel said to Della, firmly, but in a kinder tone than he'd ever used with me.

She stopped short of the cell doors. "Absolutely not. Do you know who my father is?"

"This is where those suspected of having the Scourge must wait until they can be checked by the physician. It's Governor Felling's orders."

"My father should be the governor right now! The last election was a fraud!"

I didn't know about that. By law, River People couldn't own property, and as such, weren't granted the right to vote. But if all I had to choose from was the father of a girl like her and a governor who would house sick people—or those suspected of being sick—in a cell meant for criminals, then for now, I was glad not to have to vote. It was like choosing between two poisons, the only difference being the way it would kill you.

"Your father can take up the matter with Governor Felling tomorrow morning," Gossel said. "Now walk in, miss, or I'll push you in."

Push her in, I thought. I would've liked to have seen it.

But Della stepped inside and the door behind her clanged shut. Gossel looked my way and said, "We'll be watching this cell very closely now. Try to run again and you won't return to this cell. You won't return anywhere."

I turned away from him to lie down on the bed. I wasn't going to try escaping. I could barely walk, much less run.

Once we were alone, Della crouched down in the corner of the cell and began crying, far too loudly for my taste. Perhaps she hoped that her cries would carry across the courtyard, roads, and river to pierce those thick walls of her home and tell her father where she was. Instead, they only pierced my ears, like a hawk swooping for the kill.

I knew how to make her stop. But I wouldn't do it. I didn't hate her that much. Not yet anyway.

Back in the isolation wagon, Weevil had told me that the sound of scratching was the second-worst sound in the world. That was a joke between us, because we both knew the worst—it was me, singing. I could sing to Della now and make her cry for an entirely different reason.

Singing was the way Weevil and I had met. Four summers ago, I had been working in my family's garden, singing a tune to pass the time. Weevil had been fishing nearby and came to the rear of our garden to beg me to stop.

"I don't mean to be rude," he had said, "but that truly is the most horrible sound I've ever heard. Sort of like a chicken's dying squawk. Only that ends—yours just goes on and on. And then on and on some more, like you don't even need air while creating that blasphemy of noise."

With a smile, I had sat back on my heels. "Did you seriously think that wouldn't be rude?"

"Oh, it was rude—I agree," Weevil had said. "And I'm sorry about that. But it wasn't as rude as you singing in the first place. Honestly, if I had any money, I'd give you all of it, just to beg you to stop."

"But you don't have money," I'd said with a wink, and

then continued singing. Weevil's pretending to roll on the ground in pain—or perhaps actually being in pain—was the beginning of our friendship.

It had also given me a great idea for how my singing might be of use. Ironically, that same idea might spell the end of our friendship. I wished I knew where Weevil was now, whether he was already on his way home. I hoped so.

At least if he was gone, he wouldn't have to share in the misery of listening to Della cry. Until this very moment, I had been comfortable knowing that my singing could produce the worst sound in the world.

But Della's crying was worse, and she was getting louder.

Finally, just to get her to stop, I rolled over and said, "Would you like me to sing to you? It might help you get to sleep." Or make her pass out—I didn't much care.

"No."

Good, because I wasn't in the mood to sing anyway. Without my heart in it, I'd probably end up sounding only mildly horrendous.

I said, "Listen, for whatever it matters, I don't have the Scourge."

"Stop talking, grub."

I sat up. "My name is Ani, not *grub*. And I'm just saying that I understand you're scared. I am too, but I'm not sick. Even if I was, one slap on the cheek probably won't get you sick either. We're going to be all right."

She stopped and sniffed. "You don't know anything. You are going to test positive tomorrow, just like I am. And you might as well accept that now, because sometime after that, they'll ship us both off to the Scourge Colony. Neither of us will ever go home again."

I hesitated a moment. "Does everyone who gets tested end up at the Colony?"

"No. But we will. The governor hates my father for trying to replace her in the last election. And you're a grub. If she decides we're sick, then we're sick."

I shook my head as fear began to fill me. "The test isn't real?"

"Oh, it's real, but the Scourge is everywhere in Keldan, so unless you live under a rock—" She hesitated. "Do you—"

"River People don't live under rocks, Della." Sadly, this was not the first time I'd had to explain that to a pinchworm.

"Well, unless you live under a rock, you've been exposed to the Scourge. So I already know how my test will come out. You should accept your fate too." Now she stood and stomped over to me, saying, "It's your fault I'm here. And for that, I will do everything in my power to make the final days of your life as miserable and lonely as I can. I promise you that."

"Miserable or lonely, which do you prefer?" Yet again, my fear was coming out like anger. "Because whenever you're with me, I'm plenty miserable. I'd much rather you went to your half of the cell and let me be lonely instead."

"You shouldn't have come down to help me!" she yelled.

"And you shouldn't have asked me to come!" I countered.

She pinched her mouth shut and stomped back to the cell door, but kept her eyes fixed on me in a murderous glare. I wasn't sure it was safe to roll over and sleep, but I suddenly didn't care. Something told me that no matter how awful today had been, tomorrow wasn't going to get any better. For now, I needed to sleep.

CHAPTER
SEVEN

Early the next morning, Warden Brogg appeared at the cell door with a cup in each hand. One for both me and Della, obviously.

"Where's the other warden?" Della asked. "Your superior?"

Brogg's eyes shifted. "Warden Gossel returned to the Colony this morning as punishment for disobeying the governor's orders."

The order to take five River People, I guessed. But I didn't say anything. Brogg probably wouldn't want to be reminded that I had overheard his conversation with Warden Gossel.

Brogg pushed the cups through the bars. "Here, take these."

"Breakfast?" I asked. After missing supper last night, I was hungry. But Della seemed to know better.

She sniffed at the cups. "This is the test? I thought it was more . . . painful."

"That was the old test," Brogg said. "Trust me, you'd rather cooperate now than face the way we used to do it."

47

"How did you used to do it?" I asked, but Brogg shook his head at me, warning me not to ask again.

"What's in the drink?" Della asked, taking one cup.

"Do I look like a physician?" he replied. "All I know is it draws out symptoms that might not appear for two or three weeks otherwise. If you're sick, we'll know it within the hour. If it doesn't affect you, then you're free to go home."

He held out the second cup to me, but I remained on the bed, letting Della drink hers first.

She took a sip and murmured, "Tastes sweet."

He smiled, clearly pleased with himself. "Many people who take the test ask for more. But even if they beg, they only get one."

I doubted that was true. It seemed more likely that people were usually forced into taking this test, just as we were. Nobody would beg for seconds, no matter how good it tasted.

When she'd finished, Della handed him the cup back. "I don't feel any different."

"As I said, miss, it takes an hour." Then his eyes shifted to me. "Your turn."

I stood and gingerly tested my ankle before putting any real weight on it. The tenderness was still there, but the swelling had gone down quite a bit, and even the rash wasn't too bad anymore. That was a relief. With only a slight limp, I walked over to him and took the cup.

"How many people who take the drink show up with symptoms?" I asked.

He shrugged. "Plenty of people pass this test, including a family of nine just yesterday. If you're not sick, we'll know soon enough."

"One hour. If I don't show any symptoms, I can go home?"

"One hour."

I sniffed the drink, but couldn't recognize the smell as anything I was used to. It wasn't fruit, or herbs, or even spirits. Just . . . unfamiliar.

"Drink it," Della said impatiently. "I'll be home eating a fine breakfast of egg dumplings before you've even taken a sip."

I glared at her and then swallowed it all in one gulp. One hour.

Warden Brogg took my cup back and then disappeared into the building. I had wondered at first about why our cell was not guarded, especially after Weevil had proven how easy it was to escape. But during the night, it had begun to make sense to me. Wardens weren't immune to this disease any more than the rest of us. They were simply forced into the job. I might be afraid of what the wardens could do, but they were just as afraid of me, maybe more.

Della was back on her side of the cell now, staring at me to see if I'd explode or spontaneously burst into flame or whatever the contents of that cup were supposed to make me do. I stared back, determined to be equally rude.

"How bad is the Scourge for you grubs?" she asked, rebraiding her hair as we talked. It made me wonder if I should try braiding mine instead of letting it hang in loose tangles over my shoulders. "Has it affected many people?"

"None of our people have gotten it."

"Someone has to be first," she said. "When you fail the test, all the grubs will know your name, how you're the person who brought the disease to them."

I opened my mouth to reply, but nothing came. It was true that I had always hoped for a day when everyone knew my name. But not for this reason. Not for being the one who brought disease to the river country.

"I know several Scourge victims," she said. "A lot of times it takes our workers, sometimes even our best ones, the ones that you'd never think could get sick. But that doesn't explain why you grubs haven't been affected. I mean, you're dirtier than any of our workers."

Now I started finger-combing my hair. "Maybe the disease doesn't care about dirt."

She sniffed, as if that was too absurd to deserve a response. "Lately it's been moving into families like mine. And the scary thing is that who gets it seems so random. I shouldn't be here."

I felt like arguing that point, reminding her that she probably wouldn't be here if she had not slapped me last night. If the wardens truly believed I had the Scourge, after seeing her touch me, they had no choice but to test her too.

I definitely felt like reminding her of that, but I didn't. She looked too much the way I felt—scared, confused, and lonely.

So instead, I asked, "What were you doing in that boat last night?"

She opened her mouth, closed it, and then sighed. "I suppose it doesn't matter if I tell you now. One of our workers is a boy named Jonas Orden, who did all sorts of odd jobs around our home. I don't think of him as a worker, though. We were friends. He was taken away with the Scourge about three weeks ago. I knew it was only a matter of time before I started to feel sick too."

I felt like backing as far away from her as possible, though there was nowhere for me to go. "Wait—*you* already have the Scourge? You called me down to help you, asked me to carry you through the water, all the while knowing you are sick?"

"I'm not sick right now. I'm just . . . worried." She shrugged. "And anyway, you came down to my boat, knowing you're probably sick too."

There was nothing I could say to that. Though my intentions were good, to respond to a cry for help, it had been a mistake on my part to get so close to someone else. If I did have the Scourge, if I had exposed myself to it . . . No, I couldn't let my mind wander there. The test would answer those questions soon enough.

Della continued. "I knew that once I started to show symptoms, I'd be taken away too, sent to the Colony like a common person. So I decided to run away, but I didn't get far in the boat before I realized I'd never survive on my own. I didn't even know how to row it! So I changed my mind and meant to go home, but the boat had already started down river. I couldn't let my father find out I tried to leave. He'd ask why."

"If you were already exposed to the Scourge, then why do you hate me so much?" I asked. "I didn't give it to you."

Her eyes filled with tears. "I don't hate you for giving me the Scourge. I hate you for letting them find me. Wardens were already after you. Why did you stop to help?"

It was a good question. Or a better question might've been, why did I stop to help *her*? "Della?" A man came running into the courtyard, dressed in a long black coat, gold vest, and a gentleman's hat. His face was square with a wide mustache, and he looked kinder than I'd have expected, considering what I knew of his daughter. Della ran to the bars. "Father?"

"They told me what happened." He nodded at me. "Is that the girl who tried to steal our boat?"

"Yes," I said. "A worker friend of mine got the Scourge, and I was afraid I'd get it too. I didn't want to go to the

Colony like some common person, so I was using your boat to run away."

Della flashed me a glare, and I smirked back at her. She turned to her father. "You must get me out of here."

"I'll do everything I can," he said. "I'll speak to the governor at once."

When he hurried away, Della seemed to breathe easier, and she returned to her half of the cell.

I walked over to the bars myself, wondering if anyone would come for me, to beg the governor for my release. My father would come, if he knew where I was. But he didn't know, and no warden would be sent to notify him. Even if he did come, none of my people had the kind of power to demand a meeting with Governor Felling. We didn't have enough money to bribe our way in, and if my father fought me out of here, we'd only bring the battle back to the river country.

The only person who could do anything to help me was probably miles from here now, headed upriver to where it was safe.

At least, I hoped that's where Weevil was.

And at the same time, I hoped not.

I wanted him far away. I needed him here.

CHAPTER
EIGHT

If someone asked one of the River People for the time, the answer would be something like "daytime." Which in most cases was good enough for us. We estimated the passing of hours by the movement of the sun and figured overcast days were an excuse to ignore time for a while. For the River People, minutes and hours were an afterthought.

This morning, however, my entire life depended on the passing of time. I had watched the changing angle of the sun so much that my eyes were beginning to burn.

It had not been an hour yet when Della cried out behind me, "Ah!" I turned to see her kneeling on the ground, clutching her stomach. "Ani, help me!"

My first thought was whether she truly wanted my help or whether this was another excuse to accuse me of a crime. But her cries were sincere. She was hurting.

I backed away, ashamed of myself for ignoring her cries. "Get to the bed," I said. "Can you do that?" I hoped so, because I couldn't bear to see her on the ground, but I couldn't force myself to get any closer either.

Della grunted and rolled onto the bed, still doubled over.

"Where does it hurt?" I asked.

"My stomach! Oh, Ani, what does this mean? What is this?"

I knew exactly what it meant and so did she. Despite the fact that she and I were as close to enemies as anyone could be in such a short acquaintance, I still felt bad for her. I worried for myself too. Was this same pain about to come to me? I'd taken my drink just seconds after her.

Yet though I searched within myself for any sign of pain, there was nothing. I was hungry—that was certain. But hunger would not leave me shrieking with pain-filled gasps, as she was.

"Sing to me, Ani," she said. "Please."

"Sing?"

"I heard that grubs—that River People—know songs that can take the pain away."

I snorted. "That's one of the old stories. It was never true, and it's especially not true about me. Trust me, my singing will bring you more pain than it takes away."

"You offered before."

Only out of a desire to be mean. But she didn't know that.

"Please, Ani," she added.

I looked around to be sure we were alone, then started humming a tune, softly at first. When Della closed her eyes to listen, I began singing. I chose one of the nursery songs my mother used years ago to get me to sleep. From my mother's lips, the song fell like dew onto grass. My song was closer to falling cow dung.

I didn't get four notes in before her eyes flew open. "What is that noise?"

"Singing!"

"Were you singing or choking to death?" She clutched at her stomach again. "Ow! Honestly, Ani, you made me hurt worse!"

"I warned you!"

I actually had tried to sing my best. If I sang the way I usually did, I could have brought her to tears. With only a little effort, I could have made her wish the Scourge would just take her before I reached the next note.

Then Della turned to me. "I know who you are now," she said. "My people talk about you. The priest even prayed for you once in church, that you'd be healed of whatever evil spirit curses your singing."

"He prayed for me?"

"He must not have prayed hard enough. You're the grub who sings in the town squares, refusing to stop singing until people pay you coins."

"Other people sing for coins too," I said. "It's an honest way to earn money."

"But they sing well. People pay coins to thank them." She scrunched up her nose. "You're paid to stop."

My smile beamed with pride. "Either way, they pay."

"What do grubs need money for anyway?" Della asked. "You eat bugs and build your homes from logs and clay, and steal from us whenever you need something."

"That's not true," I said. We didn't eat bugs . . . very often. Only our nicest homes were made from logs and clay. And we didn't steal. However, like Weevil, some of our people were very good at borrowing. Some borrowed for longer than others. Rumor had it that sixty years ago, old Farmer Adderson even borrowed one of the pinchworm women to marry him, though she already loved him back, so she refused to be returned.

"It's so warm already," she said. "Can't you feel it?"

A warm day was coming, but nothing hot enough to cause the beads of sweat on her brow. The wardens had left us a fresh pitcher of water last night, but I'd already finished it. I regretted that now. Della's tongue was moving inside her mouth as if she was thirsty.

Della cried out and clutched at her stomach again. I wanted to cry too, but not because I felt any pain. It's only that we'd been in this same cell all night. Every contact I made with her increased my chances of getting the Scourge as well.

Della's eyes were closed, but she had calmed a bit and she whispered, "You should be feeling just as awful by now."

"I don't." Then hope flooded into me. "I'm not sick! I don't have the Scourge!" If Della hated me before, this wouldn't help things.

"Congratulations," she murmured, and a tear slipped beneath her lashes. "My father won't be able to get me out now. There's no chance of that."

My voice softened. "Everything will be all right." Though we both knew that was never the way the Scourge ended.

Suddenly, Della sat up, though her hand was still pressed against her side and her teeth were gritted. "Wait, I have an idea! Maybe I'm hurting, but there are no outward symptoms, right? No rash or fever or green dots all over my face."

For some reason, I thought about Weevil then. If the Scourge put green dots on a person's face, Weevil would probably try to get the disease. He'd find that entertaining.

Della grabbed my arm. "We can help each other."

"I don't need your help," I said, pulling away from her. "The drink didn't affect me. They'll let me go home."

Della shook her head. "You've been in this cell with me all night. You're going to get the Scourge now too, sooner or later. But if we work together, we can both walk away from here."

"You can barely walk now. And I'm not sick."

"You'll have to do the talking, Ani. You have to, because when I talk, I sound like I'm in pain. Tell them we're both fine. I can nod and agree with you."

"Della, this is the Scourge, not some simple flu. You know what it does to people."

Her voice raised in pitch. "My father will take us both away from here. He can put me in seclusion, where I won't give the disease to anyone. And he'll help you get home, offer any reward you want to bring you home to your family." She hesitated. "Grubs do have families, right?"

"Those of us who don't spring forth from the mud have families, yes."

If she even heard me, she missed the joke. She hesitated a moment to deal with another wave of pain, then said, "This can work."

"It cannot work. It must not work, Della. If you leave, you'll get others sick too."

Her face darkened. "I know about the Colony—you don't! The things the governor says in her speeches, they're not true. Why do you think I considered running away? I don't want to spend the last days of my life in the Colony."

Governor Felling often talked about the Colony in her speeches. Scourge victims were housed in the old prison, but that was only out of necessity and it did provide a single place to care for the growing population of victims. Besides, the prison had been redesigned to feel like rooms, not cells. Though Keldan had little money, the governor had redirected what resources she could to provide food for the victims, and care was provided by shepherds—volunteers from the churches who had dedicated their lives to caring for Scourge victims in their final days. The disease always ended in death, but at least it wouldn't be a cold death, one without love.

If all of that was wrong, then what was the Colony really like? And was it true that getting the Scourge was now inevitable for me? Everything I knew about the Scourge told me I was infected now.

Yet it had been one hour and I wasn't feeling sick. I had passed the test. Warden Brogg had promised I could go home now.

"Here they come," Della said. "Think of it, Ani, you can change your life today. The prettiest new dresses, a better home for your family. Think of the best reward you can imagine, and I'll make it happen. All you have to do is tell the wardens that we're both fine."

I got to my feet, and Della stood beside me, though she was leaning on me to keep herself upright.

"Please, Ani," Della whispered. "Please. Anything you want. Just tell them I'm not sick."

Anything I wanted. What would I ask for? Money? There was never enough. My mother needed new shoes and a dress that wasn't made of patched-over holes. Food? I knew what servants for the wealthy carried out of the markets: breads and cheeses and sweets that made my stomach ache for how wonderful they smelled. The possibilities for what I might want were endless.

Warden Brogg walked up to the cell with a young warden whom I'd spotted searching for me last night. While that man fiddled with his keys to find the one for our door, Brogg hefted his oversized belly over the top of his britches, looking at me first, and then his eye rested on Della. Her hand was pinched around my wrist. Based on the way her nails dug into my skin, I knew it must've been extraordinarily painful for her to even stand upright.

"So," Brogg said, "how are you both feeling?"

"Excellent," Della squeaked out.

Brogg arched a brow and looked at me. "Ani, perhaps you can tell me."

Della's nails dug in deeper, a reminder that the right kind of lie could change my life. If I told the truth, she would ruin it.

CHAPTER

NINE

The fair-skinned warden unlocked the cell door and held it open, though neither of us moved. Della was at serious risk of falling over if she did, and I was having trouble keeping my thoughts together. Her offer was more tempting than I wanted to admit.

Brogg walked up to me. "How are you feeling?"

"Perfectly well," I said. "I don't have the Scourge."

His eyes brushed over me again. "You seem to be all right, though the physician must make the final judgment."

That didn't worry me. Unless he was as stupid as a stone—always a possibility—he'd see that the drink in that cup had failed to produce any symptoms from me.

Della, on the other hand . . .

"I'm fine too," Della said. "Tell him, Ani."

She sucked a harsh breath of air in through her nose. Even if the wardens couldn't hear the pain in her voice, I certainly could.

Brogg folded his arms and looked back at me. "She says she's fine, but her face is pale. You'd know if she was having symptoms, grub. Is she?"

Surely he knew that Della was sick, so if he was asking my opinion, it was only to test whether I'd lie. My heart was pounding, but I lowered my head and murmured, "She has the Scourge. She's sick, sir."

In rage, Della's nails clawed against my arm. I snapped my arm away and held it with my hand, waiting for the sting to pass. Now that she didn't have me to support her weight, Della fell on the ground and screamed with pain. "If it's the last thing I do, Ani, you will pay for that!"

"Sir Willoughby has just finished meeting with the governor," Brogg told his companion. "He'll try to come back here for his daughter, so it's best if you bring her to the dock another way. Don't let her be seen."

"No!" Della screeched. "My father promised to get me out of here! You can't send me to the Colony!"

Considering how much pain she was in, she put up a fair fight before the warden scooped her into his long arms and carried her out of the cell, into another nearby building, one I now suspected led to a dock that would take her to the Attic Island colony.

Brogg said to me, "I won't have to tie you up now, I hope. We'll go to see the physician. Maybe he can figure out why you're not showing symptoms."

"I'm not showing symptoms because I'm not sick. You told me that I could go home now."

"I can't release you without the physician's permission," Brogg reminded me. "Let's go to his examination room."

I figured it was better to follow him than to fight. After all, there was no longer any reason to hold me. I'd passed the test. If I cooperated for a few more minutes, I'd be free. Even I could manage to behave for that long. Besides that, my ankle was still a little sore. Attempting to outrun him would only inflame the injury again or create new injuries for at least one of us. Hopefully him.

We walked toward the large brick building at the far end of the courtyard. This was where the wardens had come from and where Della's father had entered to speak to the governor. As I got closer, I was surprised to see so much decay in the building's foundation. This place would surely collapse one day, and probably sooner rather than later.

I stole a glance at Brogg, who was walking me forward like I was sure he must've done hundreds of times before with others who were suspected of the Scourge. That family of nine had passed the test. How many others had too? And how many had failed and were taken away just like Della?

"Sir," I said, "Della told me the Colony is not what the governor describes it to be. How is it?"

His teeth were clenched as he replied. "She told you that, huh? Has she been to the Colony before?"

"I'm sure she hasn't. But her father seems well connected. Perhaps he's heard things and shared them with his family."

"Sir Willoughby is not to be trusted, nor any of his

wild-eyed claims. Governor Nerysa Felling is saving our country from the Scourge, not him. Her decisions might not always be popular, but they are necessary. Besides that, our country has been doing much better in recent months— other than the disease, of course. But when Keldan flourishes again, like in the old days, it will be under Governor Felling's direction. She is saving us, not Sir Willoughby."

That all sounded very nice, but it wasn't an answer to my question. And perhaps the fact that he had used so many obviously rehearsed words to not answer me *was* the answer. The Colony was not as pleasant as the governor would have us believe.

He opened a door and directed me to walk down a dark and narrow hallway. Sconces were set into the wall, but few of them were lit, and the doors we passed as we walked were either closed or their rooms were bare. This could not be a government building, as I had suspected. If so, where was everyone?

"To your right," Brogg ordered, and we entered a small examination room. A single table stood in the center, but it looked too much like a slab for a dead body, so I refused to lie on it, as the warden clearly wanted me to do. Instead, I opted for a chair against the wall. Near me was another small table with a tray of tools on it. A magnifying glass. Something like scissors, only without sharp ends. A knife. I'd remember that item, if it became necessary. Brogg took up a post at the door, crossing his hands in front of him and watching me.

"Don't think your friend got away last night," he said. "We'll find him soon."

"If you haven't found him by now, then he got away," I said. "You and I both know he never should've been in that wagon in the first place. You only grabbed him because you had orders from the governor to take five grubs." My eyes narrowed. "For what kind of punishment? Whose uprising?"

Brogg's eyes widened. "You did hear us, then!" He started toward me, but stopped when another man entered the room. He was older, with graying hair and a stiff beard that came to a point below his chin. A pair of round glasses made his eyes look larger than they were, and he seemed to hum when he wasn't speaking.

"My name is Doctor Thomas Cresh," he said. "I am in charge of all Scourge patients inside Keldan. You were given a cup of my formula over an hour ago, correct?"

"Yes, sir. I don't have—"

"Hush." He grabbed my face and turned it side to side, then pressed his fingers into my stomach. "Does that hurt?"

"Well, you poke hard for an old man. Otherwise, I'm not hurting."

"Before last night, have you come into contact with any person who has the Scourge?"

"No, sir." Not as far as I knew. Was that good enough?

"And you have no pain?"

"None." Except for him. He was a big pain.

"Then I suppose I have to let you go."

"Wait a minute," a woman said, stepping into the room. "You're Ani Mells?"

The doctor turned, and I looked around him to see a woman with dark hair dressed into an elaborate bun. Her eyes were wide, deep set, and intelligent. Her long dress was elegant, yet designed to show her as someone to be taken seriously. In every way, she evoked power, which I'm sure was exactly how she wanted it. This was the governor, though I'd never seen her up close. I'd sometimes been singing in towns where she came to speak, though.

When I didn't answer her question, Governor Felling stepped toward me. "Ani, my name is—"

"I know who you are," I said as I stood for her. "I've just passed the Scourge test. My parents don't know where I am, and they must be terrified for me. Please, can I leave?"

Her smile was cold and empty. "River People certainly are short on manners." Now the governor looked to Warden Brogg. "You told me that this girl tried to escape last night. After she encountered Sir Willoughby's daughter, what did Ani say to her?"

Brogg cleared his throat. "It wasn't meant—"

"What did Ani say?"

"She told Della Willoughby that she had the Scourge and that she was already half-dead from it."

My heart slammed against my chest. "I only said that to be mean. Della had just accused me of theft and slapped me. I was lying, but only to scare her."

"So you admit that you are a liar and have shown a willingness to threaten our citizens." She tsked with her tongue.

"I have no symptoms, Governor Felling. They promised I could go home."

"Tell me, Ani. The River People have an herb they often use to flavor their stews. It's got long, thin leaves, and it's almost unheard of in Keldan, except in the rivers near your home. What is its name?"

"Thrushweed." I knew it well, in fact. Flavoring stews was the least of our uses for thrushweed. The leaves could be boiled until soft and used to make creams to cure skin conditions, or dried and crushed for teas that could help a person sleep. All women kept a bottle of thrushweed oil in their homes in case of food poisoning, though Weevil's mother had given it to him once and he swore the cure was worse. Most infants spent their first year sleeping on bedding filled with thrushweed leaves rather than feathers. We believed it made us stronger from birth.

"Ah yes, thrushweed." She turned to Doctor Cresh. "Didn't you once tell me that the problem with testing River

People is they often have too much thrushweed in their systems?"

His eyes widened behind his glasses. "Oh yes, indeed. Thrushweed masks Scourge symptoms from my test."

As fiercely as possible, I shook my head. "I've eaten no thrushweed for over a week. I've eaten nothing at all for almost a day. There's nothing in my system."

The governor smiled at me with the sort of sympathy that could only be faked by a bad actor. "Is that true, Ani? Or another lie?" She moved closer. "You see, I don't think you're telling us the whole truth. Let's start with the question of how you were exposed to the Scourge."

"I was never exposed!" I said. "River People don't socialize with pinchworms."

The governor raised her hand, and I flinched, fully expecting her to slap me. But she stopped herself and only said, "How dare you insult us? To have such a limited vocabulary lowers you and all your filthy people. Besides, it is townsfolk who have no interest in socializing with you." To the physician, she added, "Isn't there another way to determine for sure whether this girl has the Scourge?"

"There is the old way of testing," Doctor Cresh said. "But I'd rather not—"

"Yes," the governor said firmly, "give her the older test." Her eyes sharpened as they returned to me. "I'm sorry, Ani. This test is not as pleasant as simply drinking from a cup.

But obviously the doctor's formula does not work on River People."

I stepped back from her. "The test worked. It showed I'm not sick."

"It should have done something to you. Raised a mild rash or a slight fever. Something to show it reacted with your body. But it did nothing. That means it didn't work. Thrushweed is a very strong herb after all."

"I won't do another test." I pointed to Warden Brogg. "He promised that if I didn't show symptoms, I could go home. He promised!"

The governor lifted her chin. "Yes, well, the River People promised they would not cause any trouble for Keldan, didn't they? And now you're here."

I had no idea what she could possibly be talking about. No matter how Keldan had pushed us, our people had stood firm on the idea that fighting back would only make things worse for everyone. But I didn't have time to ask what she'd meant. Brogg darted toward me. I backed away from him and grabbed the knife from the doctor's tray.

"I'm leaving," I said, wielding the knife in the way my father did when wild boars got into our garden. "None of you had better dare try stopping me."

Governor Felling remained calm as she took a single step toward me. "Someone has to be the first of the River People to get sick. What if I'm right, Ani, and it's you? Would you return home with even the slightest question in your mind that you might spread the disease? If you knew your return would kill them all?"

"I'm not sick," I said, though her question was already nagging at me. The slightest question in my mind? Yes, I did have questions, just as I had secrets, and they weren't slight.

The governor advanced another step. "If you leave, I will have to figure out whether you've already spread the disease. You will force me to bring your family in, and your friends, and their families, and put them through these tests. I will go through the River People one by one to figure out who is infected"—she leaned in to me now—"and who is simply a useless grub."

"No!" I slashed the knife through the air, with no intention of touching her, but simply to warn her away. In that moment, Brogg grabbed my arm and twisted it behind my back, then forced me to drop the knife.

"Leave us alone," I said. "We are not sick!"

The governor's smile turned wicked. "Three hundred years ago, your people first brought the disease to Keldan, spreading it without having the decency to let it kill you off."

"Those are old stories," I said. "We were never responsible for the Scourge."

"That's where you're wrong, Ani. River People *are* the Scourge."

Then with a slight nod of her head, Brogg pressed my arm to the table while holding the rest of me in his grip.

Doctor Cresh picked up the knife off the floor and stepped toward me.

"Do not move," he warned. "I'm sorry, but this is going to hurt."

And he pressed the knife into my flesh.

CHAPTER
TEN

The knife didn't go deep, but it hurt enough to raise a well of tears in my eyes. I gritted my teeth to keep from crying out—either from fear or the pain.

It sliced along my forearm, instantly drawing blood. I didn't mind the sight of blood; I wasn't squeamish in that way. I was more concerned about what the doctor would do next.

While Brogg continued pinning my arm to the table, Doctor Cresh turned behind him to pull a rag from a jar. It was wet, and he handled it with only the tips of his fingers.

"What's on that rag?" I asked, panicked now. "Don't do this!"

"Calm down," he said. "It's the same ingredients that were in the cup you drank. But they go directly into your blood, so it bypasses any thrushweed in your system. We'll also see a quicker reaction."

That should have calmed me. I had passed the test with the cup; surely I would pass this one as well. But I was more frightened than ever. There was a slight sting in my arm when he tightly wrapped the rag around the wound he had made. At least it would stop the bleeding.

"How long?" I asked. "Until you see a reaction, how long?"

"Within minutes," Cresh said. "Can you feel any difference now?"

"No," I said.

But that was a lie. Blood was already rushing through my veins, sending a deep ache inside my head. Was that because of the wound, because of the fight I'd just put up? Or was the wet rag doing something to me?

"You're beginning to sweat," Cresh said.

"It's warm in here," I said.

But he shook his head. "It's not."

I looked from the governor to Cresh to what I could see of the warden's face from this position, searching for even a bead of sweat on them. It shouldn't have mattered to me. After all, the warmth I felt could be explained by my fear, and the fact that the warden had been so rough on me.

Or it could be the start of symptoms. What did sweat mean? The governor had said everyone should have some reaction to the test. Was this simply one of those reactions, innocent and meaningless? Because if so, I wanted to admit I was warm, to prove to the governor that this test had worked on me and that I still had no sign of the Scourge.

Or was this the Scourge beginning to show itself? Della had complained of the heat, and if she had been thirsty before, then it could not possibly compete with the thirst that parched my throat now, as if all that stood between my life and death was a single drop of water.

"Let her sit down," Doctor Cresh said to the warden. "She looks like she needs to sit."

"I don't," I said.

But I did. My legs were shaking beneath the weight of my body, as if I had suddenly turned to lead and was standing on only twigs. Brogg pulled me away from the table and pushed me onto the chair. He didn't need to. I would've fallen just fine on my own.

Doctor Cresh grabbed my face again, turning it from side to side as he had done earlier. But whatever he had been looking for then, he found now. His thumb rubbed up the side of my head along the outside of my eye.

"See that vein?" he asked the governor. "The way it's darkened? That's our sign."

"A sign of what?" I grabbed his hands, forcing him to look at me. "I feel—I felt perfectly fine. What have you done to me?"

"I only brought out symptoms that would've appeared anyway, in time. Without this test, the Scourge would've destroyed Keldan by now. Hopefully, we caught this before you could spread the disease to anyone else."

"I don't have the Scourge," I said, and the tears flowed. Because I was only saying it now as something I *wished* could be true. The way I felt, I knew something was terribly wrong.

The pain in my stomach hit me next, coming on like being blindsided by a rogue wave. I clutched my side and tried to swallow my scream. Was this how Della had felt? If so, then I had been wrong to stand back when she begged for my help. This was horrible.

Cresh wiped my sweat-drenched hair from my face, and his tone turned kinder. "I have medicine, Ani. It can't cure the disease—nothing can do that—but it can dull the pain. Do you want some?"

I nodded, though my vision was blurring and I couldn't really see him. Maybe when my tears dried, the focus would return. Maybe this was the start of blindness. I didn't know. Or maybe—I stopped there. Unable to complete any rational thought, I clutched at my side again. Either I had become possessed by a monster determined to burst out from my skin. Or else I had the Scourge.

I had the Scourge. Moreover, I knew where I had gotten it, and how, and why, and it was entirely my fault.

I had the Scourge.

My life, in effect, had just ended.

CHAPTER
ELEVEN

The medicine from the physician helped a lot. While it didn't take the pain away completely, it calmed it enough that I could breathe evenly and pull my thoughts together.

I started with the most important thought—the fact that this really was for the best. The last thing I wanted was to have any responsibility for my family becoming sick, or Weevil, or any of the River People. Or anyone, anywhere, for that matter. I wouldn't wish this kind of pain on my enemies. Well, not *most* of them.

Second came the rush of questions about what would happen to me now. Was the Colony the way the governor had described it, a place of peace and rest? Or the way Della seemed to think of it? Would I be cared for, looked after in my final hours? Would the final few weeks of my life be pleasant?

Doctor Cresh had me laid out on his table now, not to examine me, but to let me rest. I felt like sleeping and my eyes were closed, but my mind was still fully involved in my surroundings.

The doctor and Governor Felling were discussing me in the corner. They must've thought I was asleep or they'd never have talked so openly. Maybe Brogg was with them, or maybe he wasn't even in the room anymore—I didn't know. My eyes were too heavy to check.

"Who else might she have exposed?" Cresh was asking.

"Her family, obviously," the governor said. "I'm told that her father is a strong man, well respected amongst the grubs. There will be a fight if we try to take him for testing."

Yes, there would. My father had once fought a whole pack of wild dogs that had gotten too close to our home. In the end, they'd called it even, though if the dogs had not run off, I had no doubt my father would've eventually won.

"All the River People will fight if we start taking them," Brogg said. So he was still in the room. "It was no small thing to get this girl and her friend, and they were caught off guard."

"It was too hard for you and Warden Gossel, obviously," the governor said. "Perhaps I should have sent you to work in the Colony too."

Brogg's mouth snapped shut—I actually heard that, which made me want to smile. He was afraid of the governor.

"The girl is sick, so she's no threat," Doctor Cresh said.

The governor added, "River People are strong. If she gets better, then we'll see what she can do."

My ears perked up. Get better? There was a chance to recover from this disease?

"But you lost the boy," the physician said. "Won't he try to return to his people?"

"If he does, it'll mean trouble," the governor said. "I can't deal with the Scourge and face an uprising from the River People at the same time!"

Brogg said, "Governor, if that boy gets back to his people and explains what's happened, an uprising is certain. With two of their children gone missing, they will be prepared for us when we return for more grubs, if they aren't on their way here already."

"Then find him," the governor said. "Search for him everywhere, but especially on the trails leading back to his home. Don't worry about bringing him in for testing. Just kill him and be finished with that."

I drew in a sharp gasp, which Brogg must've heard because his footsteps came over to me. I felt his hot breath near my face as he got close enough to check on whether I was indeed asleep. I tried to stay calm, to keep my breathing low and even, but after hearing that, how could I?

Weevil was fast. He might've made it home already. But there was also a chance he'd lingered in the area, hoping I'd find a way to escape a second time. Of course that's what he'd do—he'd never leave me behind. Which meant he might have sealed his own fate.

A tear had formed in my eye, but I couldn't let it fall. Brogg would see; he would know that I had overheard everything. He put a hand over the rag binding the cut on my arm. It was dry now, probably the only reason he dared touch it. Then he squeezed on the wound.

I gasped with the pain of it, and my eyes flew open. I sat up on the table, instantly dizzy, but I pulled my arm away and kicked at his legs.

"I knew she was awake," he said.

"I am now, thanks to you," I said, trying to cover for all I'd overheard. My vision was still blurry, though not quite as bad as before. Maybe I wouldn't go blind after all. "How long was I out?"

Before anyone could answer, a voice called from outside the examination room, "Governor Felling! I demand to see you!" That was Della's father.

The governor sighed and started to open the door, but before she could, Sir Willoughby burst through it.

"There you are!" he said. "You promised we'd continue our conversation, and then you disappeared."

"I told you I had to witness a Scourge test." The governor motioned toward me. "You shouldn't be in here. This girl tested positive for it."

He glanced my way, but as soon as he determined I

wasn't his daughter, he forgot entirely about me. "Where's Della? I checked the cell where you were holding her and she's gone."

"Your daughter has the Scourge," the physician said. "The test results were clear."

Willoughby's face paled. "No! I saw her only a couple of hours ago, and she was fine."

"She must go to the Colony." The governor couldn't even pretend to care about the words she was speaking. "It's the law."

"It's *your* law." Willoughby's tone raised in pitch. "She's already exposed my household, so let me take her home."

"And then your household will infect the surrounding households, who will infect the rest of Keldan," the governor said. "Be grateful I am not bringing all of you in right now for testing and isolation. Because I could, and if you keep fighting me, I will."

I'd expected him to back down at that, but instead, Willoughby seemed to grow larger in the room. "Do you think I haven't noticed who gets brought in for testing? Is it any coincidence that your enemies seem to get sick more often than your friends?"

"Call it a coincidence if you'd like." The governor's smug grin seemed to infuriate Willoughby further. "You opposed me in the last election, I remember. Didn't I warn you back then that it would be a mistake?"

Willoughby started to say something, then changed his mind and said, "I've heard there are other medicines. Stronger medicines that can protect us from the Scourge."

"Dangerous rumors. Ignore what you've heard." The governor's voice had a strange edge to it. Was she mocking him, or simply not lying well enough?

"I will pay you for the medicines." Willoughby's voice was choked up now with sadness. "If they prevent the disease, perhaps they can treat it too."

Governor Felling remained calm. "It's too late for your daughter, and the law must apply equally to everyone who tests positive. But for the rest of your family, you are entirely dependent upon my mercy now. Who does your daughter spend the most time with? Her mother perhaps? Shall I bring your wife in next? Don't you have other children as well? Does Della ever play with them?"

That gave Willoughby pause. He had raised an arm in a threatening gesture toward the governor, but now he lowered it.

"Please don't take my daughter away," he said softly. "Governor, I'll give you anything you want."

Her tone softened as well. "There's nothing I can do, Sir Willoughby. If I release your daughter, who then infects someone else's daughter, how do I explain that to their family?"

Willoughby nodded and clumsily brushed tears from his eyes with the back of his hand. Then he walked over to me.

"Tell my daughter—" He swallowed hard. "Tell my daughter I loved her."

Loved, as in the past tense. Used for those who have already passed on.

"I will on one condition," I said, holding back tears of my own. "You must get word to my family on the river, of where I've gone. Tell them I've already died and that it was peaceful." That was the most kindness I could offer them, to believe this was over for me.

"One more thing, Sir Willoughby." The governor's voice was low and menacing now. "If I hear you're the person spreading those rumors about different medications, I will immediately start testing the rest of your family. Do you understand?"

Willoughby swallowed hard on whatever response he clearly wanted to make. He then nodded and backed out of the room, though none of us missed his icy glare aimed at the governor.

Doctor Cresh picked up a metal flask from his desk and handed it to me. It was small and silver with a thin rope attached to sling it over my shoulder, which I did.

"What is this?" I asked.

"It's your medicine, and there isn't enough to go around so be careful with it. Once your flask is gone, that's all you'll get."

My smile was faint. "Medicine for us common people, huh?" Then, with only a brief glance at the governor's angry, pinched face, I stood and turned to Warden Brogg. "All right, I'm ready. Let's get this over with."

He replaced his hat, nodded respectfully to both the governor and doctor. And I left the room with him, on my way to the Colony.

CHAPTER
TWELVE

We crossed through the mostly empty building and out a rear door heavily guarded by other wardens. Perhaps this was why no one guarded any other part of the building—everyone was needed here. Even if Willoughby had known Della was on the other side of this door, he still wouldn't have been able to get past so many armed men.

The door opened to a small dock on the Scuttle Sea, an unimpressive saltwater inlet that lacked the beauty of our freshwater rivers. Several more wardens here watched over ten other people, who were probably also Scourge victims. Pinchworms, all of them. Della was standing near the group, but had set herself at enough distance to make it clear that she considered herself as different, their superior.

It struck me as odd. I had always viewed the pinchworms as one useless clump. It had never occurred to me that perhaps some pinchworms might look down on others of their own people too. Come to think of it, that sort of division sometimes happened amongst the River People. Maybe that was human nature, to divide groups into better and worse. I turned away from the people and looked out across the water, hoping to turn my thoughts away as well.

Attic Island loomed on the horizon, a place I had never expected to go. Like the neglected room of a home, Attic Island was the overlooked part of Keldan. It was isolated, surrounded by choppy seas, and prone to terrible storms. Nobody had ever escaped from the prison there. Even when Dulan was shouting about a coming war, they had never asked for the island. They didn't want it. It was the natural place to build the Colony. Away from the healthy population. Forgotten.

"Is there anything to drink?" I asked Warden Brogg. "Please, I'm so thirsty."

"You'll get more than enough water soon," he said without looking at me.

"What about food? I haven't eaten since yesterday."

"I haven't got any food here," he said. "Besides, what do the dead need with food?"

My temper rose, but I kept my voice calm. "Nothing," I said innocently. "Except a ghost with a full stomach is less likely to haunt your nightmares. You haven't seen the last of me."

"Yes, I have." He pushed me forward and walked along behind me. The flask from the physician bounced against my chest while the liquid sloshed inside. Beneath it, I felt the rhythm of my heart, beating far too fast. I had to keep talking, to keep myself from thinking too heavily about my situation.

"Where's your medicine?" I asked Brogg. "You don't seem nervous about catching this disease. Is it the same medicine as I have, or was Sir Willoughby serious before; are there different medicines that can prevent people from getting the Scourge? Why don't you give that to everyone in Keldan?"

"You heard the governor. It's only a rumor." He nodded to the flask I wore. "You're lucky to get any medicine at all, grub."

"You know my name. Why don't you use it?" I asked.

"I don't have to care about the things I don't name," he responded.

Which, in a strange way, made sense. We didn't want to know their names any more than they wanted to know ours. The wardens were nameless men who harassed my people for crimes we had not committed, and corralled us into smaller territories to make room for growing numbers of pinchworms. Not knowing them made it easier to resent them. And pinchworms . . . I supposed most of them were people too.

Once we reached the shoreline, I saw a long rope stretching out over the water and extending for as far as I could see. Attic Island was in the distance, and if I looked carefully, I could barely see the top of the old prison. I guessed the rope went all the way to the island. Attached to the rope but near the shore were three rowboats.

The method for delivering us to the Colony was clear. We would row ourselves in the boats to the island, and then these wardens could pull the boats back to the mainland. Nobody but Scourge victims had to touch the boats. Everyone would stay on course through the rough waters because there was no other choice. The only thing I didn't understand was how we were expected to get out to the boats. Some of the victims around me looked in far worse shape than I felt, which was no small thing considering that I felt like I had been trampled over.

"Wait!" a familiar voice called. "Don't leave without me!"

I swung around to see Weevil running down the hill toward us. It was all at once the best possible sight and the worst. I didn't want him to be here, doomed to my fate. And yet it meant he was still safe, for now.

I started forward, but Brogg put a hand on my shoulder to hold me back. "Only you and I know the governor's orders," he whispered. "If you make him leave now, I'll have to go after him." I glanced back at the warden's expression of warning. Brogg wasn't on my side, but maybe he wasn't a murderer either.

By then, Weevil had spotted me. Normally, he'd have greeted me with a friendly wave, but these were far from normal times. Instead, he only nodded. He knew something was wrong.

"He'll have to come to the Colony now," Brogg said, more loudly. "It would've been better if he'd stayed out of sight. Your friend is insane to show up here."

"He probably is," I said, brushing Brogg's hand away. "But that's better than dead." In a strange way, Weevil might have just saved his own life.

I began walking toward Weevil, but other wardens had surrounded him, twisting his arms behind his back as if he had come here threatening them. If I were not so unsteady on my feet, I would have challenged them.

"I'm sick!" Weevil said, far too cheerfully. "I'm really, truly sick, just like the others. I need to go to the Colony."

"Have you been tested?" a warden asked.

"Ow!" Weevil said as his arm was pulled again. "Really, is all of this necessary? I'm asking to go to the Colony. I don't see what the problem is."

"What are your symptoms?" the warden asked.

They had him on his knees by then, and someone was holding his arms behind his back. Weevil only looked past the men at me and tried to frown.

He cleared his throat. "Well, I've had all the symptoms. You know, pain, fevers, rash. You name it, I've had it."

"He doesn't look sick," a warden said. "Take him to the doctor for testing."

I pushed to the center of the group and immediately knelt beside Weevil and put a hand on his forehead. "There you are! I was so worried about you, all the pain you were in before you left. You must've been so delirious, you didn't even know what you were doing."

Which was a ridiculous thing to say, of course. I never knew a person so plagued by delirium that he was sent into fits of lock picking.

"Whether he's sick or not, he will get sick now," another warden said. "Put him on the boats. He'll be useful on the island."

Weevil jumped to his feet—more quickly than any actual Scourge victim could—and we immediately started walking to the docks. We hung back from the rest of the group, and Weevil leaned in to talk to me out of the others' earshot.

"I've seen you look better," he said. "Yesterday, for example. Or any other day ever."

"What were you thinking, coming back here?" I hissed.

"You and I always wanted to see new places," he replied. "I wasn't going to let you have this adventure all alone."

"Are you sick?" I asked him. "Have you—felt anything wrong yet?"

"At this point, does it really matter?"

No, it didn't matter. Nor did it lessen the guilt already weighing on my shoulders.

"Eat these." Weevil took my hand and pressed into them some leaves. Just by their feel, I recognized them as thrushweed leaves. "I found a small patch by the river last night. They'll keep you from getting sick."

"I'm already sick." I pushed the leaves back at him. "You take them."

"Then they'll keep you from getting sicker. I already ate some, this morning. Now hurry, eat them while no one's looking."

I did. Most of our people enjoyed chewing on fresh thrushweed leaves, but I hadn't liked them since I was a young child. Still, I was sure they'd do me some good now.

The dock was already crowded with other sick persons, and no doubt all of them were wondering the same question as Weevil asked aloud: "How do we get out to the boats?"

He was immediately answered by a warden who raised a pistol and said, "Anyone who is not in the water by the time I count to ten will be shot. One!"

Della turned. "My father, Sir Willoughby, is arranging with Governor Felling for me to stay here. I've told you a hundred times already, I'm not supposed to go on those boats."

"Stay if you want," the warden said. "I have enough rounds for you and anyone else who thinks they're too good for the Colony. Two!"

That was enough for Della, who jumped into the water and began swimming for the boats. Others still on the dock seemed to be less certain about which was worse—attempting to make the swim while fighting their pain, or facing the pistol.

I marched over to the warden. "You have the rope. Pull the boats closer to the dock!"

"We have our reasons."

"But those people could drown!"

He smiled wickedly. "Then you'd better get in to save them. Three!"

And he pushed me into the water.

CHAPTER
THIRTEEN

The old legends say that the River People came from the union of a mermaid who had swum too far inland and a handsome young farmer who rescued her. Though I didn't put much faith in most of the old stories, I believed this one. It explained why I had a singing voice that made people want to drown themselves. It also explained why all River People were excellent swimmers.

But none of that protected me from the foot pushing down on my head every time I tried coming up for air. Whoever was kicking me, they probably didn't even realize it. Their legs were thrashing around so wildly that I wondered if they were fighting just to stay at the water's surface.

Eventually, I swam far enough away that I could come up. I first looked for Weevil, who was already clinging to one of the boats, helping some other Scourge victims get inside.

Della was already in the boat farthest from the shore. The silk ribbons on her pretty dress, I noticed, were ruined.

Perhaps if she had been less concerned about them before, she wouldn't have been here right now.

A woman behind me screamed for help, and then her voice gargled in the water. Ignoring the dizziness in my own head, I swerved around and noticed her sinking beneath the surface. I dove for her and heard Weevil calling behind me that he was coming too.

She was one of those who had looked sickest while standing on the docks, and she was bent over in the water as if the swim had sharpened her pain. She kicked me hard as she tried to get to the surface, reigniting my own aches. I gasped too, swallowing a mouthful of water, then raised my head to get more air.

Weevil had one of her arms now, which he wrapped over his shoulder, and I took the other. We raised the woman to the surface and, as she calmed down, helped her float on her back. That position would be less painful, at least for me.

By then, the rest of the victims had climbed into the boats, and the only spot available was in the farthest boat, where Della was still alone. Little surprise. After her stand-off attitude on the shore, I understood why no one else would want to share a boat with her. I still reserved the right to dislike her the most.

Della stood as we swam closer. "Look how sick that woman is! She'll make me worse!"

"The other boats are full," Weevil said.

"Ignore her," I muttered.

I gripped the side of the boat, but the woman we were helping was too weak to lift herself into it. Della made it even harder by shifting her weight to the opposite end of the boat, preventing us from tilting it down for the woman.

"I refuse to ride with grubs, or with people too sick to swim!"

I'd had enough. "Have it your way," I said. Then I pushed my end of the boat up, toppling Della back into the water. If she had been able to swim here once, she could swim back again.

The people on the other boats laughed and there was even some applause, but Weevil only frowned at me. "This isn't the place for that," he scolded.

"She deserved it," I told him.

"She's sick too," Weevil said. "She's scared."

Maybe she was, but if anything, sickness had only made her more selfish than before. So I didn't feel any guilt, or at least, not that much. When the boat rocked back toward us, we were able to tilt it down enough to let the woman slide in. She sank to the floor of the boat, unable to even sit on the benches.

"Thank you," she whispered.

Della's head popped up over the side of the boat, though her face was so red I wondered if she'd swum through a patch of dye while underwater.

"My flask of medicine fell off my neck," she screeched at me. "That's your fault, Ani!"

"Has anything in the last day *not* been my fault?" I countered. "Add this to your list against me."

"There is a list," Della said. "And I will get revenge for every single thing on it."

"Let's just get in the boat," Weevil said. "The others are ready to go."

He helped me in and then climbed in himself while Della rolled in from the other side. As she had said, the flask was gone from around her neck. She began eyeing my flask, as if staring increased her chances of getting it. A part of me sympathized with her plight. I knew how valuable the medicine was and how awful the pain that was coming for her if she didn't get more.

Yet Weevil hadn't been given any medicine, and sickness seemed inevitable for him now. If I gave any medicine to Della, I wouldn't have enough to share with him. So I put my hand on my flask, just as a reassurance that she would not take it from me. Weevil and I needed it too.

Oars were in the boat to help us row toward the island. Although we were all attached to the rope, that only prevented us from getting pulled out to sea by the strong currents or from some desperate victim taking their boat in another direction in an attempt to escape. I took one oar, and Weevil took the other. Della nestled into a spot near the front of the boat and turned her back to us, which was about the best thing I could've hoped for. The woman we had saved was still on the floor of the boat. She had already taken a sip of her medicine. She'd feel better soon.

While we rowed, Weevil began whistling a cheery tune. Every time he hit one of the higher notes, Della shuddered, as if his song caused her pain. For my part, I rather liked it. With the whistling, our fate didn't seem nearly as awful. Some of the people in the boats behind us picked up the same tune, and with that came more chatter and even a little laughing.

Except for Della. She turned around a couple of times, and at first I thought she was glaring at us. But that wasn't it. Tears were running down her cheeks, reminding me again that for all her rudeness and superiority, she was terrified.

When we were about halfway across, the woman in the center of our boat managed to prop herself upright on a bench. Her face was still pale, and she was clinging on to the wood slat as if it were life itself, but at least she was facing the right direction.

"You saved my life," she whispered.

Weevil stopped whistling long enough to say, "You'd have done the same for us, if you weren't busy drowning."

She smiled briefly, and then said, "I *will* do the same for you. My name is Marjorie. Listen, I've heard things, I know things . . ."

"And I know you," Della said. "You're a server at a filthy tavern. You don't know anything."

Marjorie swallowed, looking as if even that caused her pain. I wondered if she was naturally a sickly person, or if not, then how long it would be before I felt as bad as she did. Turning farther away from Della and with a quieter voice, Marjorie said, "I serve drinks to the wardens, both those in Keldan and those who come over from the island. The things they say about the Colony, the things they know, some of it sounds terrible. From what I've heard, you don't want to stay in the old prison."

"Where are we supposed to stay?" Weevil asked.

"I don't know. I don't understand everything they talk about. Most of it makes little sense. I only knew I walked away from them with that warning: Stay anywhere else."

"I can't stay elsewhere," Della said, as if the conversation had been about her. "My father will come for me on the island. He'll look for me in the old prison."

That wasn't possible. Surely she knew that. I bit my lip, and now I did feel the smallest hint of compassion for her. Shaking my head, I said, "When I was in the physician's examination room, your father came in, trying to persuade the governor to let you go."

"You're lying," Della said. "The governor doesn't sit in for Scourge tests, especially not for a grub! My father never would've gone in there!"

My fists clenched, but I took another breath and said, "Why would I lie about this? He did come in, and he tried to get you back, but the governor refused him and threatened to bring in the rest of your family for testing if he didn't leave. He had no choice, Della—he had to let you go. But he asked me to tell you that he loves you."

Loves. Not loved. I couldn't say it to her exactly as her father had done.

Della scooted back in the boat until she sat directly beside Marjorie, facing me. Tears had welled in her eyes again, but her expression was so full of fury, I knew the tears were a sign of her rage, more than of her pain.

To Marjorie, she said, "A friend of mine was sent to the Colony three weeks ago. He was a worker in town about my age, named Jonas Orden. Did you happen to overhear anything about him? Anyone who mentioned his name?"

"I'm sorry." Marjorie shook her head. "Perhaps he will be there to greet you when you arrive."

Della's spine stiffened. "Yes, and then when my father comes, he will take us both back home again, and he will find a way to cure me."

Weevil and I looked at each other. Della, friends with a worker? I couldn't understand that.

She leaned toward me now with a frosty glare, adding, "And then you will pay for your lies!" *That* Della, I understood.

"Move back," Weevil said more forcefully. "Della, move back to where you were, away from Ani. If you don't, my oar might slip out of my hand and accidentally spank you out of this boat. I'm very clumsy, and my accidental spanks are really quite hard."

Della's glare went from him to me and even to Marjorie before she returned to the front of the boat, where she refused to turn around again for the rest of the journey.

I should have been angry with her. She had caused me nothing but trouble, and even worse trouble was no doubt on the way. And yet, as I searched myself for the proper word for the emotion I felt, it wasn't anger. If anything, it was pity.

For the first time in my life, I truly felt sorry for a pinchworm.

No, not a pinchworm. I felt sorry for Della.

CHAPTER
FOURTEEN

The old prison loomed even greater as we neared Attic Island. The battlements that had once surrounded it were mostly rubble now. Yet the prison itself seemed no less foreboding for their loss. The thick stone walls had been gray once, but time had blackened them. Any trees that might've been there before were long ago chopped down, perhaps to prevent their use as weapons by invading armies. *What invading armies?* I thought. No one had ever stepped foot on this island who wasn't forced to be here. The prison looked more like the ancient fortress it once was than a place to hold criminals. We were neither invaders nor criminals, but it was home now.

The rope to which our boats were attached ended at a wood post, while a fair depth of water still remained below us. I had only barely dried out from my last swim, and I certainly didn't feel up to another one, but there was nothing else to do. Weevil and I splashed into the water first, then helped Marjorie get safely to shore. She whispered her thanks and promised to repay the service somehow.

Della had gone directly to land. And though I hadn't cared about getting there first, once I arrived on land too, I realized I might've made a mistake. Because Della was at the end of a conversation with the warden waiting for us on the shore, who was glaring at me as if I'd done something wrong. I already didn't like him—oily black hair stuck out from beneath his hat. If I were the governor of Keldan, I'd have sent him here too, as far away as possible.

As I approached, the warden asked Della, "Is this the girl who pushed you out of the boat?"

The sneer on her face was so triumphant I wanted to slap it off. But it was obvious I was in enough trouble already. Slapping wouldn't be the best way to prove I didn't start fights. "She wouldn't let us lift a Scourge victim into the boat," I said.

"Any Scourge victim who can't get into the boat would probably be better off just drowning," he replied.

Thus the reason for the boats departing and leaving in deep water, I guessed. To get rid of the weakest people first. I already hated this place.

"My flask of medicine was lost," Della added. "If it had been a mistake, I wouldn't be complaining now, but this grub meant to do it."

The warden frowned at me. "Is this true?"

The problem was that yes, technically it was true. Even if Della had deserved what happened, that didn't excuse the fact that I had absolutely intended for her to fall into the water. I hadn't wanted her to lose her medicine, though. No more than I wanted to lose mine. I grabbed hold of my flask, hoping the punishment for what I'd done wasn't being forced to give it to her.

So I nodded, but added, "Would it matter if I tell you that she is a genuinely horrible person? Literally, the worst person I've ever met?" That might've been an exaggeration, but not a big one, and I figured it might help my argument.

"No," he said. "It does not matter."

"Where can I get more medicine?" Della asked. "The ride over in the boat was so difficult, I'm already feeling pain again."

"Was it truly difficult, the way you sat there doing nothing?" I asked.

"There is no more medicine," the warden said. "You were warned to take care of what you were given." Then he turned to me. "What is your name, grub?"

"Ani Mells."

He humphed, then called out to the other newcomers, "Everyone report to the food tent at the top of the hill. You'll be given instructions for your new life here, for as long as you have it. Accept what is required of you, and you will be provided with food and shelter in your end days."

I started forward with the others, but the warden put a

hand on my shoulder and held me back. His hand felt just as oily as his hair looked. "Not you."

"I haven't eaten since yesterday morning," I said. "If you want to punish me for what happened in the water, that's fine, but could you do it after I've eaten?"

He only frowned. "Follow me."

I glanced back at Della as I followed the warden. She was gloating over her victory and telling everyone around her that I deserved whatever was coming for me next. Maybe she was right about that, because if I were in that water with her again, I'd do exactly the same thing as before.

I looked at Weevil next. He'd been standing near Marjorie until she obeyed the orders to go to the food tent. I knew the determined expression on his face now. The last time I'd seen it, he and I had ended up repairing a big hole in Farmer Adderson's barn roof. It turned out my parents were right—gunpowder was not a toy. To be fair, we had expected a much smaller explosion.

Now Weevil took a deep breath, then suddenly charged at Della, picking her up and throwing her over his shoulder and walking with her toward the water. She screamed and began pounding his back with her fists, but he was strong enough to keep control of her.

The warden turned and yelled, "You, grub—put her down!"

"Yes, sir," Weevil said, and dropped Della into the water.

He brushed his hands together as he turned around, then walked back up the beach and faced the warden directly. "I've heard that there are consequences for dumping Della Willoughby into the water."

"This is why we never wanted grubs in the Colony. Your people take a delight in causing trouble—that's how you all are. I tried to warn the governor." The warden sighed. "You'll both come with me, then."

"What were you thinking?" I hissed at Weevil as he walked.

"Did you see how angry she was?" he said, glancing back at Della, who had just climbed onto the shore again.

"Of course she was angry. You shouldn't have done that!"

"Yes, I should have." He took my hand, and this time there were pieces of dried meat in his hand. I couldn't imagine where he had borrowed them from, but I wasn't about to ask. His other hand was in the pocket of his trousers. I also noticed for the first time that his pockets appeared to be full.

I slipped the meat into my skirt pocket, surprised to find a few wheat kernels there. Bothered by that discovery, I withdrew the meat and kept it in my fist instead, eating the pieces as quickly as I could. It wasn't a lot, but in that moment, it was enough. Weevil had given me more than a little food. He gave me hope and friendship, and maybe the feeling that in the end, everything would be all right.

Once I was finished, I took his hand again and gave it a squeeze. Wherever we were going, I'd try my best to lighten the burden of Weevil's punishment. I owed him that much. But I also knew full well that nothing I could do would ever repay what he had just done for me.

CHAPTER
FIFTEEN

We followed the warden past the old prison on our right and saw the food tent even farther away. But instead of going there, which I'd have been perfectly happy to do, we entered a large yard that had been cordoned off by a split log fence. Other than a few crates that probably contained supplies for the care of the people here at the Colony, the area was empty.

Thin grasses were scattered around the yard, but otherwise nothing meaningful was growing here except for a single vinefruit tree, which must've been transplanted here years ago. They weren't native to anywhere but river country, and most townsfolk considered them hugely oversized weeds. I immediately wanted a vinefruit, though they were all out of reach. The meat had taken the edge off my hunger, but it had also whetted my appetite for something more. A swallow of medicine perhaps. It felt like a hecklebird was pecking at my head.

Hanging high in the tree was what could only be described as a round wooden cage, one that'd barely be large enough for me, a painful proposition for Weevil, and an impossible fit for the both of us. It couldn't be our intended punishment.

The warden pointed to two worn dirt spots on the ground and said to each of us, "Stand there, facing each other."

Weevil and I did as we were told. We weren't far apart, but still wouldn't be able to touch even if we had both reached forward. While we exchanged quizzical looks, the warden went over to a crate and opened it, withdrawing a long, stiff rod.

Now the punishment was becoming clear, and I didn't like it one bit.

If I had groveled at Della's feet and begged forgiveness for existing, perhaps Weevil and I could've avoided this fate. It might've saved us from being struck with that rod. Yet even to avoid punishment, I was not that girl. I hated the idea of having to beg, from Della, or from anyone.

"If this is the punishment, they don't know River People," Weevil muttered to me as the warden walked back toward us.

River People were strong, that was true, but this didn't feel like a test of strength. At least, not physical strength. Was my heart equally strong?

The warden stood between us with the rod balanced in his hands. I tried not to look at it, and instead kept my eyes locked on him, daring him to find any fear in my expression.

Truly, though I was nervous for him to raise that rod against me and Weevil, that wasn't my biggest problem. More concerning was the growing pain inside my gut to accompany the ache in my head. I didn't want to take any medicine yet—once it was gone, there'd be no more—but the way I felt now, I knew I wouldn't make it to the end of this day before I gave in and took another sip.

The warden said, "There are very few wardens here at the Colony. You can understand why—it's difficult to get men as stupid as me who will work with the diseased." He had looked at Weevil when he said that, which I thought was entirely unfair, since Weevil was probably the least sick of anyone on this island. Then I thought of what the governor had said, that the River People *were* the Scourge of Keldan. Maybe the warden also thought of Weevil as a disease, just because of who he was and where he was from. The warden continued. "Therefore, the responsibility for keeping order largely falls on the sick to take care of themselves. Here at the Colony, you work for the benefit of others and then accept their work for your own good. Do you understand?"

I nodded. Not only did I understand, this was the way the River People functioned. Nobody had very much, so the only way any of us survived was if we helped one another.

Weevil's family was the exception amongst us. After his father was lost on the exploration, and with so many siblings to take care of, Weevil's mother felt there was little her family could do to contribute equally. It was a foolish pride, but a pride Weevil shared too. So after refusing the help of the River People, Weevil did what he could for his family, but it was never enough.

Finally, under the warden's glare, Weevil nodded too.

"Good," the warden said. "There is one other rule here in the Colony, and that is respect. You are not free people anymore; you cannot think of yourselves that way."

"Is getting sick a crime now?" I asked. "We're no better than the prisoners who used to be here?" Of course we weren't any better. We would even be housed in the prison. All that we lacked were their chains.

"You are servants of the healthy citizens of Keldan. It is your duty to keep the disease away from them and see that Keldan succeeds."

"I'm not a servant," I said. "I'm a free person who happens to be sick. Every last bit of strength in me will go to getting better, not serving a country that has pushed my people farther away each year."

He stepped toward me. "If the River People really are free, then how have we pushed you away?"

That was something I had not considered. Were we free? My people had been known by many names over our existence, all of them signifying rejection by our own countrymen. We built temporary homes on land we could not own, paid higher prices in pinchworm markets after earning half their salaries, and when the wardens came and said it was time to move into even higher country, we went.

Weevil's father wasn't free, certainly, nor the other River People who had been forced onto the governor's expedition.

The wardens had come to us a year and a half ago, asking for three volunteers for a voyage into the northern seas in search of resources for Keldan. Their pleas were met with silence. Weevil's father stepped forward and said he had been there before, and that if we thought the storms that collected around Attic Island were bad, it was nothing compared to what happened farther north.

"The River People will not join your voyage," he had told the wardens. "Collect your volunteers amongst the townsfolk."

That speech had sealed his fate, my parents later explained. Weevil's father was taken from his home by force late that night, while his family tried to stop the wardens. Weevil had shown up at my door the following morning with a swollen eye, bruised lip, and a broken heart. It didn't matter how hard he had fought for his father. He only cared that he had failed.

"If I'd been stronger," he had said to me. "Or if any of the River People had come to help us, this wouldn't have happened."

"We didn't know," I had replied. "We thought the

wardens had left the river country, or we'd have come. But we'll help you now."

"You won't," Weevil had said. "I failed my father. I'll take care of my family now. I owe him that much."

If only Weevil knew how they survived. He would be stripped of his pride and his honor. It would devastate him.

The warden continued. "Part of your duties as a servant of Keldan is to respect the other people here. You will not harm them, not for any reason."

"Della wasn't harmed when she fell into the water," I protested. "She was already wet, so I didn't even do that much to her. And for that matter, she deserved it."

The warden's mouth tightened. "Hold out your hand, Ani. Palm up."

I licked my lips and did as he said. Behind him, Weevil had shifted his position so that he could see me. I knew Weevil's mind was working, but this punishment wasn't his to prevent. What I'd done to Della was my own fault. I didn't know how many times the warden intended to strike my hand with that rod, but I wouldn't make a sound when he did. I wouldn't give him that satisfaction.

The warden raised the rod, and Weevil cried out, "Wait! Do that to me instead. Not her."

The warden turned, lifting an eyebrow as if amused. "Don't worry, grub, you'll get your punishment next."

"I know that," Weevil said. "But I want hers first."

"No," I said. "The only reason you're even on this island is because of me. I'll take the full punishment for you."

The warden smiled. "There's no need for either of you to worry. I'll give you both as many strikes of the rod as you can stand."

"Stop!" a man called. "I know these two. The rod is not enough."

We turned to see Warden Gossel hurrying toward us. Seeing him again left the same taste as a mouthful of mud. The bottoms of his trousers were still wet, so he could not have arrived long before us, though he had obviously gotten here on another boat. A real boat that went all the way to the shore.

The warden holding the rod acknowledged him with a slight tilt of his head, so I knew Gossel was the superior officer. But Gossel was also here as punishment of his own. If Gossel had disliked us before, getting sent here because of us would hardly make things better.

"These two were just competing for who should take the other's punishment," the warden said.

"Oh?" Gossel held out his hand for the rod and then curtly dismissed the other warden. Once he'd left, Gossel nodded at us. "I'm surprised to see such honor amongst grubs. But here in the Colony, you must live by a different set of rules. There is no room for such foolish loyalties here."

"Friendship is not foolish," I said.

Gossel stepped closer to me. "Here, it is. There is only so much medicine to go around. You'll have limited food, limited beds. There are ways to keep yourself alive a little longer." He glanced at Weevil. "But not if you're always looking out for someone else first. Before you can join the others, I will have to break the friendship out of you."

Weevil and I looked at each other. "You can try, but you won't succeed," he said. "Nothing can break a true friendship."

I believed that. I also believed that Weevil had always been the truest friend to me, perfectly loyal and good. But that didn't mean our friendship was perfect. If Gossel found the flaws, he could worm in between them and divide us.

"We'll see," Gossel said, turning the rod in his hands. "Here is how this works. If you truly want the other's punishment, then you must earn it. Whoever can prove him—or *her*self—to be the worse friend will receive the full punishment. The other one is free to leave." He looked from me over to Weevil. "So who is the worst between you?"

I immediately thought of the way the River People talked about me and Weevil. Everyone knew he was the better person and, thus, the better friend. I knew the truth of that better than anyone. It wouldn't take long before that was obvious to the warden too.

I spoke first. "I'm the worse friend, sir. And I can prove it."

Weevil immediately reacted to my words, jumping in with, "I want the whole punishment. Let her go free."

Gossel arched a brow. "The first point is against you, grub. A sacrifice like that only proves you are a better friend."

I should have taken that hint and said if Weevil wanted the whole punishment, then he should get it. That would've proven I was the worse friend and, ironically, set him free. But I couldn't say it, because a part of me feared that if I agreed with Weevil, Gossel would still punish him, and maybe worse than just the rod. Did Gossel know what the governor had ordered for Weevil? I couldn't risk it.

So instead I said, "I am worse. A few months ago, Weevil was diving in the river for clams and ended up with a fish bite right on his nose. It swelled up to the size of his fist for two days. I couldn't help but laugh every time I saw him."

Weevil smiled at the memory. I'd left out of the story how hard Weevil had laughed at himself. We had joked that if the swelling never went down, his snoring would become the new worst sound in the world. But in hindsight, I shouldn't have laughed. The swelling had probably hurt more than I'd realized at the time.

"I'm the worse friend," Weevil said. "I make fun of Ani's singing every chance I get. You have no idea how bad it is, how it drives you to wish you were deaf, just to get away from it. A better friend would overlook her singing, but I never do."

He always did. Whether Gossel knew it or not, Weevil was proving again how great he was to me. Of course he teased me about my singing. Everyone else just covered their ears and tried to ignore me. I loved that he would tell me the truth and make me laugh about it at the same time.

"I'm much worse than that," I said. "My family has more food than his. There are only three of us, so it's easier to provide for ourselves. He has five younger brothers and sisters and no father in his home. Yet I never share from our table. Ever."

"I've never asked you to share, or wanted what you have," Weevil said, directly to me. "Even if you tried to share your food, we'd never accept it."

How well I knew that.

"Anyway, I can still do worse," Weevil continued. "There was this one day, a couple of weeks ago, when you looked really pretty. Not just pretty, but beautiful, like the angels in the heavens must look. I should've told you. That's the kind of things girls like to hear, right?"

"I don't care about that," I whispered. But I knew exactly which day he meant. I had dressed up in my very best to go down into Windywood to sing. He had caught me unexpectedly. Even if he'd wanted to compliment my looks, there had been no chance for it before I hurried him out the door. I didn't want him to know where I was going. I still didn't want him to know.

"I never tell you those things," Weevil said. "Such as how much I admire the person you are, your strength and your courage to do anything you believe is right. I used to think I wouldn't say those things because it might embarrass you. But that's not it. I don't say those things because it'd embarrass me. That's not a good friend."

"I don't say them to you either," I said. "And that never matters *because* we're friends. We already know that about each other."

"You seem to be a very good friend," Gossel said to me. "But when all is laid open, is he an equal friend back?"

"I'm not," Weevil said. "The other night, when we escaped the cell, I wasn't far away when Warden Brogg recaptured you. I would've helped if I could, but there was nothing I could do. A good friend would never have left you alone in that cell."

"I hoped you would go back home," I said. "I didn't

want you back in that cell with me, and certainly didn't want you here now. I wish you had not come back."

And at the same time, it was my greatest wish to never have to be here without him.

"The decision is made, then," Gossel said to me. "You are the better friend because you had hoped to spare him from the Colony." He turned to Weevil. "Raise your hand, grub, palm out."

I had hoped our game wouldn't get this far, but it had. I whispered, "I did want to spare him." Now tears formed in my eyes. "I am the worse friend. I said I can prove it, and I will."

I reached into the pocket of my dress and pulled out the few wet wheat kernels that were in the bottom, the ones I'd discovered when Weevil had given me the dried meat strips.

Weevil shook his head. "It's just wheat. What is that supposed to prove?"

"Your mother makes poor man's bread for your family every day," I said. "Where does she get the wheat?"

"We buy it."

"Who buys it? From where?"

Weevil tilted his head, confused. "We have money. I work hard every day, and I catch fish in the river whenever I can. My mother sews for the River People, and sends my sisters to the market for salt and eggs and—"

"Not wheat," I said. "They never buy wheat. It's too expensive in the river country."

Weevil's eyes darted away, then came back to me. "Your family has nothing either."

"I have no brothers and sisters. We don't need as much."

He shifted his balance on the ground, clearly uncomfortable. "We had an agreement, Ani. Whatever we found as we fished or hunted, we would keep for our own families. That kept everything fair and equal."

"It was never fair and equal." The first tear fell on my cheek. "Never."

"You took home your fish, just as I took home mine." Then his eyes locked on the wheat again. It was something, obviously, that we never fished for, never hunted for, something we never even gathered. Wheat could not grow in the river country. It only grew in the lowlands. "Where did you get that?"

"I told you that I had to be home with my family each evening," I said. "That wasn't true. Each evening I went into the town and sang. With the coins I earned, I bought wheat for both of our families. I left a jar of it outside your mother's window each night. She never knew it was me."

Weevil's expression had stiffened. "How long has this been going on?"

"Since a few weeks after your father was taken away on that ship."

His hands had formed into fists now, and his face had reddened. "You were giving us food, when you needed it too? We were your charity, your duty to the needy family?"

"You were my friend. You *are* my friend. Your family needed this wheat!"

He yelled, "How dare you? The day my father left, it became *my* duty to take care of my family. Not yours!"

I'd never seen him so angry, and he'd never been angry at all with me. But I wasn't angry when I yelled back at him, only frightened. "You were doing your best, but it wasn't enough!"

"Who made you the judge of what's enough for my family?" he asked.

"Your mother was becoming too thin," I said. "Did you notice that she wasn't eating at suppertime? There wasn't enough food, not until I brought the wheat."

"And when you were at my home and we offered you the bread from our table, did you secretly gloat over the fact that you were the one who had really given it to us?"

"Never!" I said. "Wouldn't you have done the same for me, if my family had needed help?"

"I would've respected our agreement, or if I was giving you food, then I'd have been honest about helping you."

"If I had said anything, you never would've accepted it. You won't accept help from our people because your family can't give back. I know you were doing your best, but your best could not keep them alive. You needed my help, even if you didn't want it."

"Thank you, then," Weevil said stiffly. "Thank you for taking care of my family. Obviously, I couldn't."

"And so you are the better friend," Gossel said to me. "You are saving him and his family."

Weevil remained silent and only continued staring at me, utterly wounded. This was exactly how I knew he'd react.

"I just took away his pride," I said. "And if that is not bad enough, I can do even worse. There is only one way I could have gotten this sickness, and that is from the coins the townspeople paid me each night for singing. One of the coins that dropped into my jar must have come from a Scourge victim. When I picked it up, I got the disease too. Then, along with the wheat, I brought that back to my best friend." Tears filled my eyes. "I'm so sorry about that, Weevil. It's my fault you're here, my fault that you will eventually get this disease too. I am sorry for breaking our promise. But I am not sorry for my reasons for doing it. I couldn't go to sleep every night with a full stomach, knowing you were only a few houses away and slowly starving to death."

"Then you saved me from that death," Weevil said, shrugging. "And gave me this death instead."

Silence fell between us. Then Gossel said, "We're done here. Ani, you are the worse friend. Weevil, you may go."

CHAPTER
SEVENTEEN

When he was dismissed, Weevil didn't move. He was scuffing his foot against the ground and looking anywhere but at me.

"Leave," Gossel ordered him.

"I won't," Weevil said, though he still would not look up.

Gossel grabbed my arm and pulled me to his side. "Leave, or I'll double her punishment."

"Double my punishment," Weevil said. "I want it."

I didn't care about whatever Gossel would do to me. The sting on my palm would pass quickly enough. I cared that Weevil looked so broken, and because of me. That sting, the one in my heart, might never fade.

"If you are still here when I count to five, this rod will strike elsewhere than her hand."

"Go, Weevil," I said. "We played his game. I won."

And I lost.

"One," the warden said, raising the rod again.

Now Weevil looked at me, but said to the warden, "If you really want to punish her, then let her see me be hit with that rod. Look at how she's hurting now, and that's only after words between us. Make her watch if you must, but give it to me."

"Two."

"Go," I told him. He was right about what he said. I'd much rather take the punishment than see it happen to him.

"Three."

Weevil mouthed something, but it was too soft for me to hear.

"Four." He raised the rod higher.

"Listen to me, sir. I want her punishment."

The warden's hand tightened around my arm. "Five."

"I want you to leave!" I yelled at Weevil. "I broke my promise to you, I lied to you, every single night. It's my fault you're here, my fault you'll get the Scourge." I choked back a full sob. "My fault you're going to die. Just leave!"

The warden stared at Weevil. "Stay here and I promise that it will only get worse for her. Now what will you do?"

Weevil nodded at me and stepped back to leave the yard. I was so sad by then, and in so much pain from the disease spreading through my body, that my legs collapsed beneath me. The warden released my arm, which I used to wrap around my aching side. If I were smart, I would eat the wheat kernels still in my other hand. Now that they were wet, it wouldn't be long before they were ruined.

Yet, I couldn't eat them, so I merely dropped them onto the ground and held up my palm. "Get it over with," I said.

Gossel's voice was calm. "The rod was never going to be the punishment. The punishment was ending your friendship." He pointed to the wooden cage high in the tree. "You're going to stay in there until tomorrow, high enough that everyone in the Colony can see what happens to those who defy our rules."

Other men appeared in the yard, not wardens, but Scourge victims. I could tell because of their common clothing and the medicine flasks hanging from their necks. They untied a rope to lower the cage to the ground, and then one man stuck a key into a lock to open the door. It was the only metal piece of the cage, nothing I'd be able to break, even if I were feeling in perfect health.

I didn't get to my feet, not yet. And it wasn't because I was afraid to go into the cage—I didn't care about that. It's because I had decided for sure to take another sip of medicine. Not much, I knew I had to preserve it, but enough to take the edge off the pain. So I unscrewed the cap and took a swallow. More than I should have swallowed perhaps, but not nearly all I wanted.

Once I got the cap on, Gossel reached down and snatched it from my hand. "No medicine while you're in the cage."

"What if I need it?" I asked.

"Then it will motivate you into better behavior once you're released." He crouched down beside me. "To survive the Colony, you must be broken. You're a grub, so maybe you think you can outlast me. But I've broken your friendship, and now I will break you, just as we do to everyone else here."

"I'm not like everyone else." Now I stood and squeezed into the cage, which was even smaller up close than it had seemed while dangling in the air. Then, just to make him angry, I said, "It's a lucky thing that nobody will feed me. One meal, and I might not have fit so comfortably."

He said, "If withholding meals makes you comfortable, I'm sure we can arrange to make your stay in the Colony very comfortable indeed."

"It's pinchworm food anyway," I said. "No taste to it."

Then the door shut in my face, and the men began hoisting my cage into the air. Other than being cramped inside, it wasn't the worst punishment. The tree gave me some shade, and the cool breeze was a welcome relief from the heat. It wouldn't be pleasant, but I could endure this.

Once I was in place, I became aware of the Scourge patients wandering the Colony, turning their eyes to me. Likely, word was already spreading throughout the camp about what I had done to Della. Hopefully, at least a few of those words were the truth about what had happened. If not, being in this cage was probably the best treatment I'd get here.

"Be good, and you'll be out by tomorrow," Gossel said.

Of course I'd be good. What other choice did I have? My mind was already swirling with possibilities. The knife was still in my boot, for example. If I cut the rope . . .

No, that was incredibly foolish. If I cut the rope, then the cage would fall.

"Where's my medicine?" I asked.

He draped the rope across a low-hanging branch. "Here, waiting for you. Try not to get any sicker."

Then he and the other men walked away, leaving me suspended in the aerial cage. I leaned my head against a thick wood bar and let the medicine work inside me. I wasn't sure how long it would last, but I figured if I remained calm, that would preserve its effects for a while longer.

Slowly, the pain eased, leaving me with only regret for what had happened with Weevil. Even after I'd hurt him, he still tried to take my punishment, and I knew his offer had been sincere.

I scanned the Colony for any sign of him. Had he gone inside the old prison to find a room? Had he gone to the beach to stare at the shoreline of Keldan, regretting his decision to come here with me? Well, of course he'd be regretting that right now. I just wondered where he was while he was regretting it.

Not here, that was certain. He wasn't here, beside me, making jokes, telling me everything would be all right, assuring me that I could fight this disease, just as I had fought everything else.

He wasn't here, so I would have to comfort myself. But no matter how I tried, I could never believe my own lies.

I'd always liked having Weevil for a friend. Indeed, he was one of the few people who seemed to understand me for the person I really was deep down.

Yes, I'd always liked Weevil for a friend. But now, I realized, I needed his friendship too. Only I realized that one conversation too late.

CHAPTER
EIGHTEEN

For the most part, I didn't mind the afternoon and evening in the cage. Yes, I was cramped and desperately needed to stretch my legs. The gnawing hunger within me was worse than ever, and I had yet to see Weevil anywhere. Thanks to the medicine, I was managing the pain all right, though it didn't take it away as well as it had done in Doctor Cresh's office.

I didn't care about the stares from the people on the ground, or at least I didn't mind the more sympathetic glances my way. I ignored the rest, and figured this was a rare opportunity to see the Colony from an angle few people ever would.

Unfortunately, I wasn't high enough to see past what I was calling the Colony's square, the main gathering area in front of the prison. Everyone seemed to pass through the square at one time or another, bustling about at whatever task they had been assigned. As the warden suggested, every Scourge victim did their part for the Colony. Many people worked in a large garden to the east, and several others seemed to be preparing food for the next meal, served under a wide tent. Six or seven men in an upper corner of the Colony were working behind a fence, walking a treadmill while other men fed wheat grains into the grinder below them to be ground into flour.

The treadmill caught my attention for some time. It was an incredible waste of energy. In the very same area, a river was flowing. Its current looked reasonably strong—I could see that from here. If they widened it enough for the entire treadmill to sit inside the water, the current would do most of the work in rotating the mill. That's how we did things in the river country.

Instead, they were using the far weaker human strength. The treadmill was a long, round tube with steps on all sides. As the men climbed it, the treadmill turned downward, forcing the men to step up again and again, like a never-ending stairway. Their work ground up the grains that had been fed inside the tube, but there were so many better ways to accomplish that. These were sick men, diseased men. It was wrong to make them do such difficult work, just to grind wheat.

Before long, I turned away. The wheat reminded me of Weevil.

As evening fell, I saw something that struck me as interesting. With the sound of a ringing bell from the food tent, most people headed that way. But not everyone. Some people disappeared behind the prison and never returned to eat.

That made no sense to me. I probably wouldn't have even noticed their disappearance if I had been on the ground. But here, it was a curious thing. Maybe the Scourge left people without an appetite.

I frowned at that, wondering exactly how sick Weevil would have to get before he wasn't hungry anymore. As far as I could tell, he didn't go to the food tent either. It bothered me that he had disappeared so completely. Was he already sick too?

If that wasn't bad enough, I heard a caw to my left and saw a hecklebird headed straight for me. Miserable creatures—they were on this island too? I wanted to reach for my knife, but if I could see so many people, then all those people could see me as well, and this wasn't the moment when I wanted my knife revealed. So I hissed at the bird that pecked back at me, for no reason other than that I was there. If only the wooden bars of this cage were wider apart, I could reach through them and strangle that thing.

I finally shooed it away and, in doing so, rotated my cage to the opposite direction, with my back toward the Colony. I liked it better this way, where I didn't have to look at the passersby staring up at me. I didn't want either their sympathy or their judgment.

When I turned, I saw another building to the south that was more curious than anything else. It was only a single story tall but wide and unfriendly looking. Nothing decorated the building, or softened its sharp, square corners. The river that had meandered around the treadmill came near one corner of the building, though it was narrower there. As I watched, a warden escorted a middle-aged man inside. The man was holding his side as if in pain and didn't look particularly happy about going to the building. Minutes later, only the warden went out. Perhaps the building was a sort of resting place for the sickest ones or those closest to death.

I was so intent on studying the building that I failed to notice someone had entered the fenced yard beneath me. I might not have noticed, in fact, if the intruder had not tripped in the lower light of evening.

At first I couldn't see who it was because the cage didn't allow me to change positions enough to look down. But I recognized the voice immediately.

"This is your own fault, you know." It was Della, come to gloat. "You could have avoided all this trouble."

"Are you sure of that?" I called to her. "Because I tried my best to avoid you, and it didn't work."

Her voice rose in pitch. "The problem with grubs is you don't know your place. Well, now you do."

"Has your father come for you yet?" I asked. "Didn't you say he'd be here to get you? Or what about your friend Jonas? Is he still here? Maybe he heard you were coming and dove into the sea to escape you."

There was a long pause, so I knew I'd hit a nerve. Finally, she said, "This is only our first day here. I'll find Jonas soon. And my father will probably come tomorrow."

If her father came, it'd only be after he also tested positive for the Scourge. I had a feeling that the governor would love any excuse to send Sir Willoughby away from Keldan. Besides, if Della had the disease, her father probably did too.

Which led me to another thought, of whether I should expect to see my family here soon. If Della could spread it to her family, then I could've spread it to mine. And if they pulled in my family, then the wardens would start to look at who my parents had associated with over the last few weeks, and bring them in as well. Della had already warned of this. My name would become known as the girl who destroyed the River People. As the one who did far more damage to them than the governor and her wardens ever could.

"Did you come here expecting that I would apologize?" I asked. "If so, then I'm glad because I do need to tell you how sorry I am. I'm sorry I tried to help you the other night. I'm sorry you got back in our boat after I dumped you out of it. And I'm sorry you came all this way to see me, because it was for nothing."

She chuckled. "I wouldn't forgive you, even if you gave me a real apology. Because if I forgave you, then I'd feel bad about getting my revenge."

"More revenge?" I asked. "I'm already in this cage, so if I deserved any punishment, I'm getting it. And what happened was your fault anyway."

"As you say, the wardens are already punishing you for

dumping me into the water. But you do need to learn some respect for who I am."

"Really?" I said. "Because I think I understand you far too well."

"I have a special status in Keldan. My father is—"

"We're not in Keldan anymore. We're in the Scourge Colony. And here, you are alone, just like me. You have a terrible disease, just like me. And this disease will probably kill you."

"Just like you?" she asked.

I smiled down at her. "No, that won't be at all like me. I intend to recover."

"Nobody recovers from the Scourge."

"What if it's true, that my people started the Scourge three hundred years ago? We didn't die from it then, and we won't die from it now!"

"It's a different disease now," Della said. "My father told me that the symptoms are so much worse than what are in the old records. And you have no medicine this time."

"Yes, I do."

Or did I? Suddenly, I understood why Della had come.

I twisted around enough to look down and saw her pouring the medicine out of my flask and into another flask. She must've stolen it, because hers was somewhere in the not-so-shallow part of the Scuttle Sea.

"Where'd you get that flask, Della?"

She shrugged indifferently. "An old woman in the room next to mine is getting very sick. It's only a matter of time. I took her flask before someone else did."

"Was there any medicine in it?"

"A little, but I need more."

"There's a shortage! You should save as much as you can."

"There's no shortage for me, not anymore."

By then, she had finished emptying my flask and sealed up the container, letting it fall back against the tree. She took a swallow of her flask—filled with my medicine—making sure I saw it.

"I'll stop the pain before it comes back," she said. "That'll keep my body strong enough to fight off this disease."

I grabbed the bars of the cage, wishing I had enough strength to break them. "That medicine is mine!"

"It would've remained yours too, if my medicine wasn't fish food right now." With that, she skipped out of the yard below me. Literally skipped, as if she didn't have a care in the world.

I wished I could say the same. Because with the knowledge that I no longer had any medicine to fight off this disease, the pain in my gut suddenly returned. Worse than ever.

CHAPTER
NINETEEN

The Colonists had long settled in for the night before I fell asleep. I'd learned from watching the people that a curfew was strictly enforced, though the wardens didn't need to be strict. The people worked hard all day—very hard—and seemed almost grateful to be ordered into the prison for a night's rest.

As I drifted off, I wondered what awaited them inside the old prison. It couldn't be anything that nice, certainly not the place of peace the governor had assured us of in her many speeches.

In those speeches, she never mentioned that the sick were shoved into the water, without care for who could swim or who was too ill to get themselves into a boat. She never discussed Scourge victims having to labor for their own welfare or being punished by hanging them in a wooden cage for public scorn. When she described the shepherds who offered love to the victims, she might've forgotten that church volunteers didn't carry pistols and wear the cocked hats of the wardens. Somehow, between praising herself for her compassion and expressing love for everyone in Keldan but the River People, she'd left all those things out.

Those were the last thoughts in my head as I fell asleep that night. It had been too warm in the day, but now, without the sun, the sea breeze sent a chill right through me. I'd even sneezed a couple of times and smiled at the irony that I'd probably catch my death of the cold before the Scourge got me.

At first, I thought the sounds I heard next were only part of my dreams, so it took a while to pull my senses together. Everything around me had become very dark, though thanks to the stars, it didn't take long for my eyes to adjust. I was glad to see the stars. It meant there'd be no rain tonight, which was a possibility I had dreaded.

But there—the sounds came again. The groan of a branch beneath someone's weight. I was not alone in this tree!

That worried me. If anyone released the knot for this cage, I'd go crashing to the ground with no way to slow the fall. Maybe Della had returned, this time with a far deadlier revenge than simply stealing my medicine. I couldn't imagine she was capable of that, but someone had their reasons for coming up here.

I felt for the knife hidden inside my boot, but was too cramped now to get it out. If I had been smart, I'd have found a way to get it out earlier. Of course, I couldn't have predicted someone would break curfew to climb a tree in total darkness to rob a person who had nothing to her name.

While I struggled to get the knife out of my boot, I also faced the problem of the sea breeze that, with occasional gusts, rotated my cage. It was doing that now, sending me slowly spinning to my right, and then the rope correcting itself to spin to the left. I was already dizzy and now unable to get a fix on whoever was climbing this tree.

I closed my eyes to let the dizziness melt away, then opened them and saw a face staring back at me. My first instinct was to scream. The face came closer, revealing Weevil's bright eyes, glowing in the starlight.

"Shh," he said, pressing a finger to his lips.

Suppressing a squeal of happiness, I clutched at the bars. "What are you doing here?"

"I just happened to be in the area."

"But I thought . . . the wheat . . ."

He sighed. "You kept my family from starvation, Ani. If that makes you a terrible friend, then you must promise to continue being terrible."

"What good are any promises after I lied to you? I promised never to share our food with you, and began ignoring that promise the very next night."

The corner of his mouth turned up. "Well, that's a relief! Had you broken your promise the same night, that would be unforgiveable. It's a good thing you waited a whole day."

"I'm serious, Weevil!"

"So am I." Now his eyes met mine. "You said it yourself. Sometimes friendship is doing what's right for a person, even if it's not what they want." He grabbed the bars to keep my cage from rotating away from him. "Earlier today, I began thinking about a time eight or nine months ago when we were fishing. There was something you wanted to tell me. Was this it?"

I nodded. That day was perfectly clear in my memories. "I started to tell you about the wheat, but then you interrupted with a story about a woman upriver who had brought your mother a meat pie and how that upset you. That was only one meat pie, Weevil, just given as neighborly kindness. I knew how angry you'd be if I finished my story."

"I would've been angry—that's true."

"I tried to tell you other times too. I did try."

"I know, and I'm sorry for being so stupid at times. I owe you more than I can ever repay."

"You owe me nothing. When you get the Scourge, it'll be my fault. That's much worse."

"But I don't have it yet, so until then, you're the better friend." His brows pressed together. "I know the warden never used the rod. But how are you feeling?"

It was hard to think of the right word to describe the pain inside me. It wasn't as severe as it had first been in the doctor's office, but overall, I could feel myself getting weaker. Thanks to Della, there was no way to make it better now.

My eyes darted to the right while I searched for what to say, and as it turned out, he didn't need an answer. Weevil reached into his pocket and pulled out a few more thrush-weed leaves. "It's all I have left, but they'll spoil by tomorrow anyway."

I pushed them back at him. "You need them too. Besides, you already gave me some."

"You need more." He crouched closer to the cage. "Let me pay you back for the wheat. Let me be your friend, as much as you are mine."

I stared at him a moment before taking the leaves and putting them into my mouth. I still didn't like the taste, but there was a chance they might help with the pain.

While I chewed the leaves, Weevil withdrew the lock-picking needles that had been stuck in the fabric of his pants.

I shook my head. "They'll expect to find me here in the morning. If I escape, I doubt there's anywhere to hide on this island."

Because of the darkness, it took him several tries with the lock before he found the place to stick the first needle in.

"You can go back into the cage at dawn, but that's hours away. You need a better place to rest."

His second needle went into the lock, and within seconds, the shackle popped apart. I waited for him to safely scoot back along his branch before I opened the cage door, and then he held my hand to guide me onto the branch with him.

"Are we climbing down?" I asked.

"Actually, I thought we could go a little higher. It'll be hard to avoid the thorns below, and there won't be many higher up. Besides, there's a nice branch above us that looks comfortable enough. No hecklebird nests—I checked!"

I gave his hand a squeeze. "Let's go!"

Weevil led the way, carefully explaining where to put my hands and feet. I'd climbed plenty of trees in my life, though never in so much darkness or with the pains that still twisted my side into knots. I should've been more nervous, but I wasn't. Not with Weevil as a guide.

We didn't have far to climb before he announced we were there and asked me to sit. The branch was sturdy and didn't protest under our combined weight. It also formed a sort of hollow where it joined with the tree's trunk. Weevil settled into that hollow, and I sat beside him. When I did, he reached into a satchel around his side and pulled out a couple of bread rolls.

"Are you hungry?" he asked.

I snatched the first one out of his hand and inhaled it without saying a word. I was two bites into the second before I mumbled a "thank you."

"Your manners have gotten terrible since leaving home," Weevil said in a fake stern voice. "I hope you won't turn out as bad as all the other River People."

"I intend to be worse," I said, finishing the roll. He then produced a sugar apple. It was small and a little soft, probably left over from last fall's harvest, but I didn't complain a bit. I ate the whole thing, core and all. River People never wasted anything.

With that, I told him I was full and suddenly sleepy.

"Rest against me," Weevil said. "If you fall asleep, I'll keep you in this tree."

I leaned against him, but more than feeling tired, I was relieved to have my friend back. No, not back. He'd never stopped being my friend. It was me who had stopped believing in him.

"Why did you come with me to the Colony?" I asked. "You were free."

Weevil pondered that a moment, then said, "When we're apart too long, everything starts to look sideways, as if the whole world has shifted. It hasn't, of course, but then I realize that I'm the one who's walking crooked. You balance me, Ani."

An ache poked at my side, as it had all night, but I smiled anyway. "Do you suppose Della Willoughby has any friends? Whenever I saw her today, she was alone."

He gave a low whistle. "We could balance her, I think."

"That's not why I was asking. I won't be her friend."

"Someone has to. I don't think she's as bad as she seems. I saw her earlier, bringing food to a few people too sick to get it for themselves. She's just scared, Ani. She needs a friend."

"No, Weevil."

"But—"

"Hush!"

I leaned forward and crept farther out on the branch. Weevil cautioned me to be careful, but I told him to hush again. Somewhere to the south of us was the sound of movement. A lot of movement.

I couldn't understand it. Everyone was supposed to be in by sundown—I'd seen the wardens hurry the Colonists back into the prison. Who was out there in the darkness?

CHAPTER
TWENTY

Weevil joined me out on the branch, and for the first time, it creaked. I barely took notice of it, though. My attention was too heavily focused on the sounds to the south of us. If only it were a little less dark. Not enough for us to be seen, but just so that we could see what was going on down there.

I guessed that the noises were near the building I had seen to the south—the one that people entered but only wardens exited. Perhaps it was wardens out there now, but what were they doing?

I wanted to climb up higher, where I hoped I'd be better able to see, but the ache in my side had spread now, sending throbbing pulses to the tips of my fingers and toes. My balance was less steady than when I had first climbed out on this branch, though I wouldn't tell Weevil. I didn't want him to know how bad it was getting for me. I didn't want him to think about how bad it would get for him too, eventually.

"We won't see anything while it's this dark," I said. "Let's go back and try looking again when it's lighter."

Weevil followed my cue and scooted back first. He took his place in the hollow, but when I went to sit beside him, a wave of dizziness hit me.

"Careful!" He grabbed my arm and steadied me, then let me lean against him and put his arms on either side of me.

I closed my eyes and let him do the work of ensuring I didn't fall. "Thank you," I mumbled.

"I saw your flask of medicine at the base of the tree," he said. "If you can keep from tipping over, I'll go down and get it for you."

"It's empty," I said.

Weevil squeezed on my arm. "It's already gone? There's a shortage—"

"It was stolen while I was in the cage. By that girl you think we need to befriend."

"Della? But she—"

"May the gods help me, Weevil, if you defend her for stealing my medicine, I will sing to you, or something worse."

"There is nothing worse." He leaned his chin against my shoulder. "Listen, she lost her medicine because of you. Maybe she started this fight, and maybe she deserved it, but you did dump her into the water."

"And I could dump you out of this tree!" I smiled when I said it. Of course I'd never hurt him, but I still didn't want him making excuses for *her*. No matter how wrong they sometimes seemed, my actions were defensible. Not hers.

He chuckled and squeezed my arm again. "You River People, always putting up a fight."

That reminded me of something the governor had said while I was in the physician's office. She had said that the River People had promised not to cause any trouble in Keldan, and then we'd broken that promise.

I told Weevil that, and then asked, "Do you know what she was talking about? Has there been an uprising? Because if so, no one invited me."

He shrugged. "No one invited any of the River People." He drew in a breath. "Unless she's talking about an incident a few weeks ago. Your father traveled to Elmdale for some reason, and when he went into the market, they threw him out, saying the River People's money was no good. He was so angry he tossed a stool at the window, shattering it. That wasn't an uprising, but I'm sure the governor heard about it."

By then, my heart had stopped cold in my chest—and considering that I was a Scourge victim, that could almost be taken literally.

"They accept my coins in the market—they figure it's one way of getting back their money. My father didn't know how they'd treat him." I sat up, ignoring the dizziness that washed over me. "I remember that night. I'd been down in the towns, singing. It was late, and my father had become worried so he went looking for me."

Weevil reached for my arm and brought me back to the center of the branch. "Relax, Ani."

"I will not relax! Don't you see? The governor thinks the River People are involved in an uprising, but my father only went into town because of me. All of this is my fault!"

"It's not your fault!" Weevil said. "Your father shattered that window, not you. And maybe the governor meant something else entirely. Keldan has never respected our people. If they want reasons to blame us, they'll find them."

"Why do they hate us so much?" I mumbled.

"Because they don't know us, and we don't know them," he said. "It's easy to hate what you don't understand."

I considered that a moment, and then a harsh reality hit me, like a slap across the face. As sick as I felt with the Scourge, the tightening of my throat and clench of my hands right now was not a result of this illness. It was knowing that recovering from the Scourge was only the smallest part of surviving the Colony.

I fully intended to get better from this disease . . . somehow. And if Weevil was sick by then, I'd figure out a way to help him get better too. Afterward, we'd have to find a way to leave this island, something no other Scourge victim had yet done.

For that, we'd need the help of a pinchworm. And not just any regular townsfolk. We'd need the help of someone with an influential father who was powerful enough to stand up to the governor herself.

We needed Della.

Just at the thought of it, a sour taste filled my mouth, but I swallowed it, just as I'd have to swallow my pride in order to escape this island. "I hate to say this, Weevil, but you were right before. Somehow we've got to make Della Willoughby our friend."

CHAPTER
TWENTY-ONE

I slept for most of the night after that, though I doubted Weevil even closed his eyes. Every time I awoke, he was there with his arms around me, keeping me safely in the tree. Most River People thought I was the stronger one in our friendship, but that wasn't true. Weevil was always stronger than me.

Normally, I would have at least tried to stay awake, but without the medicine, I was hurting more than I wanted to let on. Based on my constant squirming, I'm sure he knew, and he was obviously worried, but there was nothing he could do except let me sleep.

I did feel a little better once I woke up. My side was still burning, and it felt like someone was using my forehead for a drum. But the dizziness was better, which was a good thing, since dawn was coming fast and I needed to make it back to the cage before anyone realized I'd cheated on my punishment.

When he saw I was awake, Weevil didn't ask how I was

feeling, something I appreciated. Instead, he said, "It's about time you woke up. You snore."

"No, I don't!" I countered.

He chuckled. "Well then, perhaps you were singing in your sleep. It sounds about the same."

I sat up and from out of nowhere, Weevil produced a vinefruit for me. He must've plucked it while we were on the outer branch last night. Before taking it, I eyed him. "Where's yours?"

He shrugged. "I'll eat as soon as I get down from this tree. I'm not sure when they'll let you out."

So I took the vinefruit and bit into it, making sure not to drip juice on myself this time. That'd be hard to explain to Warden Gossel when he returned for me. Vinefruit were always delicious, but never more so than this morning.

While I ate, Weevil stared off into the distance, lost in his thoughts. Finally, he said, "I admit that when you told me about the wheat yesterday, I wasn't sure how to react. All this time, I thought I was doing better for my family than I actually was. One of the last things my father said to me before he left was that I was responsible for my family now. He trusted me, and I let him down."

"Your father would be proud of you! Nobody could've done more than you've done for your family."

"I needed your help, even if I didn't know it before." Weevil shrugged. "It should be me in the cage, not you."

"Stop this," I said. "It shouldn't be either of us in that cage. The truth is that I was always going to be punished because of what I did to Della—all the rest was just Gossel's game for his own entertainment. He told me they want to break us, that they have to break everyone here in the Colony."

"Then the best thing is to make them think you're broken," Weevil said. "We have to stay out of trouble."

My smile turned mischievous as I glanced back at him. "Now when have you ever known me to stay out of trouble?"

In return, he only frowned at me. "You should try it, for once. There's a building south of us, probably where we heard all that movement last night. It's called the infirmary, though from what I've heard, nobody who goes in there is ever seen again. You keep getting in trouble, and that's where you'll end up."

"I'm still curious about those noises we heard."

"No you're not, and it'd be best if you forget you ever heard them. Listen, people will be waking up soon. You need to get back in that cage before you're spotted."

With the little available light, it was easier to stand on the branch, holding on to higher limbs for balance. My legs were shaky when I first stood. The Scourge must have moved into the muscles there too, but I was steadier than when I'd scooted along the branch earlier.

I turned southward, in the direction of last night's mystery sounds. Everything in that direction was quiet. But from this height, I was able to see behind the infirmary where a tall fence was made of posts dug into the ground and lashed together. The fence was probably left over from when Attic Island served as a prison. Maybe the prisoners were sometimes allowed to wander, just as we moved about here in the Colony. That fence was apparently the line nobody was supposed to cross. So from which side of the wall had I heard all that movement? And who was making it?

From that very moment, I knew that all I really wanted was to get behind the fence. My curiosity nagged at me like an itch, one I knew I'd eventually be forced to acknowledge. I decided not to tell Weevil, though. He had interpreted my silence as agreement.

Weevil helped me back into the cage, and though I hated being cramped up again, the truth was the short climb here had put a fierce pain in my gut, so even if I had all the space in Keldan, I'd still be curled up somewhere in a ball. For all it mattered, I might as well be in the cage.

He apologized as he shut the cage door, and I didn't answer. I wanted to. I needed to thank him for risking so much to give me a better night, and for bringing me food, and for giving up a night of sleep. But my teeth were gritted together so tight that I couldn't say a word, and I hoped he understood.

"I'll be waiting when they bring you down," he said.

I nodded and waved him away. He needed to get out of the tree before he was seen. And before he could see the tears forming in my eyes. It was cruel for Della to have taken my medicine.

And cruel for me to have refused to offer any medicine to her, after I had been responsible for the loss of her flask. This was probably exactly how she had felt on the boat ride over here, in pain but with no one offering sympathy, and with no hope of things getting easier. Meanwhile, I had sat almost right next to her with a full flask of medicine, indifferent about offering her even a sip. No, *determined* not to offer her help of any kind. In many ways, I was no better than she.

It was only minutes later when the Colony began to awaken. Della was one of the last to leave the prison and looked worse than I felt, which was no small accomplishment considering that my insides were knotting themselves into ever tightening loops. The medicine was doing her no good. Or maybe even harming her, if she was drinking too much of it. Even the River People's mild herbs could be dangerous if we took too much.

This was going to become a problem. If I wanted to become her friend—which I didn't, by the way—the truest act of friendship was to take that medicine away and control its dosage for her. But if I did that, she would hate me even more, and then I'd have no choice but to do something unkind back, earning her revenge. Also a deadly cycle.

It was another few hours before Warden Gossel returned for me, along with two other men, to lower my cage. Once it was on the ground, he crouched beside me and checked the door to be sure it was locked.

"Were you in here all night?" he asked.

I nodded up at the tree. "I was up there, yes, sir." That was truthful enough.

"Most people start crying after the sun goes down," he said, then muttered something under his breath about River People. A compliment, I thought.

I smiled at that. We had the reputation of being stronger than the townsfolk, but maybe we weren't. Maybe we just didn't follow the same rules. Because if I had remained in the cage, I probably would've done worse than just cry to get out.

He helped me from the cage, and though I was unsteady on my feet at first, I realized that I felt better than I had earlier that morning. I still had some pain, of course, but less than before.

"You've been given a job assignment," he said. "Laundry. You'll be responsible for collecting used linens from the old prison and bringing them to the wash." His eyes narrowed. "Do grubs know about washing, or do you all just stand in the river to get clean?"

"Actually, we avoid cleanliness," I replied. "Our smell keeps you pinchworms away."

He smiled, though it instantly darkened. "With that attitude, I bet you don't last a week here, grub."

"You're pronouncing that word wrong," I said. "It's not 'grub'; it's 'Ani.' Hear the difference?"

"No." Gossel had roughly the same sense of humor as a cornered snake. None.

"I'm not as sick as when I got here," I said. "I intend to get over the Scourge."

"Nobody gets over the Scourge," he said. "Not when they understand how bad it really is."

I turned on my heel to walk away from him. "Pinchworms might not get better. But River People do."

Weevil was waiting for me right outside the gate. "Why is your face so flushed?" Then he added, "You were arguing with that warden, weren't you?"

"He started it."

"I doubt that. Here, take this." He handed me some flapjacks. They were cold and slightly burnt, but I didn't care. "Don't miss any more meals, all right? It's getting harder to steal for you."

I nudged his side. "When we get home, I promise not to tell everyone how good you're getting at stealing and sneaking around. They'll think I've corrupted you."

"You corrupted me a long time ago." His smile was mischievous, but he didn't nudge me back. He was probably worried about how sick I might still feel. "Now come on. Let's put some distance between us and that cage."

I followed Weevil toward the Colony's square. "Where are we going?"

"We need to find rooms. I waited to claim some until you were out."

"In the boats, Marjorie warned against staying in the old prison."

"Where else would we go? Besides, the wardens were very clear that everyone was to stay in there. The upper floors are quieter, but since they're farther up, it's harder to get help as the sickness worsens."

"I'm going to get better," I said. "We can take an upper floor."

"Don't take any floor," someone behind us said.

We turned and saw Marjorie staring at us. Although she looked just as ill as when I'd first helped her into the boat, at least she was standing, so the medicine had to be helping a little.

"Don't take any room, on any floor," she repeated. "I am warning you. If you want to survive this place, do not go to the old prison."

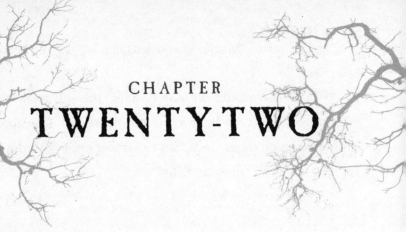

CHAPTER
TWENTY-TWO

Questions immediately rushed through my mind, so many that I didn't know where to start.

Why shouldn't we stay in the prison? Where else were we supposed to live?

Would the wardens allow us to stay elsewhere? I doubted that.

I wondered again what was wrong with the prison. Were there rats the size of pigs but with larger teeth? Big gaping holes in the floor? Or too much disease, crowded into one place?

And most important, did Marjorie know a better way to survive?

In cases like this, Weevil had a talent for summarizing. He whispered, "Tell us everything."

Marjorie motioned us away from the prison and over to a clearing past the food tent. Then we stood facing north. Marjorie said, "As soon as I got here yesterday, I started asking around, to see if anyone knew a place to live other than the prison. I met a woman at suppertime, and I'll tell you what she told me. There's no way to go south on this island. Past the infirmary is a tall fence that used to keep the prison inmates trapped here."

"I know about that," I said. "I saw it last night."

"You saw that from the cage?" Marjorie asked. "I didn't think you were up that high."

Weevil looked like he wanted to give me a kick right then, just to stop me from saying anything more. However, Marjorie was clearly breaking rules by telling us her story. She'd hardly turn us in for hinting that we had already broken rules too.

Marjorie shrugged and continued. "The shoreline to the north is harsh, with sharp rocks and a lot of wind. But there is also a cave, almost impossible to see until you're right on top of it. If we go inside deeply enough, then the cave walls will protect us from the winds and we can even build a fire for warmth. The smoke from the fire simply gets sucked out to sea. The caves do flood every afternoon and evening, but we're working during the day and eating in the evening, so it's easy to miss those waters. When I went to the caves, I found other people living there too. They are much healthier than those in the prison. Some claim they've even been cured. Maybe it's the salt water, or maybe the prison's air is too infested with the Scourge, but the caves are your best chance to survive."

"The wardens don't mind?" I asked.

"The wardens don't know, and we want to keep it that way. We have to be careful coming and going, and we do as we're told so that we never draw their attention."

"Why not?" Weevil asked.

Marjorie nodded in the direction of the infirmary. "Get the attention of the wardens, and you're likely to disappear from the Colony. They say only the sickest people go into the infirmary, the ones that need extra care, but from what I saw yesterday, that isn't always true."

"And nobody comes out again," I said. "I heard that too."

This time, Weevil did give me a light kick, which wasn't fair. He was the one who had told me that.

"Do your chores for the day and then have your supper," she said. "When it starts to get dark, find a way to casually slip away from the group. But be careful, because if you're caught, the cave dwellers will be a bigger problem to you than the wardens could ever be. They were very clear about that when I met them last night. They will not accept mistakes that risk giving away their secret."

Weevil and I nodded, and then we all headed back toward the Colony square. As we walked, I said to Weevil, "What is your assigned job?"

"I'm a gatherer," he said. "They know River People are good with herbs and plants, so I'm assigned to find some of the ingredients they use in making the medicines. Most of them are familiar, but there's one I don't know—

spindlewill—so it'll be tricky to find it at first. But I'm glad to have the job. The more ingredients I find, the more medicine they can make. I'm hoping to get access to where it's made so you can have some."

I liked that idea. Though I was feeling better at the moment, that was really only in comparison to the fact that death had me in its clutches last night. As long as nothing got worse, I could manage this. Then I could get to the caves and figure out what those who claimed to be healthy were doing. I wished I had my medicine back.

"Come with me," Marjorie said. "I was assigned to work in the laundry too, though I do the washing. You'll be collecting it."

Weevil went in one direction, and Marjorie and I went toward the prison again. "Collect any dirty laundry from the prison rooms," she said. "A large bin should be just inside the prison's entryway, on the main floor. You'll carry the linens down from the upper floors and load them into the bin, then roll it outside for us to wash."

"Sounds like fun," I said, in a tone that suggested this job would be anything but fun.

Marjorie missed the sarcasm. "Be careful in the rooms with those too sick to leave their beds. Their linens are sure to be infested, and that can't be healthy for you."

She left me there, to enter the prison on my own. Staring at the entrance, I fought the urge to run. It felt like walking into a nightmare, dark and full of unexpected monsters that would leave a person shaking in their bed. Perhaps it wouldn't actually be that bad, nor did I believe in monsters. Or at least, I was in serious doubt of their existence. But in the moment, that's how it felt.

I took one step in, clutching at the door's frame as a wave of nausea flooded over me. Right inside the door was the collecting bin, large enough to hold a grown man, though that was hardly its purpose. As I looked around, I realized this was as far into the prison as I ever wanted to go.

A set of narrow steps was to the left of the entry. They'd be barely wide enough for my father's shoulders if he ever came here. I closed my eyes and shook my head. No, my father would never come here. I'd submitted to Doctor Cresh's second test so that they wouldn't have to test my father. He was not sick.

Not sick . . . yet. I'd exposed him to the Scourge. And my mother, and countless others. I had to prove it was possible to recover from this, for them.

Looking ahead, the main floor had a low, heavy roof, just as I was sure every other floor had. Rows of cells were on either end of a long dark hallway lit by a single oil lamp at the far end. At least the bars that had once defined this place as a prison were gone and dim candlelight in the rooms flickered through empty doorways.

Much as I already hated my work, this was what I'd been assigned. As Weevil said, our best plan was to not cause any further trouble. I knew myself too well to believe the plan would last for more than a day or two, but I had to be good for as long as possible. The fact was that my life now depended on me staying out of trouble. Every ounce of strength within me had to focus on getting better, and for that, I needed access to medicine, and rest, and food. None of that would come if I was back in the cage, getting pecked by hecklebirds.

I wasn't sure where to begin with the laundry. The collection bin wouldn't go up the stairs, so obviously I'd have to carry everything down. Start with the hardest part of the job; that was what my mother had always taught me.

So I made the climb to the top floor, up four flights of crumbling stairs. A small window was on each landing but they were all closed, making the air stuffy and thick. The odor was unbearable. Was this the smell of death? If I'd done nothing else but smell this place, I'd still have refused to stay here. More than ever, I missed the river country: the fresh, moist air and the scent of wildflowers in the fields where Weevil and I lay to dry off after every dive for fish.

Once I arrived on the fifth floor, I saw the long corridor of rooms that had once been prison cells. Without doors to replace the bars, there was no privacy, no shield between the very ill and those who still had some shred of their former strength. For that matter, there was no hope, no joy, and no sign of living. Everything was an awful shade of dirty gray.

I went into each room and gathered up any piles of linens in the corners of the room. Fortunately, there weren't many people staying on this floor, so there wasn't much to gather. I bound it all in my arms and went back down the stairs. About midway down, I almost tripped on a person sitting right in the middle of the stairs.

Della.

Naturally it was her. If anyone in this entire camp would be in a place to cause me to nearly trip and roll down three flights of stairs, it'd be Della.

I dropped the laundry and stood tall, ready to fight if that's what she wanted. She must've heard me coming and didn't move out of the way, which meant she was probably here deliberately.

Or not.

Della looked up to me, her face so pale and gaunt that her eyes looked like they'd shrunk in their sockets. "Help me, Ani. I can't do this. I'm going to die here."

CHAPTER
TWENTY-THREE

I eyed Della for a moment, waiting for whatever trap she was baiting me into. It wouldn't work. I intended to obey the Colony rules now, or at least, most of them. Besides that, I wanted to remain angry with Della, assuring myself that I had been right all along, that Weevil was naïve in expressing any sympathy for her, and that she truly was the most horrible creature ever to roam these lands. I tried to believe it, truly I did. But the longer I stared at her, the sorrier I felt. Maybe she was mean-spirited and rude, but maybe I was too, a little. And like Weevil had said, she was definitely scared. So was I. And maybe she was snobbish and self-centered and a lot of other things I absolutely wasn't, for the most part. But whatever Della was, somewhere in the world, there had to be at least one person who was worse than her.

Even if she was the worst, I still needed her help to escape this island. So I sat down beside Della and took her hand in mine. "You are *not* going to die in this place, do you understand me? Last night I felt the very same way—so sick that every part of me hurt. But I'm a little better today. You just have to keep going and let the symptoms pass."

"They do, when I take the medicine," Della said. "I'm taking too much—I know I am. I'll run out in only another day or two, but I can't help it. Nothing else works."

"Give it to me," I said, holding out my hand for the flask. "I promise to let you have a sip when you really need it, but we must make it last until you're better."

She sniffed. "You think I can get better?"

"I'm feeling better today." I smiled and looked sideways at her. "Surely if I can do this, then so can you."

Her hand was still tight around her flask. "You promise I can still have this when I need it? Even after I took it from you?"

"River People have many faults," I said. "We fight over things that don't matter and back down from the fights that do matter. We work too hard and somehow still produce too little, and frankly, some of us don't bathe often enough. But we never break our promises."

She unscrewed the lid and started to take a drink from it. I went to grab it from her but she said, "This is my first sip today." She quickly took a drink, though it was hardly a sip, and then handed me the flask, which I put back around my neck.

The smell of the medicine wafted up at me, awakening the aches inside me. I wanted a sip too but couldn't take any after I had just begged the flask away from Della. She'd say

I had stolen it from her, accuse me before the wardens, who'd surely believe a pinchworm over a grub, and I'd spend another day back in the cage. Maybe I'd sneak a sip this afternoon when she wasn't looking.

While the medicine did its work, I asked Della, "What job have they assigned you?"

"The worst," she said. "Cleaning out the rooms of those who've been taken to the infirmary. Getting their rooms ready for newcomers to the Colony."

I wrinkled my nose. That was a terrible job. In comparison, gathering the laundry seemed like picking flowers. It also confirmed my suspicion that those who entered the infirmary never left it.

Della said, "There's more bad news. My friend Jonas isn't anywhere in the Colony, not anymore. When I asked about him, only a few people knew his name, and those who did said they hadn't seen him since a few days after he first arrived. One man works as an assistant to the wardens and said the wardens probably brought Jonas into the infirmary."

It was likely a place to take those who were about to die so that nobody in the Colony had to see their deaths. Upset like that could create a constant panic here. Perhaps it was better to have quiet disappearances. Out of sight, out of mind.

"I'm sorry." When she was first telling me about Jonas, I'd barely cared to listen. In fact, a part of me had doubted he even existed, because how could this girl have any friend who wasn't imaginary? But when I told her I was sorry, suddenly I was. If I heard Weevil had been taken to the infirmary, it would destroy me.

She sniffed. "We'll all end up in the infirmary, sooner or later. It's just a matter of time."

I started to tell her what Marjorie had said about the caves. More than anything, Della needed hope right now, and knowing there were people who claimed to have been healed of the Scourge would mean everything to her. However, the caves weren't my secret to share. Just as I had promised Della to return her medicine, I had promised Marjorie not to tell anyone about the caves.

I did make one more promise in that moment, a silent one this time. I promised myself never to go into the infirmary. Never.

I stood and held out a hand for Della to get to her feet also. "Here's my idea. If you help me gather the laundry, I'll help you clean out those rooms. It shouldn't matter to anyone if we share our work, as long as it gets done."

Della eyed my hand with suspicion. "Why would you help me? You've been horrible to me, and I've been almost as bad back."

I briefly considered arguing the subtle moral differences between what we had done to each other, but then remembered I might need this girl's help to escape. Also, I remembered that I was trying to be her friend. It felt like hugging a hecklebird.

So I shrugged that off. "I'm not helping you, and you're not helping me. We're sharing the work. Besides, no matter how we've behaved to each other, I'm not a horrible person, and I don't think you are either."

"I didn't used to be," she said. "And I don't want to be anymore."

She took my hand and stood, then helped me carry the laundry down the stairs. That tired her out, so we decided to stay on the main floor and collect laundry there. I let her wheel the bin while I gathered linens from the rooms.

Della showed me how the rooms designated for her to clean were marked in chalk with an X. "The X means—"

"I know what the X means," I said, drawing in a deep breath. "Let's get this over with."

The rooms were already bare of any personal possessions. Most of the people who came to the Colony had brought nothing with them, and those who did took what little they had with them into the infirmary. While I cleared the laundry from the room, Della emptied the chamber pots and straightened up. Then, after blowing out the candles, we erased the X and moved on.

We did the same on the second floor, though this time both of us had to make multiple trips down the stairs to finish our jobs. It helped that the rooms were empty, with everyone out in the Colony doing the jobs to which they had been assigned.

Well, all of them were empty except for one. An older woman lay on her prison bed, which was really just a square of concrete raised off the ground. She had a single blanket and no pillow. Della was already in there when I walked in, so I backed up and stayed in the doorway.

When she saw me, Della whispered, "What do we do?"

I shrugged. "Nothing can save her."

"Failing to help a needy person is as bad as causing the need in the first place," Della said. "My father taught me that."

I thought back to our boat ride here and felt a stab of guilt. I had caused Della's need for medicine and then failed to help her. A double crime.

The woman groaned, and Della said, "Ani, I need my medicine."

I grabbed the flask with one hand, ensuring she couldn't get it. "You've had some today."

Della picked up a dropped flask from off the floor and shook it. There was nothing inside. "I've had some. But she hasn't."

So I lifted it from my shoulders again and returned it to Della, who immediately gave the poor woman a sip. I watched that, wondering if Della had reached a delirious stage of her sickness, one that made her believe she was a kind and compassionate girl?

Or had I been delirious, thinking all along that she was more horrid than she ever actually was? While on the stairs, she had tried to tell me she wasn't as terrible as I thought. I'd figured that was the kind of thing terrible people said to make themselves feel better. Maybe she was speaking the truth.

Once we finished climbing to the third floor, Della leaned her head against the wall. "Don't you feel sick anymore?"

I did, but less sick than I would've expected. River People were stronger than the townsfolk, so this was clearly my determination paying off. Although in some ways, I was beginning to think maybe the townsfolk had their strengths too.

Taking in her pale, trembling form, I said, "You wait here. I'll take care of this floor."

When I came back with the first load, Della had pushed the window on the landing wide open. She glanced back at me and smiled. "There's more than one way to get laundry downstairs."

I shared her smile and immediately pushed the laundry through the window. It fell in a scattered pile in front of the entrance to the prison, right where I could pick it up before delivering it to Marjorie. Perfect!

With renewed energy, Della helped me again to gather the laundry, simply for the fun of pushing it out the window. By the time I had the first load gathered, the window was already open.

"Let's do the entire floor at once!" she proposed.

That sounded good to me, so we collected everything into a large clump, and then worked together to push all the laundry out at once. It fell in a giant pile, billowing down the sides of the prison walls—

"Arrrgh!"

—and directly onto the head of a warden who had wandered over to figure out what a large pile of laundry was doing in front of the prison.

Once he had pulled everything off his head and arms, he pointed up at us. "Whoever did this, stay right where you are! I'm coming to get you!"

The total time I had been able to stay out of trouble: one hour.

Almost a record for me.

CHAPTER
TWENTY-FOUR

G o find a room to clean out," I said to Della. "Quickly. Go!"

Della shook her head. "The window was my idea."

"But it's my job, so either way I'll get the blame. You don't have to get it too."

Della nodded and hurried away. I decided the best chance I had of avoiding a second night in the cage was to be as straightforward as possible. At least, that strategy had always worked when I was in trouble with my parents.

As soon as the warden was in front of me on the stairs, I lowered my head.

"I didn't see you there, sir, I'm sorry."

"Laundry is to be carried down the stairs, not thrown out the windows where it can scatter all over the dirt."

No, we wouldn't want to get the dirt on the dirty laundry. But I only said, "Of course not, sir."

That stopped him for a minute. Obviously he hadn't expected me to agree with him so easily.

"Whose idea was this?"

I saw Della peek around the corner of the room she was in. Quickly, I said, "My idea, sir. I did it alone."

"I thought I heard giggling."

Now Della disappeared into her room. "It was only me laughing," I said. "There's no one else." To prove it, I tried giggling. It didn't sound at all like Della's higher-pitched laugh, and irritated the warden.

The warden shoved me against the wall nearest to the window. "Would you like it if I treated you the same way you just treated that laundry?"

I tried calculating in my mind how much we'd thrown out the window. Would it be enough to cushion me if necessary? No, probably not.

"I won't do it again . . . sir." It annoyed me to lower my eyes and curb the edge in my voice, but fake humility was better than really being tossed out the window. "If you let me go, I'll get it all gathered up and delivered for washing."

He loosened his hold. "You will, and tomorrow you will be assigned different work, harder work. Clearly, you are not fit for laundry service. And as punishment, you will miss the evening meal tonight."

That was better news than it could have been. Besides, I had yet to get food from the tent, so another meal shouldn't make much difference.

"Yes, sir." Hopefully, no argument meant no further punishment.

I followed him down the stairs and immediately gathered up all the laundry I'd thrown out the window. Regardless of what he'd said, I still thought throwing it out the windows had been a fine idea. Walking the individual loads downstairs would've taken far more time and cost me valuable energy. It was like the treadmill I'd seen last night—extra work expended for no good reason.

After delivering the laundry to be washed, I decided to explore the Colony on my own and, with a little luck, bump into Weevil along the way. I didn't know what job I'd be assigned tomorrow, but if it was harder, then I figured I should enjoy today the best I could.

Northwest of the old prison were the garden and stables for a few dozen chickens and four miserable-looking cows. I didn't stay there long, mostly because I figured the workers there would ask for help. Nor did I go any farther north. Regardless of what I might find along the way, the caves were somewhere in that direction, and I didn't want to accidentally lead anyone there.

So I moved south, briefly looking around the fence at the treadmill where men were still exhausting themselves with the relentless climb. I wanted to stop and tell the nearby warden about my idea to have water move the treadmill instead. It would probably grind the wheat better because water didn't wear out like muscles, and would preserve the health of these men. But I didn't say anything. I was already in enough trouble.

I didn't want Weevil to learn I'd lost my supper again. He'd try to split his food in half, like he'd no doubt done for the last two meals. Not this next one, that was only for him. I'd eat tomorrow.

I passed the fenced yard and noticed there was no one in the cage today. That seemed like both good news and bad. Bad because it would've been comforting to know I wasn't the only person here who struggled with rules. And good, because if anyone had nearly entered that cage tonight, it was me.

I didn't want to get too close to the infirmary either, so instead I went as far east as possible, almost to the beach. As I walked, I passed barracks that were probably for the wardens and several other supply tents. Maybe some of them held food, a possibility I certainly would have investigated if I were not determined to avoid trouble.

So I slipped past the buildings and tents, all the way to the tall fence posts on the south end of the Colony. They were thick and bound together by wide leather straps. Not even a fly could squeeze between them. They extended out from the beach into the water, beyond where a person could reasonably swim. From the beach, I could see Keldan off in the distance, including some of the homes near the beach there. Yet even in perfect health, I couldn't make it across. These were rough waters. Still, looking at Keldan made me miss my home too much, so I decided not to return to the beach until I was cured and in possession of a boat to take me home.

From the beach, I followed the fence inland, knowing full well I shouldn't be here—although no wardens had warned me away, it seemed perfectly obvious. Curiosity burned within me for what could possibly be on the other side of this fence. Maybe it was nothing in particular. This was a leftover fence from when the island had been a prison, and obviously the prisoners had needed some sort of border.

If anything was on that side, it was likely just barren countryside, and perhaps graves for the people who had already been lost to the Scourge. In fact, the more I thought about it, the more that made sense. That's probably what Weevil and I had heard last night—wardens out digging grave sites. Those souls lost to the Scourge had to be buried somewhere. If that was the case, then maybe I didn't want to cross this fence anymore.

As I continued to walk inland, I saw a deep river that ran beneath the fence posts, its current coming in from the other side. I dipped my hand into the river, testing the waters. The current was strong enough that it'd be difficult to get beneath the fence this way. Difficult, but not impossible. If I ever changed my mind and decided to cross the fence, this was my way out.

But not today. Not when I'd have to explain how I had gotten so wet. Then I'd be in far more trouble than the loss of a meal.

Instead, I had to wait until I wouldn't be caught. Or

when I was already in so much trouble that testing myself against a strong river was better than remaining here.

On my way back to the Colony square, somewhere ahead I heard the crunching of footsteps on gravel and ducked behind a tree. From there, I saw the warden who had caught me with the laundry earlier. He turned into the barracks, forgetting to close the door behind him. The familiar voice of Warden Gossel greeted him with, "What are you doing here so early?"

"I'm taking a break. That grub girl is still causing problems. We should send her to the infirmary today."

Gossel mumbled his sympathies, then added, "I'd have taken her directly there if I could have, but that goes against orders. Governor Felling is clear about who goes to the infirmary. No one goes for misbehavior. Rule breakers are our problem."

"Well, we've never had a grub here before. If the governor is sending us grubs, then our rules have to change."

"That boy who came with her hasn't been a problem."

No, I thought. That's because Weevil is more clever than I am about getting caught. If anything, since coming here he had done far more wrong than I had.

"The boy isn't even sick, no matter how hard he tries to pretend when we're watching. Who let him come over in the first place?"

"Doesn't matter," Gossel said. "He'll end up in the infirmary too, probably sooner than the girl. They all do."

They laughed at that, which made the hairs of my arms bristle. Obviously, the longer he was here, the more likely Weevil would get sick. But for Warden Gossel to be so callous about sending people to a place they'd never leave—sending them to their deaths—that angered me.

"Listen," Gossel continued, "the same boat that brought me here is leaving the island tonight to get supplies. I'll send along a note to the governor about the grub girl, warning that we'll have an uprising if we can't get her under control. Personally, I'd be fine just to take care of things myself, but it must look like an accident. If we lose the people's trust, we'll have an even bigger problem on our hands."

I drew in a sharp breath, then clapped my hand over my mouth in hopes they hadn't heard. Were they really discussing a way to get rid of me? Why? I didn't need to be controlled. I'd already promised Weevil to obey the rules here, or at least, the rules that made sense.

"I know just how to do it," the warden said. "She's getting assigned different work tomorrow. I'll make sure an accident happens then."

CHAPTER
TWENTY-FIVE

As quickly and quietly as I could, I hurried away from the barracks. Once I was back in the Colony square, surrounded by others, I still didn't feel safe. What job did they intend to assign me tomorrow, and how would they make my death look like an accident?

More important, why was that necessary? I hadn't done anything all that wrong, not really. Surely, others had spent time in the cage or had done a poor job with their assigned duties. Why had I been singled out? This wasn't their hatred of River People—if so, they would have targeted Weevil too. No, this was just about me.

Gossel and the other wardens reappeared when the dinner bell rang. Of course they did. The wardens always ate first. They ate Scourge-contaminated food prepared by the hands of Scourge victims and then wandered around us while we ate. Never worrying that they might get the disease too. Never becoming sick. Never entering the infirmary while wondering if they would ever come out again.

If they weren't afraid of the Scourge, then they were somehow protected from it. Della's father seemed to believe there were some medicines that could prevent a person from getting the Scourge. If that was true, maybe he was also right that they'd heal a person who was already sick. Della looked even worse tonight than when I'd seen her only a few hours ago. If those rumors were true, then the special medicine must be kept inside the wardens' barracks. Inside their *unguarded* barracks.

All the wardens were here, eating.

Sometimes I hated the way my brain worked, like a magnet to thoughts I should not have and actions I should not take. My mother said I was born backward and that probably explained how I'd gotten this way. Maybe she was right—I didn't know.

"Where have you been?" Weevil asked, appearing beside me. "I looked for you in the tent. You need to get in line as soon as that bell rings or there isn't much left at the end."

I shrugged. "I'm not hungry. You get in line."

His eyes narrowed. "What did you do?"

"Nothing! I'm not hungry. Now go eat before it's all gone."

"You lost meal privileges. How, Ani?"

I turned to him, using as much anger as possible to make him go away. "Maybe I'm not hungry because the Scourge has taken my appetite! Maybe I'm not like you, someone who begins thinking about his second meal before he's even finished his first. Maybe I don't like the food here! Not everything happens because I'm in trouble!"

Weevil looked taken aback at first, then nodded at me with a smile. "You must've really done something wrong. All right, I'll go eat. Can you at least manage to stay out of trouble until I finish?"

No, I thought. That was definitely not my plan.

"Yes," I said.

He casually raked a hand through his hair. "I'll save some of my supper for you."

I sighed. "Go eat, Weevil. Go eat as much as you can."

He winked at me and ran back to the food tent. The minute he disappeared, I left too. I made it look as if I were headed to the old prison, then cut from there down to the beach and went southward, back to the barracks.

I studied the barracks for several minutes, making sure no one remained inside. If they were planning an accident for me tomorrow, then getting caught here would save them the trouble. I could think of few things that would warrant a greater punishment than for me to be caught inside the wardens' living quarters.

Finally, I snuck up to the barracks door and pressed my ear against it, listening for any sound inside. Nothing.

I knocked. "Sir," I said. "Did you not hear the supper bell? The other wardens sent me to get you."

No answer.

Taking a deep breath, I looked around to be sure no one was watching me, then opened the door and slipped inside.

The barracks weren't fancy, but the room was clean and orderly. It had beds for twelve men, all of them stacked in twos. A table in the center served as a sort of desk, and each man had a trunk for his personal possessions. A window was in the far wall, over one of the beds. If necessary, that would be my escape. Just like the laundry in the prison.

I glanced at a half-written letter on the table, addressed to Governor Nerysa Felling. My name was on it, near the top, but thanks to the conversation I'd overheard earlier, I already knew what it said. I was a problem and might cause an uprising here if I wasn't stopped. No need to waste time reading it. I knew everything I'd done, and it was far more than what was written in that letter.

No medicine flasks were hanging from the men's bunks, and no wardens carried medicine over their shoulders, as Scourge victims did. So their medicine must be in the individual trunks.

I searched the one closest to me, as quickly and carefully as I could. There was a change of clothing, stacks of letters, probably to that man's family, a holy book, and some personal grooming items. But no medicine.

The second trunk was nearly the same. Clothes, letters, books, and grooming items. No medicine.

I started into the third. This one might've been Warden Gossel's or maybe even his commander's. Beyond the same items as the others, it held a thick key, letters from the governor, and lists of names. Scourge victims' names perhaps?

Suddenly, I heard voices approaching the barracks. It was time to leave. I quietly closed the trunk, then climbed up to the bed and looked for the latch to open the window. Where was it? River People didn't have windows in our homes, so I didn't have much experience with them, but the prison windows opened wide. How did this one open? *Did* it open?

It had to! The voices were getting closer. Even if I escaped now, they'd see me running away.

I jumped off the bed and looked beneath the lower bunks for the best place to hide. How long would I need to stay in here? Not through the whole evening, I hoped, but I would if necessary.

In my panic, a pain shot up my side, the first time I'd felt sick all day, but returning with a vengeance. Doubling over from the pain, I got to the floor to crawl under the nearest bed, hoping against reason that this would work.

The barracks door opened. I wasn't yet all the way under the bed, and nothing else was down here to help me. Not unless I could hide behind tiny grains of sand and someone's missing sock. Thinking about the punishment surely headed my way made my brain want to explode.

Then I heard a voice. "Pardon me, sirs, can you help?" That was Weevil.

Weevil? He must have followed me here.

"What is it?" one warden answered. Hopefully the other wasn't Gossel, who'd be more suspicious.

"I feel warm. Do I have a fever? Can you check?"

I heard the shuffling of feet as one warden moved away from the door. The other guard must've continued holding it open, though, obviously signaling his desire for Weevil to leave so they could go inside.

With hands pressed against my aching side, I crept to the open door. I couldn't see through it to know whether the warden holding the door was looking at Weevil or not, but I had to take the chance that he was.

"You're not warm," the warden said. "Now go away, grub, you shouldn't be down here."

I snuck out the door and backed away from it. Almost instantly the other warden walked around the door to enter the barracks. He spotted me.

I looked at Weevil as if I had just come from the opposite direction. "There you are! I already told you that your head wasn't warm. You didn't need to bother these nice wardens about that."

Weevil frowned at me. "I just wanted to be sure, since I know that sometimes you tell me what I want to hear, instead of what's really going on."

I grabbed his arm and started to pull him away. Looking back at the wardens, I said, "Sorry he troubled you. Boys can be such babies about deadly diseases, don't you think?"

The wardens didn't laugh, but they did let us go. And as soon as they went inside, I found myself leaning more heavily on Weevil's arm.

He stopped walking, and when he did, I closed him into a hug, clasping my hands around his neck so he wouldn't know how bad they were shaking. "Thank you, thank you."

He pushed me back, clearly angry. "You'd better have a good reason for doing that."

"I thought they'd have more powerful medicines, ones I could share with Della and this old woman I saw in the prison today, and everyone here who probably needs more than what the governor gives us. But I didn't find anything. Where are the wardens' medicines?"

"Maybe they don't have any!"

"They have to! Why aren't the wardens sick? Or the physician who tested me for the Scourge? Or the governor, who sat in the testing room with me? They know how to keep from getting sick. Whatever that secret is, the wardens must have it in their barracks!"

He sighed. "You checked everywhere?"

"I only had time to check three of the twelve trunks. And there were probably other places I could have looked too. Next time I go in—"

He grabbed my hands and looked me directly in the eyes. "No, Ani, you cannot keep doing this! Eventually, you are going to push things too far, to the point where nobody can save you."

"What I just did is the first actual rule I've broken. The rest are just bad circumstances."

"Maybe, but why do all the bad circumstances involve you? You're always in the middle of everything that goes wrong!"

"That's my point. Something is wrong in this whole Colony, Weevil, very wrong! Everything I see brings up more questions with answers that don't make sense. If we melt in with everyone else, pretending not to see the problems, do you think they'll just go away?"

"We don't have to make the problems go away! All we have to do is get you better and then find a way to escape this island. That's our only job. But if you go sneaking into the wardens' barracks, getting yourself banned from meal-times, and making enemies with people whose help we might need to escape, you won't last here for a week. Don't you understand how dangerous this is? They will find a way to get rid of you."

I understood perfectly. Getting rid of me was, in fact, their plan for tomorrow.

But I couldn't tell Weevil that. So instead, I lowered my head. "You're right. From now on, I'll be the model Scourge victim of this Colony."

Weevil brushed his knuckles across my arm. "I doubt

you could do that, even if you tried. Just . . . try harder. Now come on—we've got to find those caves before it gets dark."

That was what I loved about my friend. No sooner had Weevil gotten me to agree that I would not break any more rules, than he was proposing that we hurry and break yet another rule.

CHAPTER
TWENTY-SIX

When we returned to the Colony square, Della immediately found us. Her hand was shaking when she reached for me, as if the muscles had already given up. The Scourge was taking her, far too quickly. She needed a stronger medicine. If I had discovered even a single sip of something that might help, the risk would absolutely have been worth it.

"Here," she whispered. "This is for you."

She pressed two rolls into my hands. They weren't enough to cover the hunger I felt, but they were something.

"Why?" I asked, giving one to Weevil.

Her eyes filled with tears, then drifted to the prison walls. "When we first met, I blamed you for stealing my boat, just to keep myself out of trouble. But today you took the blame for me. You could have used me to keep yourself out of trouble. Why did you do that, Ani? Why would a River Person do that for me?"

For the first time, she hadn't referred to me as a grub.

And I vowed at that moment never again to call her people pinchworms.

I took her hand in mine. "It can't be you and me against each other anymore. It must be you and me against the Scourge." Or against the wardens and Governor Felling, who I was beginning to think were the far greater dangers here.

She squeezed back, as well as she could. "Agreed."

After a sideways glance at Weevil, I said, "You shouldn't stay in the old prison anymore. Come with us, Della. There's another place we can sleep tonight."

She shook her head. "My father will come for me in the old prison."

"He's not coming. I know he wants to, but they won't let him come."

Her mouth pinched together. Then she said, "If your father knew where you were, how far would he go to get you out of trouble?"

Tears welled in my eyes to think of him. "He'd split the earth to save me," I said. "*If* he knew."

"That's what my father is doing too," Della said. "He does know where I am. I'll wait in the prisons until he comes."

She lumbered away. Weevil took my arm and nudged me along with him. "We'll see her tomorrow, but for now, we should go," he said. "No one's watching." And we slipped away.

Our plan for finding the caves wasn't particularly complex: go north. Eventually we'd find the caves or hit seawater. But no matter what we found, we were both firm that we would not stay in the prison. Aside from the fact that it was utterly depressing, I had a feeling that avoiding the infirmary required us to avoid the prison too.

The infirmary. That's where Della was headed soon, and nothing I could do would stop it. Maybe if I got back inside the wardens' barracks and searched the rest of the trunks. Maybe all the medicines were kept in one trunk and I hadn't found it yet.

Weevil seemed to be thinking the same thing, only in a far less dangerous way. "As I was searching for their herbs today, I tried to figure out which one was the most important for making their medicine, and I think I know which it is. It's the one ingredient I hadn't heard of before, spindlewill."

I wrinkled my nose. "We don't have spindlewill in the river country, at least not by that name."

"It probably can't grow in the higher lands. But if I could find some and sneak some away, we might be able to offer it to Della. Maybe in a more concentrated tea, the medicine would help her. We could make our own medicine."

"We don't know anything about spindlewill."

"No, but the wardens were very insistent on how much we needed to find it. If they do have a stronger medicine, I'm guessing it involves spindlewill."

"I'm sure another medicine exists. When we were together in the physician's office, Della's father accused Governor Felling of giving that medicine to her favorites. And Sir Willoughby tried to take the governor's job in the last election, so let's assume his family is not amongst her favorites. By withholding that medicine from Della, the governor is punishing her father."

Weevil grunted. "Get better, Ani. Get better and we'll take this fight right to the governor's front door."

I pretended to be shocked. "Ever since coming here, I've done everything I can to stay out of trouble. Are you trying to corrupt me now?"

Since he had accused me of the same thing only yesterday, he seemed to enjoy the retort. "Every chance I get."

My hope was that once we reached the north shore, it would become obvious where the caves should be, but the reality was just the opposite. From where we stood, nothing could be seen except for sea, the shore, and the sharp rocks beneath our boots. Certainly there were no signs of a place where people could live, hidden from the eyes of the wardens. Everything was rocky here and I guessed the cave entrance was where the waves crashed, but guessing wrong could get us carried out with the tide. The shoreline was wider than expected, and the caves could just as easily be anywhere along this northern coast. It was already getting dark, and the evening breeze was picking up. I didn't like the idea of being out here overnight. Except for the caves, there was nowhere here to take shelter.

Weevil touched my arm. "How are you feeling?"

"I'm all right." His brows pressed together but I nodded. "Really, Weevil, I feel good." Maybe it was only my growing hope to leave this Colony one day, but I hadn't felt this good since leaving the river country.

Then, from the corner of my eye, I saw movement to my left. It was quick, and my eyes might have been deceiving me, but I could have sworn I saw a head poke up from the rocks, right at the beach.

I pointed it out to Weevil, and we went in that direction, crawling over the wind-carved rocks to get to the beach.

When we were nearly there, Weevil pointed to a wisp of smoke drifting out to sea. It was very windy now, with competing currents coming inland and then out again. But the breeze carrying the smoke was our clue.

We followed the smoke to an overlook with the beach a long way below us. Weevil lay on the rock and dipped his head down, then raised it again with a smile. "It's here," he mouthed, pointing right below us.

Looking around, I saw a ladder made of uneven sticks lashed together with beach grasses. We climbed down the ladder and stood at the entrance of a cave. The entrance to our new home, if they would have us.

"Marjorie!" I called inside. "Is Marjorie here? She invited us to come."

Moments later, Marjorie came out to greet us. She hugged me first and then Weevil. "I'm so glad you're here."

With a hand on each of our shoulders, she said, "Listen, I'm very new here, so I have no way of convincing them to let you stay. I barely convinced them to let me stay here, and I'm townsfolk while you're—well, you'll have to do this on your own."

An earlier version of me might've told these people if they didn't let us stay, I'd go back to the wardens and tell them where this cave was. But that was the old me, the one whose quick tongue and slow judgment always led to problems.

The new me understood that I would never threaten these people with any secrets I already had. Not for any reward or under any risk to my own safety. I would be as dependent upon them for my survival as they would be upon me.

Marjorie led us inside. The entrance was narrow, requiring us to scoot along sideways. Nature had given these people a brilliant place to hide. The tight entrance protected them from the evening breeze but still kept the air from going stale.

That led to a wider room with another tunnel that we had to crawl through. Once we did, we were there. In a large room filled with a dozen people, most of them rolling out beds for the night. Their mattresses were made of stolen linens stitched together and filled with grasses. Lit candles were set into posts on the cave walls. Although there wasn't much light, it was enough. Another fire was around a corner, in a separate small room. It kept the cave at a comfortable temperature, and I guessed there was some sort of ventilation to carry the smoke outside since the air smelled clean in here.

"It's perfect," I whispered.

This was every bit as nice as any home a River Person had, and except for the twice-daily flooding, it might've been an improvement on our homes. Not only could Weevil and I be comfortable here, I felt we could also contribute to making this cave even better.

Weevil cleared his throat and said to the group who had stopped working to stare at us, "We just came to the Colony yesterday. We ask permission to stay with you all. We'll do everything we can to help. We're good at fishing and gathering food, and—"

A man in the back of the room stood and pointed at me. "Get out, grubs. You'll bring nothing good our way. Get out, or we'll toss you out with the tide."

CHAPTER
TWENTY-SEVEN

Weevil reached for my hand, but I didn't need it. I stepped past him. "What if we are River People? We're also prisoners of this Colony, same as you."

"You're not the same," the man who had spoken before said. "We do everything we can to avoid the attention of the wardens. And from the minute you stepped foot on this island, you have broken every possible rule."

I raised my voice, making sure everyone in this cave could hear me perfectly. "Is that your judgment of us, that we're rule breakers? How dare you?" I moved deeper into the room and grabbed one of the stitched blankets. "Were these linens gifts to you, or are they stolen? Is that why you allowed Marjorie to stay here, because she works in the laundry and can steal more when you need them? What about those candles on the wall? Who carried the candle wax here when you were brought on the boats? Or did someone steal them too, perhaps from the old prison? For that matter, which of you in this room has the wardens' permission to be here? Who is the greatest rule follower in this group? Stand and identify yourself!"

There was silence for a moment, and then a woman said, "We're all breaking rules here—that is true. But the wardens are keeping an eye out for you. What happens when they look for you tonight and can't find you in the prison?"

"Ani snuck into the wardens' barracks earlier tonight," Weevil said, crossing over to me. "She got in and out, right beneath their noses. If she can do that, she can sneak in and out of this place."

More silence. Another younger woman said, "Why should we trust the word of two grubs?"

Weevil's fist clenched, but I said, "There are skills River People have that can benefit you. We're no different from you townsfolk, not really." I felt Weevil's eyes on me then. He had never heard me refer to these people as anything other than pinchworms. Never again, I reminded myself. "Weevil doesn't have the Scourge, and I'm feeling much better than before. We won't be a burden here. River People are strong."

The man who had spoken first shook his head. "River People are cowards."

"My father was in the exploration ship that was lost last year," Weevil said. "He died for this country."

"Where's the heroism in his being forced to go?" the man asked. "Why don't your people fight for your land; why don't you fight to vote, to be full citizens of this country? Anyone who's learned their history knows the River People didn't start the Scourge, yet you all just accept the lies and let us treat you with no more respect than we'd give an actual grub."

I said, "Every time Keldan pushes us, there is talk of pushing back. But we don't fight, and it isn't because we're weak—it's because we know our strength. We know what would happen to Keldan if we took up weapons against our own countrymen. We love our country, the same as you. Times have been hard and they are getting harder. The only way our country will survive is if River People and townsfolk come together. Not if we fight one another. Please, let us stay now."

Yet more silence followed. The people in the caves looked at one another, as if trying to come to an unspoken agreement for what they would do. Then a boy stood up from the shadows. He was a few years older than me and Weevil, with dark eyes and darker hair. His clothes were those of townsfolk, though they were nothing fancy like Della's, and time had worn down the fabric.

He said to the group, "You know me, and by now you trust me. But perhaps you trusted me too much, for there was one secret I've kept from you since coming to the Colony. I worked for the townsfolk, as if I'd always been one of you. But what I am, and what I always shall be, is one of the

River People. If you turn these two away for that reason, then you will have to turn me away as well."

An older woman said, "That would be a death sentence, Jonas."

I didn't know why he couldn't leave the caves, but my instincts had already guessed that was his name. Jonas Orden, Della's friend.

He nodded and stepped closer to us, standing right next to Weevil. "You trusted me, and you can trust them too. They will never lead the wardens to us. They will never betray us."

Although some grumblings were heard, the man from the back, who seemed to be the leader, said, "All right, grubs, you can stay."

"My name is Ani," I said. "This is Weevil. You'll use our names or not refer to us at all."

He smirked, amused at my boldness. "Very well, Ani and Weevil, my name is Clement Rust and I'm in charge of everyone in these caves. Betray us in any way, and I'll toss you into the sea myself. Other than that, this is your home now. If you need refreshment, get yourselves a drink of some hot tea. We have extra mattresses." Even as he said it, two thin cloth mattresses were handed over to us—I wasn't sure from where.

Once we were settled in a corner, Jonas came over to sit beside us.

After thanking him for defending us, Weevil asked, "Are you sure you're River People? There's no one by the name of Orden amongst us."

"I changed the name, to fit in better with the townsfolk," he said. "My original name was Jonas Ord."

I nodded. "Several years ago, the Ord family sent one of their sons to live with the townsfolk, in hopes of giving him a better life."

He nodded. "How's my family? I miss them."

"Life is hard," I said. "We help them as best as we can, but—"

"Baked bread," Weevil said. "Twice a week, our family goes without our baked bread and my mother gives it to your family." Then he winked at me. "Ani supplied the wheat for that bread."

"Thank you," Jonas said, sincerely grateful.

I hadn't known that, but I should've guessed. Weevil's mother never would've continued accepting my wheat if she had not found a way to take my gift and turn it into an even greater gift for someone else.

Weevil said, "I overheard the woman say that if you left these caves, you would be taken straight to the infirmary."

Jonas nodded. "I can't ever leave. Not if I want to survive."

"Della's here," I said. "She came with us to the Colony."

Jonas's eyes widened. "What? She's here?" He brushed a

hand through his hair. "She must have gotten the Scourge from me. She and I were so close—"

"Friends?" Weevil asked.

"More than friends," I said. "Correct?"

After a pause, Jonas nodded again. "She never cared that I was a worker, though that might change if she knew I was from the rivers. Still, I think she genuinely cares about me."

"She does," I said. "It would do her a lot of good to see you."

"I want to see her too. But I can't leave."

"She's been looking for you everywhere," I said. "She thinks they've already taken you to the infirmary."

"And if I come out, that's where I'll go," he said. "One of the men here even works with the wardens. Pretended to look for me for days until he convinced them I'd probably fallen in the sea and drowned. He asked a warden what they'd do if they found me and was told if I'm still alive, I was going to the infirmary."

"Why?" Weevil asked. "You don't look sick."

"I don't feel sick. For the first week that I was here, I was terribly ill. Every day got worse, so much so that at one point, I could barely get down the prison stairs. The wardens stopped me one day and said it was time for me to go to the infirmary. I didn't want that. I've seen the people who go into the infirmary doors."

"And never come out again," I breathed.

"Exactly. So I ran and hid. I lay in some underbrush for a whole day, knowing I would probably die in that exact spot." Jonas pointed out a woman in conversation with someone else in the caves. "Her job is to gather herbs. She found me and brought me here, then mixed some herbs into teas. They saved my life."

"Like a stronger, more powerful medicine?" I asked. "Made of spindlewill?"

Jonas shrugged. "I don't know what she found, only that it really helped me."

"Are you fully healed?" Weevil asked.

"It's only been a couple of weeks, but I don't feel sick anymore. Many of the people here don't feel sick either. I want to show myself to the wardens, to tell them there is hope for everyone else at the Colony, but I'm afraid of what will happen if I do. I can't risk them finding me."

"So you'll live out your life here?" I asked. "Why not build a boat and get back to Keldan?"

He rolled up the sleeve of his shirt, revealing a long, thin red line running up his forearm. "They call it the scar of health. Everyone who seems to have recovered from the Scourge has one of these. We think it's the sign the disease has left the body."

"So hide your forearm and go home," I said.

"A few months ago, there was a group of people who believed they had healed," he said. "They snuck aboard a supply boat returning to Keldan and went ashore. Within a month, every one of them was turned in, most of them by their own families. They were brought back here along with many of the people who had helped to hide them. Everyone who claimed to have been healed was tested again, and they still had the Scourge. Then each escapee was sent straight to the infirmary. None of them have been seen since that day."

"What happened to them?" Weevil asked.

"I don't know." Jonas's eyes darkened. "But I will never go to the infirmary. Sending them there was an obvious punishment for escaping. The wardens told the people here that even if we think we are healed, the Scourge can still be passed to others."

"So it's true," I mumbled. "There is no cure." My heart sank at the thought of it.

"Even if there is, you will never be healed enough for anyone in Keldan to accept it," Jonas said. "We don't dare go back now. Maybe you'll feel better for a while, but you can always start feeling sick again, especially if you push yourself too hard before you've fully recovered. And even when you're sure it's over for you, after seeing how awful this place is, would you return to your family if there were even the slightest risk of them being forced to come here next?"

I shook my head and so did Weevil. At least we now had a place to stay that was a thousand times better than the old prison. And I felt reasonably healthy and had every hope of continuing to feel better. Yet all of that was not enough. We would never get any farther away from the Colony than in these caves. This time we were prisoners of our own choosing.

CHAPTER
TWENTY-EIGHT

Although the mattresses were far more comfortable than even my mattress at home and the cave felt warm and safe, I didn't sleep well that night.

I hadn't told Weevil of the warden's plans for me the next day, nor would I tell him. There was no point in it. If he knew, he would likely try to convince me to remain in hiding, like Jonas. But if I failed to show up for work duty, the wardens would surely come looking for me. I could not be the reason they found the caves.

We were awakened early and told to thread ourselves back into the Colony slowly, and from various directions so that we did not stand out to the wardens.

Weevil was close beside me as we walked toward the Colony. "Are you feeling sick?" he asked.

"No."

"Then what's wrong? I can always tell, you know."

"You can't always tell," I lied. "I'm only . . . nervous. They're assigning me to a different job today, and I wonder what it might be."

He smiled, always the optimist. "Maybe you'll get to gather herbs with me."

That was hardly dangerous enough for the wardens. Not unless the requested herbs were only found on the thinnest outer limb of a brittle tree branch overlooking the deepest part of the sea, and could only be gathered during a violent storm. If that were the case, then yes, I might be assigned to gather herbs.

Weevil shrugged. "You're strong, Ani. You can do any of the jobs here. Just remember to do exactly what they say and you'll be fine."

No, the very opposite was true. Whatever they told me to do would be designed to end my life. I would only survive the day if I did my job without obeying their instructions. Which, ironically, would get me into even greater trouble with the wardens. There was no way to win.

The morning after his father had been taken away last year, Weevil had described their situation with a similar conclusion. "What was he supposed to do?" Weevil had said. "If my father refused to go on the governor's exploration, she would have him imprisoned for denying service to his country. So we'd lose him. If he is successful on the governor's exploration, she will demand even more explorations from him. So we'll lose him. And if he is not successful, then he'll die. And we'll lose him. There is no choice for my father that ends with him back at home with my family. No way for him to win."

Only weeks after his father's ship left for the northern seas, word came of the storm they'd encountered. That news had opened up a wound inside Weevil's heart that I doubted would ever fully heal. I would not deepen the wound by telling him about today, when the wardens would make things nearly as impossible for me. Except I intended to survive the day's challenge.

We easily blended in with the other Colonists, and for the first time, I got to go through the food lines. I took as much food as I was allowed, hard-boiled eggs, and bread, and a small sugar apple. Weevil took a lot too. Of course he did. He had shared half of everything with me since coming here, and had missed his supper last night to follow me to the barracks. He was already looking thinner, which worried me. I was finally beginning to feel better. Maybe he was starting to feel sick, and hadn't told me yet. When that time came, I would do everything I could for him.

If I was still around in another week or two. If I was still around at the end of this day.

When I was nearly finished with the breakfast, Warden Gossel put his hand on my shoulder. "You'll come with me now for work duty."

I faked a smile at Weevil, and then stood. "Yes, sir."

Weevil's brow furrowed. He knew something serious was happening. For that reason, I didn't dare glance back at him. Every time he looked at me, he saw more than I wished he could.

We didn't have far to go, and once we rounded the fence, it quickly became obvious what they had planned for me: the treadmill.

Although I had intended not to make any argument today, I immediately stopped cold on the ground. "Only grown men work the treadmill," I said.

"Grown men and one young girl who thinks the rules do not apply to her."

"My legs are shorter. I can't climb fast enough to keep up with the others."

He cocked his head, as if that admission was some sort of victory for him. "Get on your knees, then. Get on your knees and beg me for mercy. Tell me you will do whatever is asked of you. Then tell me how I can make all of you proud River People fall to their knees when they start coming here. Tell me all of that, Ani, and you will avoid the treadmill."

Silence fell between us while he waited to see what I would do next. I wasn't sure what it'd be, but I knew for a fact that I wouldn't get on my knees and beg for mercy from *him*.

So instead, I squared my shoulders and stuck out my chin. "You're in luck. When I woke up this morning, I felt like climbing a mountain today. I'll do that on your treadmill."

His eyes narrowed. That wasn't the response he wanted. Then he waved me forward. Only two men were on the treadmill so far, though I figured more would come through-out the day. From what I had seen while in the cage, the men rotated through in fifteen-minute shifts. Climb for fifteen minutes, then rest for fifteen. I could do this. My only challenge was exactly as I had warned the warden. The steps of the treadmill were not made for legs as short as mine. They were built for a man's much longer legs. I didn't know if I could scale the distance in time for the treadmill to rotate down again, but since I had no other choice, it was a fine day to find out.

I took a deep breath, and with the warden behind me, I climbed onto the treadmill. The men on either side of me looked curious about why a girl my age had joined them, but sweat was already pouring down their faces. It was going to be a warm day.

"Happy morning!" I said good-naturedly.

They grunted.

I could do these steps. It required a full stretch of my legs, but it reminded me of the many trees I had climbed back home, of how far I'd sometimes had to reach to get to the next safe branch. Granted, I'd had time then to calculate the distance, but the work itself was the same. I could do this.

A few minutes later, three more men came to the tread-mill. The two on either side of me got off for the rotation, so I started to get off too.

"Not you, grub," Warden Gossel said. "You keep going."

I pointed to the one man who had not rotated in. "He's done nothing yet!"

"You told me you wanted to climb a mountain today. You've only just started. I hope you don't slip from exhaustion and fall under the wheel."

"Not today." I returned to work at the treadmill, my strength powered by raw stubbornness and a desire to get revenge on the warden. But how? He sat there watching us, smugly resting in the shade, sipping a drink that probably contained special Scourge medicine that supposedly didn't exist and enjoying the cheerful chirps of the birds overhead.

Ah, the music of the birds. Here was the revenge, wasn't it?

I glanced back at him. "If it's all right with you, whenever I'm climbing a mountain, I like to sing."

He shrugged. "Go ahead. I've heard the River People have songs that do magic."

No, we didn't.

With an apology to the men on either side of me, I opened my mouth and began screeching. It was a rousing tune my people often sang together as we worked our fields. I applied the best of my talents to it now. From my very first note, Gossel's head looked as if it might split apart.

"Stop that at once!" he said.

"I can't," I said. "This is the only way I know how to climb."

The men on either side of me had seemed offended at first by my singing, as all people were. But seeing how much it irritated the warden, they began joining in.

Obviously, these men were only faking their bad singing. None of them seemed to be as gifted as I naturally was in producing sounds that should only belong to the undead. But they should not blame themselves for lacking my talents. I knew they were trying the best they could.

And it was working. Warden Gossel finally stood and yelled, "You know how much grain must be ground up today. None of you will stop until it's finished. I'll check on you at suppertime!"

The instant he was out of sight, all of us left the treadmill and took a rest. One of the men resting beside me was Clement Rust, from the caves.

"He could have claimed your singing was a sign of sickness and dragged you away to the infirmary," he warned.

But I shook my head. "I overheard the wardens talking. They don't take anyone to the infirmary until they believe they've been broken. I don't know what happens to the people once they're inside, but they don't want anyone who fights back. The best chance we have to stay alive is to continually fight against them."

"They won't tolerate rebellion," another man said, taking a sip from his medicine as he rested. "The best thing we can do is finish the grinding and stay out of their way."

"Staying out of their way isn't the problem," I said. "We have to keep the wardens out of *our* way as we heal."

"There is no healing here!" a third man said. "I go to bed each night in so much pain that I can barely climb the prison stairs. It's only worse the morning after. The wardens don't have to control us. The Scourge does it for them."

I pointed to the river, an easy distance away. "If we widened that just a little, we could drag this treadmill into the water. We'd need a different way to collect the flour after it's been ground up, but we wouldn't have to climb anymore."

The men looked at one another with eyes that lit up at my suggestion. Then Clement said, "I know a way to collect the flour."

"I know where there's a good shovel," another man said. "We can do this. The wardens aren't here to stop us, thanks to the grub."

"No, not 'the grub,'" Clement said. "Her name is Ani."

CHAPTER
TWENTY-NINE

The riverbank was softer than I'd expected, and while we worked to widen it, Clement built a collection tray from broken treadmill steps that had been tossed against the fence. The men sang as we worked and asked me to join in every time someone spotted a warden getting too close. As far as the wardens knew, we were still behind the fence, climbing.

Within only an hour, we were ready to begin moving the heavy treadmill toward the river. Although I was much smaller than the men, I wanted to do my part, so I found a place at the back where I could help to push.

The work was slow and hard—much harder than it had been to simply climb the treadmill that morning. But if we got it into the water, no one would ever have to climb again.

I strained every muscle I had in the process. Though we moved forward by only finger widths at a time, the treadmill was sliding across the dry ground. We had emptied it of all grain and even carried the grinding stone separately, yet I was still amazed at the weight of this great wooden beast.

By the time we slid it into the water, I felt the Scourge rise again inside me. Pain rippled throughout my body, and I felt dizzier than ever before. Jonas had warned me of working too hard before I'd fully recovered.

However, the water immediately started rotating the wheel for us. The men cheered—softly, of course, as nobody wanted the wardens to hear—and began loading it with grain to see if it really would grind.

I could only sit while they did, letting my feet cool in the river water. Although the wardens had intended for my life to end in the mill today, either from exhaustion or from me slipping beneath its heavy wheel, that would not happen. The mill would never harm anyone again, in fact, for nobody needed to climb it anymore. And yet the warden might still get his wish for me. I truly felt awful.

The men let me rest while I told them the most entertaining stories of Weevil's and my adventures in the river country, which they enjoyed but probably didn't believe. When I tired of that, one man made a paste for me to eat from the fresh-ground flour and a little water. It had no taste and stuck unmercifully to the roof of my mouth, but it was something to eat and I was grateful for it.

Since the water never slowed, the work of grinding went much faster than it had before. By the time Warden Gossel returned for us that evening, all of us were rested and the grain was entirely ground up.

His face went into shades of purple before he pointed a shaking finger at me. "Was this your idea, grub?"

I stood, though I still felt weak. "Yes, sir. As you can see, it's a much better—"

"It's not better."

"It is! The water is doing the work, and it goes faster than we ever could."

"Pull it out of the water, now."

"We can't," Clement said. "It was nearly impossible to carry the treadmill in, but with the weight of the water, it'll never come out of the river again. It's not a treadmill any longer, warden. It's a water mill, and that's the way it'll stay."

"How dare you refuse my orders?"

"Your orders were to see that the grain was ground," he replied. "We obeyed you perfectly."

Another man stepped forward. "If you want to punish Clement for refusing to carry that back onto dry ground, then you'll have to punish all of us."

Warden Gossel stomped over to me and grabbed my arm. "I only need to punish the grub. She gave you the idea. She is the one who refuses to cooperate."

But the men surrounded the warden, closing in around him and me. If it was their intention to intimidate Gossel and make him believe his life was in danger, it worked. As one of the larger men not-so-accidentally bumped into

Gossel, even I was nervous for him. Clement took my other arm and drew me away from the warden, then said, "She's one of us, sir, a climber. You can try punishing the lot of us, but you will not take this girl."

As the men edged closer, Warden Gossel straightened his back and pushed his way out of the group. "I've just decided that the mill can remain where it is. You'll receive new job assignments soon. However, for your rebellion, none of you will eat at supper tonight. And tomorrow when you come, twice the amount of grain will be waiting for you."

As soon as he left, I turned and hugged Clement. Last night he had been skeptical about whether to accept me at the caves, and now he had defended my life. Tears were in his eyes when he released me. "You make me think of my daughter," he said. "I've been here for almost a month and had just about given up. You remind me that I want to live, for her."

I wanted my life back too. Coming to the caves, to see all the people who claimed to be getting better, had given me hope.

Yet at the same time, I had checked my forearm at least a hundred times that day for any sign of the thin red line. Nothing of the sort had appeared, and the way I felt now, I knew it wouldn't. I was as sick as before, though I hoped this flare-up of pain was due to my exhaustion from a day of such hard work rather than a worsening of the disease.

Clement brought me back into the Colony square, where we were immediately met by Weevil. He put an arm around me, and before I could say anything, he mumbled, "I heard what you did. That was a good kind of trouble, Ani. I'm proud of you."

"Everything hurts," I said.

"I know. Come on."

"Ani, wait!" Della ran up to us, then paused to catch her breath. She looked worse than I felt, but this wasn't only because of the Scourge. The light in her eyes had dimmed too.

Weevil tilted his head. "What's wrong?"

"We had newcomers to the Colony this afternoon," she said, nodding up toward the tent. "More Scourge victims."

I hardly dared to ask. "Any River People?"

"I don't think so. But one of the arrivals was someone I knew a little. He sold meat to Jonas each week. He had a message for us, Ani."

My brow furrowed. "For *us*?"

"Before you left Keldan, did you ask my father to contact your family and tell them where you were?"

"Yes, though I'm sure your father wouldn't have—"

"He did, immediately after you left. That very night, our fathers formed a plan to come and rescue us from this island. Your father had access to one of the River People's boats. My father had money for some weapons in case a fight broke out."

My spirits lifted. "They're coming for us?"

She only shook her head. "The governor discovered their plan and sent wardens after them. They've already been sentenced for violating Scourge laws. She says she has to make an example of them, or the Scourge will spread across Keldan."

"They've been arrested?" I said, louder than I should have, and Weevil shushed me.

"No," she said, drawing in a sharp breath to hold her emotions together. "But they're in hiding, and it's only a matter of time before they're found and their sentence carried out. They won't be able to come get us. I'm sorry, Ani. That hope is gone."

I sat on a nearby rock and tried to absorb her words, but none of it felt real. In one moment, she had offered me more than I ever could have expected, then taken it away just as fast. With that sudden loss of hope came an even greater problem—the fact that my father was now in hiding, a fugitive from the law. Della was right. Sooner or later, the wardens would find him. I didn't know what his sentence would be, but I did understand the governor's cruelty now. She took me and would take my father too. My mother was now alone. How would she ever survive without us, even if she had the will to try?

This news crushed me. But it must have been so much worse for Della. The only thing that had kept her alive in this place was the certainty that her father was coming to rescue her. He wasn't coming now, and she had to accept that.

I considered telling her about Jonas, that we had found him and he was safe and healthy. But he also could not come out of the caves, and we had no permission to tell Della where he was, not yet. Until I knew that I could reunite her with Jonas, I couldn't say anything. But I did vow to ask tonight about bringing her to the caves. By now, Clement surely trusted me that much.

So we only thanked her for the news, and then Weevil led me behind the prison, out of sight from everyone else still at the food tent. If he hadn't been there to help me, I barely could've made the walk, and not because of the pains in my bones. This pain went much deeper.

"I'm sorry about your father," he said.

Tears spilled onto my cheeks. "Is this how it felt for you, when the governor took your father away?"

He looked down, scuffing his boot against the dirt. "Give it time. It won't always hurt like this."

I doubted that. Weevil still ached for his father's loss. I understood that ache now, more than I ever had before.

He tried again. "Listen, you helped me and my family. Once we're home, I'll help you and your mother too." Then he smiled, trying to cheer me up as well. "I don't have your gift for singing, but I'm thinking about taking up juggling. My plan is to throw balls at the townsfolk until they offer me a coin."

I snorted. "That sounds like a crime, Weevil."

"So is your singing, my friend." His smile was more

sincere this time. "We'll work together, and our families will survive. I promise."

"Thank you," I said as I brushed away my tears. "Thank you for believing we'll ever get back home."

"Of course we will." He began digging in his pockets. "I found a spindlewill plant today. I don't know how it's used in the medicine, but if you chew on the leaf, I think it will be almost the same."

He pulled out from his pocket a few leaves, which he pressed into my hand. I turned them over in my fingers. They looked very similar to the thrushweed leaf, which our people used all the time.

"If it works," I said, "do you have any to share with Della? She needs this far more than I do."

"They make me turn in everything I collect each day," he said. "You don't want to know how I snuck this past them, but since you ask, I do have enough for her."

I grinned. No, I definitely did not want to know how he snuck these leaves past them.

I put the leaf in my mouth and chewed on it, eager to get the juices flowing. The taste seemed familiar, something from my childhood.

I swallowed a few times and then felt a pinch inside my heart. With that came the memory.

When I was five years old, my mother had gone out with me to collect thrushweed for a stew. Like many of my people, we enjoyed the leaves to chew on as a way to pass the time. So when I found a patch of it, I'd thought nothing of chewing on a couple of leaves.

Only seconds later, I was writhing on the ground, screaming for my mother to come. She ran to me and pulled the leaves from my mouth, then saw what I had thought was thrushweed.

"This is the wrong plant!" she'd said to me.

Immediately she found other leaves, which she forced down my throat. They caused me to vomit up everything I had swallowed, leaving a fierce burning sensation behind. But it also saved my life.

We called the plant fifeberry, so rare in the river country I'd never seen it again. But now that I looked more carefully, the spindlewill leaf was very similar to fifeberry. No, not similar. It was exactly the same plant.

Fifeberry leaves, also known as spindlewill, were poisonous.

Spindlewill was poison.

I spat out the leaves and nearly fell backward in the process.

"What's wrong?" Weevil asked, grabbing on to my arms to balance me.

"Are you sure?" I asked. "Are you sure that's what the wardens wanted you to get?"

"Yes! They checked it very carefully before asking where I had found it. They said they needed more because of the medicine shortage."

"Spindlewill is not medicine," I said. My head was swimming from what I had already ingested. I needed to get it out of me, but I didn't know how. Maybe diluted with other ingredients, it wasn't as strong, but I'd just chewed a full spindlewill leaf. "Weevil, it's poison! Why would the wardens want spindlewill?"

"I know where there's some thrushweed," he cried. "It's not far away. Hold on!"

He said other things, but I couldn't hear him anymore. Instead the world faded around me and turned to black.

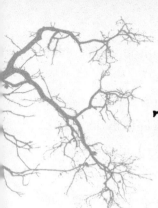

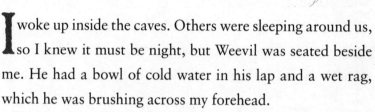

I woke up inside the caves. Others were sleeping around us, so I knew it must be night, but Weevil was seated beside me. He had a bowl of cold water in his lap and a wet rag, which he was brushing across my forehead.

When he saw my eyes open, he whispered, "I just poisoned my best friend in the world. Can we agree now that I am the worse friend?"

I coughed out a giggle, which hurt, and I winced. "Unless you want to be even worse, don't make me laugh right now."

He wasn't laughing. "That leaf could have killed you," he said. "I shoved so much thrushweed down your throat after you collapsed, I'm surprised you didn't choke on it. I'm so sorry."

"You didn't know about spindlewill. I didn't recognize the leaf either. I haven't seen it since I was five, but I should have remembered." I took his hand. "Weevil, the medicine is a poison."

"All the time you've been asleep, I've been trying to

figure this out. Why would the governor poison sick people? The Scourge will take them anyway, right?"

I swallowed hard. Weevil noticed and offered me a sip of water from a cup he also had nearby, which I gladly accepted.

"The medicine isn't meant to heal us," I said. "She never claimed that. Only that it would numb the symptoms."

"But it's also poisoning the people who are taking it," he said. "Killing them faster."

I nodded. That was why I had felt better after Della stole my medicine. I was stronger without it. I still had to recover from the Scourge, but the medicine only made the Scourge worse.

"We have to tell Della," I said. "We have to tell everyone."

"We'll tell Della. But think of what might happen if we try to tell the whole Colony at once."

"They're poisoning themselves! In smaller quantities than what I got last night, but if the spindlewill is in the medicine, then it's in them, accumulating more and more each day!"

"Everyone here has the Scourge. You know as well as anyone the kind of pain it can cause. For most of them, that medicine is all that gets them through each day. In small doses, it numbs the pain. Is it really better to take that away from them?"

"We can do better than numbing the pain," I whispered. "Jonas said that after he first came to the caves, a woman gave him some herbs that healed him. I'd guess that included thrushweed."

Weevil showed me a few other thrushweed leaves. "This is all that's left of the plant I found, and I haven't seen any others here. Even if you're right, there's not enough for everyone. We should tell Della, but for now, no one else."

I took the leaves and shoved them into the pocket of my skirt. Maybe they'd be enough to start helping Della, but what about Marjorie, and Clement, and that woman too sick to leave her bed in the old prison? What about everyone here?

"If Della improves after taking the thrushweed, then we must tell everyone," I said.

"Agreed." Weevil set the bowl of water on the ground. "How are you feeling now?"

My eyes were heavy. I took his hand and pulled him to lie down beside me. "You're as tired as I am."

"No, I'm not," he whispered. Then, with a chuckle he couldn't keep back, he added, "You've been sleeping for hours. My tiredness is much worse."

I elbowed him, and then did it a second time as a penalty for making me laugh. I fell asleep with Weevil beside me and a smile on my face.

By morning meal, I still felt the effects of the poison, making the idea of food seem strangely similar to a medieval torture. Yet I forced myself to go to the food tent, partially because I hadn't eaten enough in the last few days and hunger was starting to take its toll on me. But mostly because I was desperate to try out the thrushweed on Della.

We found her already in line, barely able to stand and clutching her flask of medicine while she waited. She appeared to be counting the minutes until she dared take more of it. Unless she had stolen again, I wondered how she could have any medicine left.

Weevil signaled for her to join us once she had gotten her food. She looked so wobbly on her feet that I doubted whether she'd be able to carry a spoon, much less the rest of her meal.

While the line edged forward, Warden Gossel walked past the people, stopping every now and then to say something to someone. He stopped and spoke to Della too, and when he did, her eyes widened. She shook her head and replied to him, but he spoke again to her and she only lowered her head and nodded.

"What do you think he said?" I asked Weevil.

"Nothing good." Weevil pointed down the line. "Look at everyone Gossel is speaking to. They all have that same expression."

As soon as Della was through the line, Weevil jumped up from our place on the ground and hurried over to her, offering one arm to help balance her and carrying her food in his other arm. Della was such a pretty girl, or had been up until a few days ago. I wondered if she was the kind of girl Weevil could ever like. Not just in a friendly way, as he thought of me, but more than that, the way Jonas seemed to like Della.

When she was seated, Weevil asked, "What did the warden say to you?"

Della wiped a tear from her eye. "I'm going to the infirmary after morning meal. He said I'm too sick to contribute. I told him that I would be fine, but he said they have better medicines in there. Ones that can help me."

"Nobody comes out of the infirmary," I said. "You can't let them take you."

"What choice do I have?" Della wiped more tears away. "I'm not strong enough to fight them. If they want to take me, then I'll have to go."

I held out my hand to her. "Give me your medicine flask."

Della gripped it again. "Why?"

"I want to smell it."

She eyed me suspiciously. "Smell it?"

"Please, Della, trust me."

She removed the flask and placed it in my hands. I unscrewed the cap and sniffed it. I had hoped to detect a whiff of spindlewill in the medicine, but whatever gave the medicine its sweetness overpowered the spindlewill's scent.

That was unfortunate, though I was still positive that my suspicions were right.

Nearly positive.

What if I was wrong, and this medicine was the only thing keeping Della and the other Colonists alive? I'd had no medicine in over two days and certainly felt plenty sick last night.

If I was wrong, I would doom the entire Colony to suffer the full effects of this disease. It would be cruel. Even if I was right, I still couldn't save them from the Scourge. There was no way to win.

"Well?" Della asked.

I looked at her. "When I was younger, my mama used to make this char bean soup. Have you ever had char beans?"

Della shook her head, obviously confused. So was Weevil, for that matter, which was odd. By now, I expected him to know where my thoughts were long before I'd opened my mouth.

"Well, char beans taste a lot like the back-end business of a bat, and they don't look much different either. I wouldn't eat them, not ever. Nobody should have to eat anything that looks like it was left behind by another animal."

Weevil giggled. "Or that left the behind of another animal."

I rolled my eyes. Honestly, some days I wondered if he was permanently six years old.

"Anyway," I said, "my mama and I used to fight about it all the time. She insisted char beans were healthy for me, that they would give me nutrition like nothing else could, and make me stronger if I ate them. I thought they were disgusting." Now I leaned in to Della. "Who was right, me or my mama?"

Della shrugged. After a moment of consideration, she said, "If they really would make you healthier and stronger, then your mother was right. You should do what she wanted, even if you didn't like it."

Gently, I placed a hand over Della's. "I agree. So please don't get upset." And I turned her flask over and dumped out all the medicine.

Della screeched and lunged for me. Who'd have thought that as sick as she looked, she would still have so much energy? Weevil got between us and took Della by the shoulders.

"It's poison," he said to her. "The medicine is poisoning you."

"It's my medicine!" she screamed. "What have you done, Ani?"

She screamed it loud enough that we now had the entire Colony looking. Wardens were on their feet and moving toward us. There was no choice now but to explain what I'd done.

I scrambled to my feet and held up the flask high enough for everyone to see. "The medicine contains a plant called spindlewill. Townsfolk don't know the plant because it's rare in Keldan. Spindlewill is a poison. In small doses, it will numb you, but as the numbing effects start to fade, it leaves you feeling worse than before. So you think you need more medicine."

"It's better than feeling the Scourge!" a woman shouted out.

"No, what's better is if we try to cure it!" Now I held up the thrushweed leaves Weevil had given me last night. "This is a plant from the river country. I think it can help us!"

"You *think*?" a man shouted. "What if you're wrong, grub?"

Weevil pulled a few spindlewill leaves from his pocket. "I gave one of these to Ani last night, thinking it would help. Instead, it almost killed her. It would have, if I had not given her some thrushweed right away. We think there's a chance thrushweed will help with the Scourge."

The wardens were eyeing one another, trying to figure out what to do. Would they pounce on me and Weevil at once, making the other Colonists wonder if there really was something to our claims? Or would they wait until we had finished speaking and then quietly drag us off? For now, they were motioning for other wardens to come up to the food tent. Something was about to happen—I just didn't know what.

"These are lies!" a boy shouted. "I remember it was grubs who first brought the Scourge to Keldan hundreds of years ago."

He remembered hundreds of years ago, really? If he was even a year older than Weevil and me, I'd be stunned.

"Governor Felling wants us to take the medicine," an older man said. "If your grub leaves could help, she'd give us those instead."

I held up the leaves again. "Maybe she doesn't know about thrushweed. Or maybe she doesn't know what's really in the medicine. But I will not take one more drink of it, and I don't think you should either."

The wardens definitely didn't like that. They began closing in on me. I looked for Della too, but couldn't see her anymore.

"You're a grub!" a woman yelled. "Why should we listen to you?"

"There are no grubs here in the Colony," I said. "And no pinchworms. No River People, no townsfolk, and, for that matter, no victims. We are Colonists, all of us who have the Scourge. We are one people, me and you. And if we work together, we can defeat this." I pointed to the wardens. "We can defeat them!"

Now the wardens moved forward, but the people had gotten to their feet around us and they were having trouble pushing through the crowd.

"Just stop taking it for three days," Weevil said. "After three days, the medicine should be out of your system. Then you can decide if you feel better or worse."

One of the men who had been on the treadmills stood and held up his flask. "I can tell you right now what I'll do." And he poured his medicine out onto the ground.

Another man next to him did the same thing. Then another woman across the tent did, and then several more people all at once.

"You have just doomed yourselves!" Warden Gossel shouted. "Fools, the grubs have tricked you! You will be screaming with pain tonight! And there is nothing you can do about it! All of you will beg to go to the infirmary, just to be rid of the pain!"

"Nobody needs to go to the infirmary again!" I held up the thrushweed again. "I have three leaves left. Will anyone try one, as a test?"

"Don't you dare," Gossel warned me, raising his pistol.

I backed farther from him and shouted, "Resist them! They have to break you first! But they will never break me!"

Or maybe they would. A warden grabbed my waist and clubbed me across the back with his fist. Weevil yelled and reached for me, but a warden had him too.

I struggled as best as I could, but I was still feeling the effects from last night and the warden was stronger than me anyway. The thrushweed leaves were pried from my hand and crushed beneath another warden's boot. Weevil said he had searched everywhere. There were no other plants on this island. No way to help the Colonists now.

They were dragging us toward the yard, and I had a feeling that this time, my punishment wouldn't be as easy as being stuck in a cage.

CHAPTER
THIRTY-ONE

So you refuse to be broken?" Gossel snarled as we arrived in the yard, beneath the vinefruit tree. Weevil was beside me, and Gossel looked at us both. "This friendship was supposed to have ended!"

"Sorry to disappoint you." Weevil looked at me, then back at the warden. "And by 'sorry,' I mean, we hope to disappoint you as often as possible."

Unamused, Gossel pulled out his rod again. "Only one of you will take the hits," he said. "Which of you will it be?"

"Me," both Weevil and I said at the same time.

"I'm stronger," Weevil said.

"You're *healthier*," I countered. "We're equally strong. Besides, this is my fault. You warned me not to say anything to the whole group and I did." I turned to Gossel. "What happened back there was my fault. It should be my punishment."

"No, it must be mine," Weevil said, and now his eyes filled with tears. I'd never seen any emotion like that from him before. "It *must*, Ani. I can't watch them hurt you. Don't make me see it."

"Then that is how we'll break you both," Gossel said. To me, he added, "Hold out your hand."

"Striking Ani with that rod will never break her." Desperation seeped through Weevil's words now. "She'll never let you see that it hurts."

"Let's compromise," I said. "Start by giving Weevil a full meal and a feather bed. I'll be so jealous it will put me into tears. Then, once you've broken me that way, you can give me the meal and the feather bed, which will break him too."

"Enough!" The lines on Gossel's face deepened. "You'll both get the rod, then."

"You won't touch either of them." It was Clement, the man from the caves, folding his arms and surrounded by a dozen others his size.

"Get to your chores!" Gossel shouted at him.

"My chores are at the treadmill." He pointed to me. "And that girl has treadmill duty also."

"She is being punished."

"For violating what rule?"

"She caused harm to you, or she will."

"She's done nothing but speak to the Colonists at morning meal. If dumping out the medicine causes us harm, then we did it to ourselves."

Gossel backed up, clearly intimidated by the many other men who had come to defend me. "All right, the girl can go. But this boy kept back plant leaves yesterday after being ordered to turn all of them in. That is a clear violation of his duties."

Weevil glanced at me with worry in his eyes. It was a violation. There was no doubt of that.

Then Gossel smiled as if he'd just had a great idea. That sent a ripple of anxiety through me. Anything that made him so happy was bound to be bad for us.

He said to me, "Yesterday, you promised to climb a mountain on that treadmill, didn't you?"

Cautiously, I nodded. "But it's in the water now, doing the climb for all of us. All we must do is keep the mill full of grain."

"The treadmill can still be climbed," he said.

"There's no point in it," Clement said. "The wheat will be ground without climbing."

"That never was the reason for the treadmill," I said, understanding now what should have been obvious all along. "It was there to bring down the strongest people of this Colony, breaking them."

"Correct," Gossel said. "So you climb that mountain, and your friend here will escape his punishment."

I couldn't. The effects of the spindlewill leaf were still weighing me down, and I'd eaten so little since arriving that there wasn't much left in me to continue fighting. I knew I couldn't climb a hill, much less climb that treadmill. But that was the point. They still wanted me to have that accident.

"This grub boy nearly got you killed by giving you spindlewill. That's a terrible crime," Gossel said. "We wouldn't want any harm coming to you, of course. So trust me when I say he is facing a very harsh penalty." He raised the rod. In anticipation of its first strike, Weevil winced.

"I'll climb it," I quickly said.

"Until all the wheat is ground for the day." Gossel lowered the rod and his eyes narrowed. "Which I believe we promised would be twice what you had yesterday."

"Then I'd better get started." For a moment, I considered being sick all over the warden's shoes. If I'd eaten anything that morning, I could have done it. As it was, I could only stand there feeling nauseous.

The warden's grin turned evil, and he pushed Weevil forward. "He gets a smack of the rod every time you stumble. If you fall, he'll get the worst of what I can do."

I shook my head. "That's not fair. Everyone stumbles, even when it's dry. Those steps will be wet and slippery now."

"Well, it wasn't my idea to move the treadmill into the river. Accept this deal, or he'll complete his punishment here, with me."

Weevil shook his head, but no words came to him. His talk of wanting my punishment had been sincere, but that didn't mean he wasn't afraid of what was coming, for him and for me.

I met the warden's gaze with the most defiant look I could manage. "Let's finish climbing that mountain."

I walked out with the men who had come to defend me. Weevil and the other wardens followed behind us.

"I can't decide whether that was stupid or brave," Clement said.

"For the River People, 'stupid' and 'brave' are the same word," I said. "One is used after a person loses. The other is for when we win."

"Then we'll call you brave," Clement added.

Thanks to the river, the treadmill was already in motion when I approached. I started forward but a warden said, "Chain her to it."

I turned. "What? No!"

"When you were assigned this job yesterday, you cheated. You got off and moved the mill."

"She improved on your terrible design!" Clement said. "That isn't cheating."

"If she doesn't walk according to my terms, then her friend will take his punishment!" Gossel shouted. "The grub can choose."

"If you fall into the water, you'll drown." Weevil shook his head. "Don't do it, Ani. I'll be fine."

But the glare in Gossel's eye told me otherwise. Whatever he intended for Weevil, my friend would not be fine when it was over. I stepped into the water in front of the treadmill.

The chain was already attached to the base of the treadmill. Another warden fastened its other end around my ankle and then shoved me onto the mill, where I was immediately forced to begin walking. Maybe it had been difficult before, with the weight of two other men constantly pulling it down, but the climb was so much harder now. There was no give in the rhythm of the water, and the wheel turned much faster than when the men had walked it.

Weevil was brought to stand directly in my line of sight with Warden Gossel behind him. At first I glared at the warden, but then my gaze fell to Weevil. He was staring back at me, looking perfectly confident in my ability to climb this wheel. The smile on his face was so ridiculously calm that I hated seeing it. And I loved it too. Without a single word, Weevil was telling me that everything would be all right.

The steps were even more slippery than I'd expected. If my foot didn't go down squarely on the next step, it would slip. Within minutes, I made my first stumble. The warden noticed, and Weevil received one hit from the rod across his back. He gasped and gritted his teeth for only a moment; then the smile returned, even if it was more forced this time.

I wouldn't do that again, wouldn't let him receive another lick of pain. So I turned my focus to the steps of the mill and climbed, and climbed. And climbed.

"You can do it, Ani," Della called.

I wasn't sure when she had arrived. She hadn't been there earlier. When I looked back, I saw she wasn't alone either. Other Colonists had come to see what was happening.

After an hour, my heart was pounding and sweat poured down my face, but in a strange way, I was also beginning to feel better too. The exercise was forcing the spindlewill poison out of my system. It was exhausting me, but strengthening me at the same time.

Until I stumbled a second time and Weevil received another hit. "Don't worry," he called up to me. "These wardens are as weak as my littlest sister."

His littlest sister was actually pretty strong, but I appreciated his attempt at an insult and so did the rest of the growing group, who laughed quietly and began murmuring. Through this show, wardens were not gaining the people's favor. It felt inevitable now, that there would be an uprising here in the Colony. I hoped I'd be around to see it.

I stumbled a third time and, above the sound of the water, heard Weevil cry out. I didn't dare look at him this time. I couldn't think about when my feet would fail him again. It wouldn't be long.

Two men walked forward as if to join me on the mill. At first I shook my head, warning them to stay back. They might have thought they were helping me, but with their added weight, the wheel would turn even more quickly. I'd never be able to keep up. However, instead, they climbed the opposite side of the wheel, the side that was moving toward the water. It was tricky because they had to step down each time I stepped up, but their weight was also balancing mine and the force of the water. They had slowed the mill for me.

"That isn't allowed!" Warden Gossel shouted.

"You have no reason to stop them!" Clement replied with equal force. "Ani continues to climb, as she agreed."

Gossel grumbled loudly, but he had no argument in return and he certainly didn't have the support of the people. If the wardens tried to pull those men down, there would be a reaction from the Colonists.

"You can do it, Ani," Weevil called. "It's only one mountain."

We did this for a long while, so long that I lost track of the time. Hours might've passed, though that didn't seem possible. I saw the ground flour emptying from the mill, so I knew we were making progress, but a slower mill also meant a slower grind. I didn't dare ask how much grain still remained.

More and more, even the slower climb became too much for me. Dark clouds had begun to gather overhead, which I took as an ominous sign. If a storm came, it would become impossible to finish grinding the wheat. Gossel wouldn't care. He would say that I had failed, and Weevil would pay for that.

Gossel was sitting now, though he had forced Weevil to remain standing. By the time we entered the afternoon hours, I guessed nearly all the Colonists had gathered here, along with the wardens, who seemed increasingly nervous. Which would happen first—my fall and failure? Or their uprising?

As the clouds grew darker, I knew it was only a matter of minutes before I would stumble again or even tumble from the wheel. If I fell entirely, the chain would pull me under the water and trap me, beyond the reach of any Colonists who'd try to save me. But even if this wheel defeated me, the Colony had changed now. The wardens would never again have the power they had only a few days ago. Did that mean my time here was a success, even if I failed?

More than anything, I had wanted to protect Weevil, just as he had protected me so far. He should never have been here, yet he had sacrificed his freedom to be with me. Couldn't I even give him a day of climbing? I looked up to Weevil as if to apologize. Then two more men climbed onto my side of the wheel. I shook my head, too out of breath to speak. It'd kill me if they moved the wheel any faster. But that wasn't their plan. They took each of my arms, raising me into the air to carry me between them, and continued the climb for me. To maintain the balance, others joined the opposite side, keeping the wheel slow and stable.

I leaned my head onto the shoulder of one of the men. "Thank you," I whispered.

"When I was a young child, I fell into an old well," he said. "The townsfolk couldn't get me out and had almost given up hope. It was a River Person who finally saved my life. Surely I can help save a daughter of those people."

The other man said, "My son loved a girl once who came from the river country. I refused to give him my blessing for the marriage and made them separate. I realize now what a mistake that was. If she was anything like you, I'd have been honored to bring her into our family."

I couldn't say anything in return. Maybe because I was more exhausted than I'd realized, or maybe because I was too stunned at what was happening in this Colony. Sometime in the last several hours, we had at last become one people.

"What is this foolishness?" a voice demanded.

Everyone turned. Even I turned, thinking I recognized the voice but unsure of what it might mean.

Governor Felling stood before us all in a long blue dress, in stark contrast to the sweaty rags we wore in the Colony. She was surrounded by her own wardens and looking perfectly furious.

Warden Brogg was with her, a deep frown on his face. Even from where I stood, breadcrumbs were still evident on his uniform. Maybe he'd been forced to leave Keldan in the middle of a luxurious lunch. Poor thing.

The governor pointed to me. "Get that girl down from there. She and I need to talk, alone."

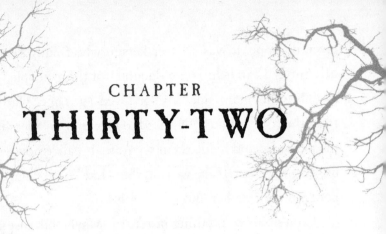

CHAPTER
THIRTY-TWO

Once I was unchained, Warden Brogg led me and the governor to a building near the barracks that I had assumed held supplies. Instead, it was empty except for some stools and a table.

"Will we be eating supper in here?" I nodded at the crumbs on Brogg's uniform. "Can I have the rest of whatever you were eating?"

"Sit," the governor said. Brogg pushed on my shoulder, ensuring I obeyed.

Not that I put up any fight. I was grateful to sit on the stool. I was grateful to sit anywhere at all because my legs felt like bags of jelly. Still, I made an effort to sit as tall as possible and look her in the eye.

Before she could ask her questions, I had one of my own. "My friend Weevil—what's happening to him right now?"

"They won't do anything until I give further orders." Governor Felling raised an eyebrow. "And what those orders will be depends entirely upon you."

"I've done nothing wrong, Governor." Since the moment I was put in that isolation wagon, I'd only tried to do what I thought was right, yet my words still sounded hollow. Here in the Colony, right and wrong were all mixed up.

"I got a letter from Warden Gossel, warning me that you were stirring up trouble. From the looks of things, I got here just in time."

"You did, but not because of me." I leaned forward. "Do you know the medicine is a poison? It's made from the spindlewill leaf, which in high enough quantities will kill a person. In low quantities, it still kills, only more slowly."

"Of course I know, but it's all we have against the Scourge!" she snapped. "Do you think you are more compassionate than me, urging the other victims here to stop taking their medicines? Perhaps you believe that you can manage the pain of the Scourge now, but what about when it gets worse? It will, you know. It will get so much worse for you, and for everyone here!'"

"It doesn't have to get worse!" I said. "If you bring in thrushweed, I think it can help. My people—"

"Grub medicine is not the answer!"

"It might be the only answer. If you would listen to me—"

"There is no cure for the Scourge."

"When a person is healed, the Scourge leaves a scar behind, up the forearm." I raised my arm to demonstrate where it would be and gasped. A thin red scar ran up my arm. It hadn't been there the last time I'd checked, before getting on the treadmill. I held it up to show her. "This. They call it the scar of health. I'll grant you, it's odd to name a scar, but they have, and it's a sign the Scourge has left the body." When the governor failed to answer, my eyes narrowed. "I know you've seen this before. Some people escaped the Colony and returned to Keldan, all of them bearing this same scar. You had them executed, didn't you?"

"They violated the law," the governor said. "No one can leave the Colony, ever, whether or not they believe they're cured. The Scourge can always be passed to someone else."

"Will you leave the Colony?" I asked. "Will you be tested for the Scourge too? Isn't it possible that you're infected now?"

"I am *not* infected!" she yelled. "What is it about grubs that compels you to fight everyone and everything?"

"You should want fighters!" My temper was rising, and I wasn't doing much to control it. "You should want the entire country of Keldan to resist the Scourge, just as we would resist Dulan if they ever invade."

"Dulan will not invade," she said. "I have seen to that. I have protected us in ways that a stupid grub like you could never understand."

"Stupid? I turned a human-powered wheel into one powered by water. I probably have a cure for the Scourge. I even found a faster way to collect the laundry here, though I admit, there were some flaws in that last idea."

A crack of thunder sounded outside and the governor froze. "What was that?" she asked Warden Brogg.

I already knew. I'd seen the dark clouds before, even if they had not.

Brogg opened the door, then shut it again. "A storm is coming this way and fast. We warned you not to come!"

Governor Felling's mouth pinched together. "I only came because Warden Gossel's letter was so urgent." She glared at me. "It's the grub's fault I'm here."

Brogg looked out again. "The storm looks pretty serious. The Colonists should be ordered into the prison early tonight, before supper. You should get to safety too, in case this results in flooding. They have a barracks on higher ground that will be safe for you."

"Not yet," the governor said. "Not until we finish with this grub."

"Ani," I said. "You keep calling me grub, but my name is Ani."

Her eyes narrowed and she leaned into me. "Your name is grub. Your name is servant. Your name is Scourge. That is what you must accept while you are here."

"My name is Ani," I repeated, leaning in toward the governor. "I am one of the River People, and I serve no one but myself. As for the Scourge, I am healed of it!"

I raised my arm again, ready to give Governor Felling an extra-close-up look at my arm, but Brogg grabbed it, protecting my fist from accidentally hitting the governor's nose. Well, accidentally, more or less.

Another crack of thunder rolled above us, immediately followed by a flash of lightning. Rain began falling as it usually did in the river country, with no early warnings of light rainfall, but suddenly, with fat, heavy drops. So much that it immediately began leaking through these thin wooden walls.

Still, Governor Felling ignored all that and only raised her voice above the storm.

"How can I send more River People here if this one can't even be controlled?" she asked. Brogg shrugged in return. Any other answer would either get him in trouble or get him sent here permanently.

"There is no Scourge amongst the River People!" I said. "But you don't care about that, do you? You told me yourself, that you believe the River People are the true Scourge of Keldan! You only want to send them here, hoping they get the disease, and to wipe us out that way!" My eyes widened. "That's why the wardens took me out of that tree. I overheard them saying you had ordered them to get five River People for testing. You didn't care which five, any of us would do."

The governor's eyes narrowed further. "If anything, I've left the River People alone for far too long," she said. "People from all over Keldan are in this Colony."

"I know that." My mind went back to the physician's office in Keldan. "Sir Willoughby knew it too. He challenged you in the last election, and you got revenge by bringing his daughter here."

"His daughter tested positive for the Scourge—you saw that yourself!"

"Unless she didn't," I said, my mind finally putting all the pieces together. "Della wasn't sick until Warden Brogg gave her that drink when she was in the cell with me. I'd stake a bet that the test was the first dose of poison. And every sip of that medicine has made her worse. The disease and the medicine are the same thing—one is just stronger than the other."

"Lies!" the governor hissed.

But I shook my head. "They are your lies, Governor Felling. There is no disease in Keldan. There is no disease here in the Colony." Now I looked directly at the woman beside me, her eyes wild with fury. "There is no Scourge."

CHAPTER
THIRTY-THREE

Behind me, Warden Brogg froze at my accusation, enough that I was able to pull my arm away from him. The governor had nearly frozen also. I knew I was right.

"There is no Scourge," I repeated. "If you want someone to get it, then they will. Or if you want someone to pass their test—maybe friends or supporters who are blind to how evil you are—then no spindlewill goes into their drink. You knew the moment you grabbed Della Willoughby that she would get it, because you planned it that way!"

"You don't know anything!" the governor finally spat out. "Three hundred years ago—"

"Maybe there was an actual disease three hundred years ago, or maybe not. I doubt we'll ever know for sure. But Della told me the disease is different now than it was back then. You know what I think, Governor? I think you wanted everyone to believe that disease had returned, and you figured out poisoning people with spindlewill mimicked the same symptoms."

"Ridiculous!" But if it was, why was the governor's face turning so red?

"No," I said, "it finally makes sense. River People eat a lot of thrushweed, and that blocks the effects of spindlewill, so I passed the first test you gave me. That's why you cut my arm—you had to put the poison directly into my blood." As the truths came together for me, I began to feel more energized. "That's why the wardens aren't afraid of getting the disease, why you're not afraid to be here. That's why I didn't find any special medicine when I searched the wardens' barracks"—the governor definitely reacted when I said that—"there is no special medicine because there is no chance of you getting the disease! There is no Scourge!"

After another crack of thunder and lightning, the governor pointed in the direction of the Colony. "People out there are sick, grub, and they are dying of something. Whether you think I gave it to them or not, whether you think it's a real disease or a poison, they are dying. Whatever you want to call it, *I* call it the Scourge. And there is plenty more of it for you."

If Brogg weren't still here, I'd have tried to run. I doubted the governor could catch me in that long dress and with all this rain. As it was, I kept my seat until I figured out a way to escape. "There's no Scourge in me. No poison in me, not anymore."

"We gave it to you once; we can do it again."

"But spindlewill is becoming harder to find. It won't be long before you have to abandon this terrible plan!"

The governor smiled wickedly. "We're developing other ways to test for the Scourge, better ways. Our solution is inside the infirmary. I'm glad to show it to you."

Brogg pulled me to my feet, getting control of both my arms this time. I wanted to kick back at him, but all my tired legs could do was just keep me from falling.

"Is the infirmary a place to kill your own people?" I asked. "Why would you do that? What could you possibly have to gain by doing all of this?"

Governor Felling looked at the warden. "Take her away. You know where she needs to go."

More lightning cracked above us, closer this time. Brogg looked up and hesitated. He didn't want to go out in the storm any more than I wanted to go to the infirmary. Of course, staying here with the governor didn't sound much more pleasant.

"Is it for power?" I asked. "Keldan is a failing country, one where your days as our leader are numbered. How evil are you, to create a deadly hoax like this, just to hold on to your power?"

She slapped me across the cheek, then yelled, "What I am doing will save Keldan! It is the only way to save my country!" She looked at Brogg. "Take her to the infirmary's back room."

His eyes widened. "The back room? No, Governor, I won't—"

"Obey my orders, Warden Brogg. I never want to see this grub again!"

"Ani Mells!" I yelled. "If you are sentencing me to death, then at least say my name!"

The governor looked me over, as if in some way seeing me for the first time. "Take this grub away," she repeated.

Brogg sighed and opened the door. Rain was pouring down, so thick that I could barely see through it.

"Don't take me there, Brogg," I said. "Please."

"Either you face her anger, or I'll have to. Sorry, Ani."

And almost the moment he stepped out into the storm, lightning hit a tree above us.

The crack was louder than I could have imagined, and the tree began to fall toward the barracks.

"Governor, watch out!" Brogg yelled. He released me to help her get out of the barracks.

The second he did, I ran.

CHAPTER
THIRTY-FOUR

I stumbled northward, almost blind in the rain. I couldn't have been wetter if I had dived into the deepest river, but that comforted me. I had been wet many times before. I had swum through waters thicker than this rain, with my eyes wide open. I could find my way through this storm.

Where would Weevil be now? The last I had seen him, he was still being held by the warden. Were they keeping him somewhere? Or would he have been released when the other Colonists were sent into the prisons early? Was there any chance he had escaped and gone to the caves?

The storm beat down on me with a violence I'd never felt before, not even in the worst storms the river country produced. I vaguely wondered if this was the kind of storm that had brought down the ship that had carried Weevil's father.

By the time I got to the Colony square, it was empty. The Colonists would all be in the prison, sheltered and safe. Weevil wouldn't be there, though. Hopefully not Della either, because I could not risk entering the prison to find her. It was the first place the wardens would look for me.

Even now, they were probably spreading out around the island to search for me.

I had to keep going north.

When I reached the rocky north shore, the winds had picked up. Raindrops felt like knives on my arms and face, but I couldn't look down or I'd be too quickly lost. Normally I could have withstood the storm, but by now, I was almost too tired to even stand. A powerful gust of wind knocked me down once, my hands and knees crashing onto the sharp rock. Ignoring the stings, I got up, only to be immediately knocked over again.

I didn't get up this time, not yet. I would in a while, but I needed more strength first. I saw the cave entrance from where I had fallen, but for as weak as I felt, it seemed miles away.

"Help!" I cried. "Will somebody help me?"

No one would answer. In all of this wind and with the growing rain and thunder, no one would hear me.

I got to my feet once more, but my legs wobbled beneath me. It wasn't the wind that brought me down. My legs couldn't do the work.

I sat on the rocks and closed my eyes. Just take a few deep breaths, I told myself. Then get up and make it to the caves.

"It's so like you, doing a job only halfway," Weevil said, wrapping an arm around me.

I opened my eyes as he lifted me to my feet. "Where did you come from?"

"The caves, of course, though don't tell Warden Gossel because he thinks I'm in the prison, right where he promised to find me after the storm passes."

"Did you hear me calling?"

Weevil smiled. "Calling? No, but I've been watching for you. Now come on, let's get inside."

He almost had to carry me there, and it seemed to me that he did at one point. The water was almost to my knees when we entered the first room of the caves, and up to my ankles in the larger inner room. I could barely slosh through it.

"You said it floods at suppertime each day," I said to a woman as we entered. "With this storm—"

"We can stay until it reaches our knees," she said. "After that, the water outside will be too high to safely leave the caves."

"How long will that be?" I asked.

The woman brushed my wet hair out of my face and handed me some smoked fish. "Eat now, child. Then rest while you can. We won't have nearly as long as you need."

I tore into the food, frustrated that I couldn't get everything in me as quickly as I wanted. As I ate, Weevil assisted me to the farthest corner of the cave, where it was driest. Someone handed him a piece of linen, which he wrapped around my shoulders to help me dry off a bit, though I knew there was little point. Maybe we had minutes, maybe as much as an hour, but I wouldn't be dry before we were forced to leave.

"The storm might pass," Weevil said. Always optimistic.

"It might." For now, I didn't care. Once I'd finished the fish, I leaned against his shoulder and closed my eyes. "How's your back?" The rod had struck him three times, hard enough I'd heard its echo in the air.

"Do you remember the time I got trampled by that wild boar?"

It had taken Weevil over a week to walk straight again. I winced. "It was like that?"

"Not really. But every time he hit me, mostly I just thought about how I wished Gossel could be trampled by a wild boar too, just once." He put his arm around me now, drawing me in closer. "The sting will pass soon."

"I'm sorry."

"Don't be. You saved me from something so much worse." He shifted against the cave wall, probably to protect his back. "What happened with Governor Felling?"

"She doesn't like me much."

"That's ridiculous, everyone likes you," he replied. "Well, except for Farmer Adderson. And the people you sing to in the towns. And the Colonists who dumped out their medicine, and the wardens and their evil governor who've imprisoned us on this Scourge Colony."

I tilted my head up at him. "There is no Scourge, Weevil. There is no disease."

He pursed his lips, then said, "I wondered about that while I watched you on the treadmill. You've never been so strong. It was like you'd never been sick."

"Because I never was," I said. "Not from a disease anyway."

He humphed. "That discovery won't endear you to the governor, I'm sure." He chewed his lip a moment while he considered that, then added, "Why is she doing this?"

I shrugged. "She claims it's the way to save Keldan, but how can it? Although she hates the River People, this started long before she came after us. Her personal enemies were brought here too, but only a few people compared to the total number who have come through this Colony. Most of them are just ordinary townsfolk, like Jonas or Clement or Marjorie. How could taking ordinary people help Keldan?"

Now Weevil shrugged. "What are we going to do?"

"If we remain here, the wardens will eventually find us. The governor already gave her orders for me, and it wasn't to throw me a party."

He smiled. "That's too bad. In this storm, it'd be an exciting party."

"After the storm passes, we have to get off this island as quickly as possible. Maybe we can sneak aboard the governor's boat, when she goes home tomorrow."

Weevil shook his head. "Too risky. Did you see how many wardens she brought with her? We'd never avoid them all."

"The boats that we used to come over here?"

"They'll have been pulled back to Keldan already. This island was designed as a prison, and the governor knows that."

I exhaled in frustration, and Weevil drummed his fingers against the cave walls to think. He said, "We'll find a way off this island, I promise. Once we leave the caves, I'll look for a boat while you continue resting."

I didn't even argue. "A rest sounds nice. I climbed a mountain for you today, Weevil. A thousand-mile mountain."

He brushed a hand over mine. "And if it takes walking this island a thousand times, I will find us a way home. Now sleep."

For the first time, possibly ever, I obeyed him without argument. If I were not so tired, I would have argued, and probably won. Yet as I fell asleep, I decided that he deserved to win, maybe just this once.

CHAPTER
THIRTY-FIVE

L et's go, Ani."

For all I knew, Weevil had been poking at me for five minutes before I finally responded to him. I sat up and stretched and only then realized that the water around us was over my legs. No wonder I had been dreaming that I was so cold. In this water, I was shivering.

As we got to our feet, everyone else was already exiting the cave.

"The storm?" I asked.

"Worse, I'm told. But it'll slow down the wardens too. How are you?"

"Better than before." My legs still ached, but as blood began flowing through them again, they were warming. And they were supporting my weight, even as we sloshed through the flooding waters. "I can come with you to find the boat. We shouldn't be separated."

"We need to separate," Weevil said. "If another boat exists on this island, I will find it, but you have to find Della. We'll all meet again on the shore, where we first landed. If there are no boats, we'll overtake the wardens and steal the governor's boat. I can handle one or two. Judging by the way you look, you could manage any warden over age eighty-nine. Maybe Della can bribe the rest." His head tilted. "Perhaps this isn't a good plan."

I gave his arm a squeeze as I followed him out of the cave. "Find us another boat, one big enough for all the Colonists, if possible. But be safe, all right?"

"Of course!" Before we left, Weevil pulled the quilting needles from where they had been stuck into his pants leg. "Take these."

I pushed them back at him. "I'm no good at lock picking."

"You might need them to get access to Della. Take them."

I did and stuck them in the hem of my dress, hoping there were no locks between me, Della, and our boat to freedom.

"Don't break them, like you usually do," Weevil said. "They're the last two needles my mother has."

"You're only saying that because I always break them," I said.

"You're going to get Della?" Jonas stepped up to me. "I'll come with you." He had been waiting for us in the cave's outer room. "I heard what you two have done today, for all of us. I'm ashamed to have been hiding here while you have proved what it means to be from the river country."

"What it means to be a Colonist," I said. "A lot of people stood in our defense today." Then I smiled at him. "I'm glad you're coming along. I'm not sure I could persuade her to go into this storm otherwise."

He smiled back, but not at me. He was thinking about her. "Most people don't understand Della the way I do. Whenever she's afraid, she falls back on the things she knows—her money and her father's power. But that's not the real her. She's a good person."

"We know that," I said. "Now come on."

Weevil gave my hand a squeeze before we left, promising to meet me at the beach in one hour. I didn't understand how that could be possible. This was a small island, but even in good weather and with no wardens out searching for him, he'd have a difficult time covering all the shorelines. He could never see everything in only an hour.

But we were running out of time. The reality of that was pressing in on me with increasing urgency.

Jonas and I ducked as low as possible to run away from the north shore toward the old prison. As the warden had predicted, much of the island was already flooding. We were fine as long as we stuck to higher ground, but one misstep and we'd slip and find ourselves with even greater problems. If that was possible.

"Be careful," I warned Jonas.

"*You* be careful," he replied. "I've stayed out of trouble for two weeks. You don't seem able to avoid it for two minutes."

I laughed. "I can easily avoid it for two minutes. It's the third minute that always seems to challenge me."

Once we got to the rear of the old prison, Jonas and I debated the best way to find Della. It occurred to me that I didn't know which of the rooms inside was hers, or even which floor she was on. Probably one of the lower floors, I guessed. Della would have chosen a place that made it easiest for her father to find her.

"I should go in alone," Jonas said. "Wardens are looking for you."

"And you too," I said. "We'll stay together." I didn't think wardens would go into the old prison unless they had to, but they might've been in there searching, thinking that's where I'd taken shelter from the storm.

We had barely stepped inside the prison when the sounds of people's moans and cries overtook the rain and thunder outside. It was as if the walls themselves had come alive with the pain from the Scourge.

Not the Scourge. No, this was the result of people not taking the medicine. People had begun feeling the effects of emptying their flasks. I understood. I knew firsthand how awful spindlewill poisoning felt without the numbing effects of the "medicine" concoction to counter the pain.

I wished Weevil were here with us too. Or maybe not. Weevil's advice had been only to test the thrushweed on Della and then slowly wean her from the medicine. Never one for subtlety, I'd convinced everyone to dump out their medicine. The consequences of that had led us here, sneaking around on a flooded island, through a raging storm, to forge an escape attempt over seawaters that no sane person would ever cross.

Considering all of that, I was very glad Weevil wasn't here. Jonas didn't know the full potential of my foolishness yet, making him a much better companion tonight.

"Let's check each room as fast as possible," I said. "Go in quick, get out even quicker."

I let Jonas look in most of the rooms on the first floor while I kept to the shadows of the hallway. It bothered me to hear so many people hurting and to know that I had played a role in their pain. Even if it was the right thing to make them stop taking the medicine, I still felt sad and wished I had a way to help them.

"She's not on this floor," Jonas reported.

So we went to the second floor, but when I glanced out the window, I saw something that made my breath lodge in my throat. Weevil was climbing the vinefruit tree in the yard, the same one that held the cage. Of course that's what he would do. If he needed a place to look around, the old prison was taller, but windows were only on one side of the building and didn't point to any of the shores. From the tree, he'd be able to see far more—if he got up high enough.

But not in this storm!

In any other circumstance, it would have been comforting to know that in desperate times, Weevil did far more foolish things than I'd ever attempt. But now, with lightning cracking almost directly overhead, that was downright stupid!

"We have to get him out of that tree," I said to Jonas, and immediately started back down the stairs.

Jonas grabbed my arm. "We have to find Della."

"Weevil will die up there!"

"And Della will die in this prison. Your friend knows what he's doing, and he's trusting us to do our job too."

My lips pinched together. "Fine, but let's hurry."

We both searched on the second floor, and I quickly realized it had been wise to keep my face in the shadows before. Because those who saw me weren't exactly offering me cheers and good wishes. One woman even welcomed me by throwing her pitcher of water at my face when I looked into her room.

The third floor was even worse. People there had heard the commotion and those shouting out my name below. Many were already out of their rooms when we walked up.

"We were wrong to listen to you, grub!" one woman shouted at me. "Until this morning, I could do my work assignments. I could manage the Scourge pain and feel I was living an almost normal life. But now I've lain here all evening, wishing the storm would just strike this building down and end all this moaning."

"If there was one thrushweed plant on this island, then there must be more," I said. "When we find it, I'll personally bring you some and let you try it. The Scourge isn't—"

"The Scourge is going to take us anyway!" a man yelled. "At least before today, it took us more gently."

"You've all been poisoned!" I called back. "That is the Scourge—a poison. But it can be cured!" Even if there was no more thrushweed on this island, I knew where it grew in Keldan. I could return here and help these people. "If you give me a few more days, I will bring you the cure myself."

"We might have a few more days," another man said, advancing toward me and Jonas. "But you don't. The wardens promised that if we turned you over to them, we'd all get new flasks full of medicine. So that's what we'll do." He snarled at those around him. "Get the girl!"

CHAPTER
THIRTY-SIX

As the third-floor Colonists moved closer to Jonas and me, we backed toward the stairs, but more people were coming up, so we couldn't get out that way. I looked out the window, still cracked open from when Della and I had dumped out the laundry. Too bad the laundry wasn't there anymore. It might've cushioned our fall if we decided to jump.

Because as risky as that idea was, jumping out of a third-story window seemed safer than where we now were.

"You're going to have a bad night!" I yelled at the growing crowd. "It'll be one of the hardest nights you've ever had to go through. I know, I've done it. But morning will come and we'll start to fix things tomorrow."

"We don't have to wait out the night," a man said. "Not if we turn you in."

He started to lunge for us, when a voice behind everyone shouted, "I forbid you to touch her!"

Hearing Della's commanding voice, the crowd turned. With so many people between us, I couldn't see her, but I was certain that everyone around us had heard. "All of you know me and you know my father, so you know that he would've done everything possible to save me from this disease. None of it kept me from getting sick, and none of it has saved me from being here in this Colony. If all that money can't save me, what hope do any of you have? Did Governor Felling save any of you from this disease? No, she only gave you a medicine that can numb you for a while, even as it makes us sicker. There is only one person who has given us any hope of survival, and she is standing there before you. Look at Ani. She was as sick as me when we came here on the boats. Now she looks as healthy as we all used to be."

"I am healthy." I raised up my arm to show the thin red line running up my forearm. "This is evidence that I've recovered. The Scourge is not a disease. You were poisoned, and thrushweed can cure it."

"Rubbish," one woman muttered. "The governor has no reason to make us sick. The Scourge is real."

"Whatever the Scourge is, I recovered from it too," Jonas said, holding up his arm. "But it wasn't because of the medicine."

"Jonas?" Della called. I saw where she was pushing through the crowd, and suddenly, she was running to her friend. She gave him a warm embrace, and then he kissed her. I felt embarrassed to look at them, but happy too.

And I wondered if one day, Weevil might ever want to kiss me. I thought if he did, I'd probably be all right with that. One day.

When they parted, he whispered something to her. Della nodded and turned to the crowd. "I demand that you let us pass."

They parted for her in a way they never would have for me or even Jonas. And as we turned and started to leave, I checked out the window again.

I wasn't one for cursing, but I did now. Weevil had made it to the highest, thinnest branches of the vinefruit tree and was looking around in all directions.

Without waiting for the people to move, I pushed through them and ran to the main floor. There, right beside the entry, was a half-filled laundry bin, probably abandoned when the storm hit. I grabbed it and pushed it with me out in the rain toward the tree. Weevil didn't see me coming. He was facing southward, looking out over the wall behind the infirmary. He was so intent on whatever he was watching that he might've forgotten all about the storm overheard.

River People understood storms better than anyone. Water from the heavens was drawn to water already on the earth, and when storms hit, we felt the worst of it. Weevil knew better than to be up in that tree.

But he had also promised to find us a boat within one hour, and this was the only way.

I charged for him, determined to get that laundry bin beneath him before he either fell in the rain or was struck by lightning. Jonas wasn't far behind me, though Della was with him and much slower than me, so the gap between us widened.

"Weevil!" I yelled. "Get down!"

He turned and reached for a rope up in the tree with him. Probably the rope that held the cage suspended from the tree. I couldn't see the cage right now, though, only the rope.

"Ani, run!" he yelled back at me.

I was already running. But he knew that, which meant he was warning me to go back, to run away from him.

I spun around, trying to see anything through this storm, and was immediately tackled to the ground by Warden Brogg. Jonas crashed into the two of us, fighting the warden off, but then Gossel came and several more wardens with him, as if they had all been searching for us together. From the corner of my eye, I saw Della creeping toward us. I wanted to warn her to stay back, but didn't dare call attention to her.

Jonas and I were both pushed into the mud. It took the effort of every warden there to get our arms pulled behind us. I made sure of that.

"I only brought enough rope for the girl," a warden said. "I didn't think we'd find another one out here."

"Tie up the boy," Gossel said. "The governor has other plans for the girl anyway."

Whatever they were, I didn't care. My eyes were on Della. She had snuck in close enough to grab the laundry bin and was now racing toward Weevil. I doubted the wardens even noticed her or cared what she was doing if they did notice. They wanted me, and Jonas had been a fugitive for even longer. Della was considered harmless.

"Two for the infirmary, then," a warden said. "Jonas, we wondered where you had gone. I figured you were dead."

"If you had found me before, I would've been dead by now," he said.

"Well, we can take care of that."

They sat us up, and my eyes immediately went to Weevil. Della was almost to him with the laundry bin, but now that she had crossed into the fenced yard, I couldn't really see her anymore. With a shout down at us, Weevil held on to the rope and jumped into the air. Now I understood. He was using the cage as a counterbalance. It would rise up as it lowered him.

But he hadn't dropped far before lightning struck the tree, exactly where he had just been standing. Weevil was thrown off the rope, and limbs from the tree exploded away from its base. With so many wardens around me, I couldn't see where he fell. The fierce rain blinded me, or maybe it was my own fear and anger doing that. I couldn't see what was happening to him or Della.

I stifled a scream in my throat. They could be hurt—very seriously hurt from either the lightning, or the fallen branches, or Weevil hurt from the fall itself. If I told the wardens, they could go check on them and . . . and then what? They'd leave my friends to die or bring them into the infirmary with Jonas and me. To die.

I lowered my head and let the tears fall while the wardens forced us to our feet and began walking Jonas and me toward the infirmary.

Where people went in, and nobody ever came out.

CHAPTER
THIRTY-SEVEN

If the old prison had been cold and unwelcoming, it was nothing compared to the infirmary. At least some effort had been made to remove the feeling of the prison having once been an ancient dungeon.

No such effort had been made here.

Without its thick main doors, this infirmary would have been heavily flooded by now. As it was, it might've been the safest place in the Colony. Despite the serious situation, the irony of that thought gave me a grim smile.

We walked down a narrow hallway, passing rows of cells with more thick wooden doors and heavy locks. There was some moaning in here, but most of the voices I heard seemed stronger than I'd have expected from the people dragged in here during recent days. One man in a cell to my right even yelled that he felt well and begged to be released. His words were echoed by others nearby, sounding equally strong. I struggled to figure that out.

The moans obviously came from the sickest prisoners of these cells, but what were healthy people doing here? They hadn't come in healthy—at least, everyone I'd seen entering the infirmary looked like they were in their final moments of life.

The Scourge was a poison made of spindlewill, slowly killing the Colonists outside of the infirmary. The medicine they took to stay numb was just a weaker form of the same poison.

Yet in here, they were getting better.

They weren't bringing people into the infirmary to die. They brought them here to live, but why?

A Colonist had to be broken before coming to the infirmary. That was the reason the wardens hadn't been allowed to bring me here before. The governor wanted broken spirits, and whole bodies.

None of this made sense. I wished Weevil were with me because he could help me sort these things out.

No, I immediately corrected myself. No, I did *not* want Weevil here with me. I wanted him safe at home, laughing and diving to the bottom of the rivers and working hard for his family, and . . . and I wanted to be there with him.

I didn't even know if he was still alive. Nor if I would be alive by the end of this night.

As we reached the final row, Jonas was led away toward a cell. I struggled against the warden's grip, desperate to see which cell they put him in. I'd need to know that for when I came to get him out again, which I fully intended to do. By the time they got control of me, I hadn't seen exactly which cell they took him into, but I had a close enough idea. As soon as possible, I would come to rescue him.

The hallway ended there with only a single door ahead of us. This was the back room, where Governor Felling had apparently ordered me to be taken. I didn't know why, but it couldn't be for anything good. We entered an examination room, not too different from Doctor Cresh's office in Keldan. A fireplace was at the far end, with a lit fire inside, making the room a touch too warm. But a kettle was hung over it, and I recognized the scent at once. More medicine was being brewed, more poison. It had worked for over a year to keep the Colonists numb. Whatever happened to me, I doubted it would be as easy to fool them anymore. By tomorrow, when the medicine was ready, most of the people in that prison would already feel better than they had. They would know the medicine was an enemy to them. They'd know the governor was their enemy too.

The wardens would never persuade the Colonists to believe their lies again, no more than they could put all this rainwater back into the clouds.

But saving the Colonists wasn't enough. The governor could not be allowed to send anyone else here. Someone had to stop her.

I really didn't want to think about who that someone might be.

Another door stood at the far end of the room, letting in rainwater, so I guessed it had to be the infirmary's rear exit. Shelves on the walls held jars of herbs, liquids, and other ingredients. In any other physician's office, these jars might contain things to actually heal a person, or to improve their life somehow. Not here.

But my attention went to a more unusual sight, a wooden grate in the floor of the room. They already had cells in the rest of this infirmary. What would they need with a caged pit beneath the floor?

Maybe it was nothing. In the old days, when this place had been a prison, that had probably been used as an isolation cell. Before that, I couldn't imagine its use, and I was certain that I did not want to know.

Yet as they led me in that direction, I figured I was about to find out. I tried digging in my feet. Governor Felling had already ordered my sentence, that I would get enough Scourge to kill me. What was in that pit? My resistance was useless. Gossel grabbed both my arms, locking them behind me.

Brogg wasn't helping. He only stood aside, staring at our fight with sympathetic eyes. But sympathy did me no good.

"Help me, Brogg!" I cried.

He didn't move to help, but shook his head at Gossel. "The tests are one thing. This goes too far. I won't help you do this."

Gossel began dragging me toward the grate, and then I had my first clue of what was down there.

I heard hissing.

Snakes.

"This is wrong!" I yelled as I struggled against him. "You know this is wrong!"

"You left the governor no choice," Warden Gossel said. "How many times were you warned? Unlock that grate, Brogg. Do it, or you'll go in with the grub."

"Throw the keys into the pit," I told him. "Then neither of us will go in."

Brogg frowned at me, looking truly sorry. "It's not as easy as that."

"Follow my orders, or I will have you put inside, Brogg," Gossel said again. "Make your choice."

Without looking at me, Brogg knelt on the floor and unlocked the grate, pulling it open.

I squirmed again, trying to get free, but with my exhaustion and hunger, Gossel was so much stronger than me.

"Why did you take me in the first place?" I asked. "I've done nothing wrong. I wasn't even sick, not until the governor made me sick. Why?"

More lightning cracked overhead. Truly, this storm was getting worse. The caves would be entirely flooded by now. The main floor of the prison would have a lot of water too. The infirmary was downhill from the Colony square, though still protected by its thick doors.

Gossel used the distraction to push me backward into

the pit, but as I fell, I grabbed the grate door, which came down over my head, nearly knocking me off as it crashed closed on the ground. Though I had a good grip on the bars, that was only a temporary solution. Not far beneath me, the dark ground was moving. I didn't know how many snakes were in this pit, but if I didn't keep holding on, I would find out.

"Lock it," Gossel ordered, and while still avoiding my eyes, Brogg did as he was told.

Gossel outright laughed at my attempt to avoid the snakes. "They say River People are strong, so maybe you'll try to stay up there for the rest of the night, but honestly, there's no point in trying. Governor Felling will be here in the morning to check on you. Even if you last that long, she will see that you get the Scourge."

"The Scourge is spindlewill," I said, almost to myself. "But you're running out of plants." Then I looked up at him. "You're going to use snake venom next?"

"Doctor Cresh is experimenting with the right dosage to mimic symptoms of the Scourge. You'll make for a good test subject, though I suspect you're about to get far too much venom to help us." Gossel's smile reflected his cruel heart, and his eagerness to get rid of me.

Behind him, Brogg added, "We'll have to use the snakes soon. If the governor brings in more River People, the spindlewill won't work."

As he talked, I'd been looking at the snakes below me, with red spots on their black bodies, different from anything I'd seen in the river country.

"There are no snakes in the towns, and I didn't think Attic Island had snakes," I said. Moisture still on my hands from the storm was threatening my hold on the bars, and there was no dry spot on me to wipe them off. Gossel laughed as I redoubled my grip. Ignoring him, I asked, "What kind of snake is this?"

"They're very aggressive," he said, almost admiringly. "Dulanian vipers."

"Dulan?"

"They were a gift to the governor. Most of them are kept here, though Doctor Cresh has some in his offices as he continues his experiments."

"Dulan?" I still couldn't understand that. "Why would Dulan—"

Suddenly, something exploded right outside the infirmary, followed by a crash and the cries of several other prisoners in the west side of the building. It startled me so much I nearly lost my grip.

Nearly. Nothing would make me let go of these bars.

"I'll wait with the girl," Brogg said. "You'd better check that out."

Gossel swatted the side of his head. "So you can get her out? I've seen your sympathies. Come with me!"

Again, Brogg obeyed, though I also saw his apologetic look as he exited the room. He never expected to see me again. Well, he could apologize to me in person, because I wasn't about to fail now. Not after all I'd been through.

As the infirmary door closed on me, I made that a vow. Yes, they definitely would see me again.

I hoped.

CHAPTER
THIRTY-EIGHT

With the crash still echoing in my ears, I guessed that lightning had struck near the infirmary and caused one of the taller trees to fall. If it landed on the infirmary, it might've smashed through the outer wall. The yelling I was hearing might be prisoners whose cells were being flooded.

But the damage must also be connected to the pit below me, where floodwaters were already seeping in, and fast. If these snakes could swim, then it didn't matter how long I could hang here. They would rise up to meet me.

I immediately raised my left foot as high as possible without tipping it upside down. Then I checked my right hand grip. It wasn't as good as I wanted, but there was no choice. With my left hand, I reached down into the boot, searching for the knife. At first I couldn't feel it, so I wiggled my foot around until the tips of my fingers touched it. I wiggled even more, letting the boot loosen. It was going to slide off, and there was nothing I could do about it. I lifted my leg even higher, and as the boot slipped, I grabbed the knife. The boot splashed into the water below, and the snakes attacked it like it was the first meal they'd had in months.

I rolled my eyes, not at all thrilled with what I now knew. Yes, the water was already high enough to make a splash. Yes, the snakes could swim in it. And yes, they were stupid enough to think a boot was edible. I could only imagine the fun they'd have with me.

With my knife between my teeth now, I kicked off the other boot next and listened to them attack that one as well. It was a necessary sacrifice, and besides, what would I do with only a single boot anyway?

I lifted both feet up to the grate. They barely fit between the bars, but by keeping them bent inward, they should hold my weight. I tested that by releasing one hand and then the next. Happily, my feet seemed more sturdy than my hands had been.

I pulled the first of Weevil's needles from my skirts, then angled myself back up and reached between the bars for the lock on this door. It was in an awkward position, so I'd have to pick the lock both backward and upside down. If I failed, I hoped Weevil would consider those disadvantages before judging my lock-picking skills too harshly.

I stuck the tip of the knife inside the lock, then with my other hand pushed the needle in to feel for the tumblers. Something moved inside the lock, but it was still closed, so I wiggled the needle around again.

And wiggled too hard. The needle broke inside the lock. I groaned and let both halves fall below me. I heard them splash and the fierce reaction of the snakes below. I hoped they tried attacking the sharper end of the needle. Then it'd be one less snake for me to fend off.

I wanted to relax my body, just for a moment, and hang upside down for a short rest. But as the dark flood waters continued rising below me, I wasn't sure how close that'd put me to the snakes. They obviously could swim. I assumed they also had a fair ability to jump, because that was exactly how bad my day was going.

So I withdrew the second needle, determined this time to be more careful. I jammed the knife back into the lock, and the needle with it. It broke immediately, though not quite in half. If I was careful, I had enough needle left, barely. So I stuck it in again, and this time wiggled it around while paying attention to where the pressure was yielding.

While I did, I thought about what Weevil had told me, that I balanced him. In our friendship, I was the knife. Swinging for everything and anything and occasionally hitting my mark. But Weevil was different. He was the needle. He identified the most specific areas to put pressure and did nothing more than was absolutely necessary. As our time in the Colony had proved, he balanced me too.

To pick this lock, I needed that same balance. While the knife was necessary to move the tumblers, if I wanted to be successful, I had to be the needle.

With that thought, I found the spot where the needle had the most give. With a gentleness that had rarely been a part of me, I pressed against that tumbler and heard a click.

Below me, something hissed, followed by a sharp tug on my skirts. A snake had latched itself on to my skirts! The last good skirt I owned, in fact, which was infuriating.

I tried to shake it off, and in the process, the needle fell out of the lock, landing somewhere below. Landing in that snake's eye, I hoped.

Luckily, the knife was jammed in more tightly. I pulled it out and then cut away at my skirt, hoping it wasn't a part of the dress I would need once I was free.

If I was free. I'd heard the lock click, but was that just the tumbler moving aside, only to fall back in place now that the needle was gone?

With my knife back between my teeth, I rose up again, higher this time, and felt above the cage bars for the lock. It snapped open and fell into the water below. This did land on a snake. I heard the clonk.

Good. They were giving me a nasty headache; it was about time one of them got a headache too.

Holding tightly to the bars, I withdrew my feet and pressed them against the side of the pit wall, near the cage door. Once I straightened my body, I hoped it'd force the door upward. It moved a little but my feet slipped. I heard the snap of a snake's jaw and wondered how close it had come to my foot.

I straightened myself again, refusing to make any more mistakes, at least until I was out of the pit. The cage door lifted, and I got one foot onto the floor, then the other. Then I rolled from there onto the floor, slamming the crate door down again.

That was good news, but my problems were far from over. Once the water was high enough, the snakes would be free of the pit. I got to my feet and ran over to the fireplace. How odd it was, to see the fire still roaring in its place, while everything around me was soaked.

Using my skirts to protect my hands, I pulled the pot of boiling spindlewill off the fireplace and walked it back to the pit and dumped it in. Poison, meet venom. I wondered which would win.

Then I quickly scoured the room for any jar marked as alcohol or with any label that might include flammable contents. As I did, I noticed one row of glass jars that had escaped my attention before. The jars were filled with dry thrushweed leaves, enough to heal every Colonist here. If they had collected these leaves, then they must know its effect on the spindlewill. Was this thrushweed the reason some of the people here in the infirmary were saying they felt better?

I stared at the jars until hissing sounds overwhelmed the roll of thunder overhead. I had to destroy this room, *now*. It meant I'd also destroy this thrushweed, which the Colonists on the outside so desperately needed. But what they didn't need was to suddenly find the island crawling with Dulanian vipers.

I finally decided to open every jar of liquid and dump all their contents into the pit. Something in one of those bottles had to burn.

Then I returned to the fireplace. One of the logs must've been recently brought in from the storm, because half of it was still wet and fire had yet to take hold there. I grabbed it and dropped the log into the pit.

Yes, something in there was highly flammable. A funnel of fire exploded from the pit, singeing the hairs on my arm and catching a piece of my hem on fire. My skirt was thoroughly ruined now. I patted out the fire from the fabric, grabbed my knife from where I'd laid it on the floor, and then ran from the burning room.

Plenty of cries could still be heard on the west side of the infirmary, so I guessed all the wardens had gathered there. I went to the quieter half instead.

I tested the first door, one with a small barred window for communication. The woman inside pressed her nose to the bars. "Hurry! Something smells terrible. Is it fire?"

"Burning snakes," I mumbled, as if that was the sort of thing everyone was used to smelling.

I tugged on her door, but it was locked. I still had my knife, but that wasn't enough. The needles probably wouldn't have worked either. These were bigger medieval locks, half rusted over. With his thin needles, even Weevil couldn't have picked these.

The second and third doors were the same way. I didn't know why I kept trying them. Of course they'd all be locked.

The fourth door was Jonas's.

"So," he casually said, "which catastrophe was you? Did you start the fire or destroy the entire west half of the infirmary?"

I grinned. "Well, I won't take credit for the west half. I can't break the lock, but you need this."

He held out his tied hands. I gave him my knife to cut the ropes and told him to pocket the larger pieces, just in case we needed it.

"The rope is useless if you can't get me out of here," he said.

"I'm working on that."

"Stop right there!" Warden Gossel shouted from behind me. Inwardly, I groaned. Gossel was the last person I ever wanted to see, but especially not now.

Jonas had my knife, and in his hurry to get it back to me, I heard it drop inside the cell. Meanwhile, Gossel pulled out a pistol, aimed directly at me. I stared down its long barrel, frozen with fear. Even if I had my knife, it wouldn't do any good.

Then someone yelled out from behind him, and suddenly, I saw Weevil. His hair was sticking out more than usual and looked a little burnt, his clothes were torn, and someone had wrapped part of his arm in a makeshift bandage, tying it off with a silk ribbon. He looked terrible, but at least he was alive.

Also, Weevil might've gone fully insane. He came flying down the hall at Gossel like a hawk swooping for its kill and with a screech just as loud. Gossel was knocked off balance at first, but then recovered and threw Weevil down the opposite hallway. I ran toward them, happy to join the fight if the wardens really wanted to see what River People could do.

But before I could get to him, a laundry bin barreled down the hallway and ran straight into Gossel. He tumbled inside it, banging his head on a low-hanging beam in the process. Still gripping the bin's handle, Della looked sideways at me and smiled.

"Is this how you River People always live?" she asked.

With a shrug, I said, "Yes, only with more fishing and fewer people trying to kill us."

Brogg ran down the hallway to see what had happened to Gossel. The pistol in his hand was cocked and ready. Instantly, our eyes locked.

I hesitated. Even if Weevil and I had a chance against him, our fight would alert other wardens to come after us.

But Brogg only nodded, lowered the pistol, and turned to disappear from where he had come.

Weevil was back on his feet in an instant. "Are you and that warden friends now?"

"He shouldn't expect gifts from me anytime soon," I said. "But I don't think we're enemies either. How's Gossel?"

Weevil leaned inside the bin. "Very sleepy," he said. "Also, with that lump on his forehead, I think he'll need a larger hat."

Then Weevil rose up with the warden's keys in his hands, which he tossed to me. "You could've used one of my needles to pick those locks."

"It wouldn't have worked. Anyway, I broke it inside a different lock."

"What lock?"

"I'll explain later, but it was for a good cause. Besides, whatever I did, I think it's worse to climb the tallest tree on the island during a lightning storm."

Weevil grinned. "It's hard to be worse than you at anything, but I think I finally did it!"

Once I finished freeing Jonas from his cell, he clumsily shoved the knife into my hands before running to Della. Then I unlocked one more cell and handed the keys to the man inside. "You must get all the others out," I said. He nodded and continued down the hall where I had left off.

"Let's go," Weevil said.

We started toward the infirmary entrance, but by then, other wardens were aware of our presence. Worse still, thanks to the hole knocked into the west end of the building by the storm, the infirmary was beginning to flood. We'd never pull the door open with so much water in the way.

"Come on," I said, leading everyone with me toward the physician's office. We opened the door to see the floor covered in water, and oddly, fire on the walls and shelves, having spread from what I had started in the pit. It made the room at once both hot and cold. "Watch out for snakes."

"Snakes?" Della asked.

"Snakes *and* fire," Weevil said admiringly. "You've been busy." He glanced down. "Snakes, Ani—where are your boots? And what happened to your dress?"

Luckily, most of what I'd cut away was an underskirt behind me. But Weevil had noticed, so maybe it was worse than I'd thought.

"Help me brace the door," I said. Though it was heavy, we pushed the examination table in front of the door, and just in time too, for wardens were already on the other side, pounding to come in.

"I see a snake!" Della cried, leaping into Jonas's arms.

"It's dead," I said. "But they might not all be. Let's go."

I pointed to the door at the far end of the room. The wooden shelves on either end were almost entirely consumed in flame, and the door itself had blackened from the smoke and heat.

"Nothing will be out that door," Della said. "Just the pole fence behind the infirmary."

"But I've got a plan." I turned to Weevil, realizing he had just said the very same thing. What was his plan? Mine would work, but his were usually better. In fact, knowing the absolute foolishness of my plan, I could guarantee that this time, we should follow his idea.

"Can we discuss this after we're away from the snakes?" Jonas asked.

"We're all wet," Della said. "If we keep our heads down and run, the fire won't bother us."

Weevil went first, using what remained of his shirt to open the hot door. Jonas ran with Della next. I followed, but not before looking back one last time to be sure nothing still remained alive in this foul room.

Maybe that didn't matter. According to Gossel, Doctor Cresh had other Dulanian vipers back in his office on Keldan.

Besides, there was no looking back now for any of us. We could not stop until everyone knew the truth about the Scourge.

CHAPTER
THIRTY-NINE

It was a good thing Jonas was carrying Della, because any strength she'd had earlier had been exhausted on that laundry bin. She'd wielded it like a weapon, though, no doubt about that.

"What now?" Jonas asked. The tall fence was right in front of us. It wouldn't take the wardens long to figure out we had left the examination room. They'd be coming for us within minutes.

Weevil pointed to a nearby door that had been built into the fence. "The other night, Ani and I heard noises back here, probably on the other side of this wall. I don't know what's over there, but it's got to be better than here. I can easily pick this lock, and we'll walk to freedom." He turned to me. "I know you broke one of the needles, but if you still have the second one and your knife—"

"I broke both needles."

"Both?" He paused, squinting at me before wiping rain off his face. "I've got to be honest with you, Ani. That's really terrible news. The worst."

"Don't be dramatic," I said. "There's another plan." I grabbed his hand and pulled him in the direction of the river that ran beneath the fence wall. Yesterday, it had been mid-sized, with a strong flow of water coming toward the Colony, but it had also been manageable. Now, thanks to the storm, the river had flooded its banks and doubled in its swiftness.

So, yes, obviously his plan had been better. But mine would make a great story one day. Or an amazing story, *if* we survived.

Staring at the river, Weevil swiped his hair away from his face. "You've got to be joking."

"We're good swimmers," I said to him.

"Not that good. I've never gone upriver in something like that."

"Me neither, not alone." I held out my hand for the rope that had tied Jonas. "If we tie ourselves close together and one of us always stays anchored on something, the other can pull us forward."

Weevil tilted his head, obviously doubtful. Then he reached for the rope. "All right, but if we live through this, you owe my mother a new pair of quilting needles."

We stood next to each other while Jonas bound together our inside hands. For anyone else, that would make swimming difficult, but Weevil and I were stronger when we worked together. It was decided that I would be the first anchor, and so before we jumped in, I took hold of the branches of a bush growing right next to the expanded river.

The current immediately grabbed us, trying to carry us back toward the Colony. Water splashed in our faces from the river but also from the heavy downpour of rain, making breathing difficult. I still kept a tight grip on the bush until Weevil reached the fence. Then he nodded at me, signaling that he was secure.

I released the branches and used Weevil's weight to help me push forward through the water. I grabbed the fence too, though it was mossy from years of standing over this river. Weevil said, "We'll both hold on and both go under."

"If you let go of that fence, I won't be able to hold on alone," I warned.

"If you let go, I'll be even angrier than when you broke both needles," he countered.

"I broke them to get away from snakes!" I shouted. "Snakes, Weevil! Big ones!"

He winked and said, "I'll take that as your apology."

I started to protest, but he drew a deep breath and ducked under the water. I immediately followed. When we both came up for air, we were on the opposite side of the fence, outside the Colony. The rain fell just as hard here, obviously, and the terrain didn't look much different. But it definitely felt different, like we had accomplished something significant.

Weevil pointed out a rock on my side of the river. That's what we'd use to help us get out of the water. We braced our heads against the pole fence behind us and scooted sideways, getting as close to the riverbank as possible.

I grabbed the rock with my free hand, searching for a place where my fingers could dig in with a firm grip. Then Weevil swung around to my side so that he could reach for the rock as well. It was a lucky thing he found a good hold, because my hand slipped along some moss and I was pulled back underwater.

"Ani!" Weevil's fingers immediately interlaced with mine. My body yanked hard against the current, then slowly moved upstream again. Once I came up for air, I saw him lying belly down in the mud, his legs tangled around a bush to keep him from being dragged back to the river. Weevil pulled me from the water, then we lay beside each other on the bank to catch our breaths.

After a moment, I managed to sit, and coughed up some water I must've swallowed badly. Instantly, Weevil was beside me, though I wasn't sure if he was concerned about my choking, or whether he was forced to sit because our hands were still tied together. I wiggled my fingers, still woven with his. Why hadn't he let go yet? Why hadn't I?

"I'm fine," I said once I'd finished coughing. "Are you all right?"

Rather than answer, he lifted his free hand to my cheek, lightly stroking the skin. When I looked at him, I found a different expression in his eyes than I'd seen in four years of our friendship. I recognized it, though. It was the way Jonas looked at Della. And how my father looked at my mother when he didn't know I was watching.

Suddenly, I forgot how to swallow.

I bit my lip, even as I let myself move closer to him. "This will change everything, Weevil."

He wiped some strands of hair off my face, and his hand continued around to the back of my neck. "It's already changed. The only question is whether we want to admit it."

I smiled, aware of how near his mouth was to mine. When he kissed me, his lips were softer than I'd expected, though maybe it was because rain was still pouring down on us. But in that moment, the chill in the air was replaced with warmth and fullness. I forgot about the storm and about Della and Jonas on the other side of the fence, and even about the Colony. As he pulled me closer, all I could think was that Weevil was here with me, and I wouldn't have him be anywhere else.

When we parted, he brushed my cheek again, this time with the back of his knuckles. "*Now* I'm all right." He shrugged and the glimmer of his eyes reappeared. "I've wanted to do that for a while."

"Well, don't wait so long for the next kiss," I replied.

He leaned forward again, but then a hand pounded on the opposite side of the fence. Jonas.

"Townsfolk sure aren't very patient about being rescued from evil wardens," Weevil said, chuckling as he started to work at the knot binding our wrists.

We tied my end of the rope to the nearest tree, and then Weevil slipped back into the water. He would return to help

Jonas bring Della under while I worked on this end to pull the rope against the current.

"Keep hold of that rope," Weevil said with a wink.

"Stay on the other end of it," I replied.

Weevil jumped in and disappeared beneath the fence. The rope immediately pulled tight, and I grabbed it, ready for his signal. Luckily, the storm above us was finally beginning to let up, or at least, the thunder and lightning had passed, even if the rain was still fierce. That was good news, except it would also make the wardens more likely to come out and search for us.

Where was the signal? Hurry, Weevil!

Finally, I felt the tug on the rope, but it was heavier than I had expected. They must've all gotten into the water at once. The rope wasn't made to hold three people. Weevil should've known that! Threads began snapping. It wasn't a question of if this rope would break, only when. If I let it break too soon, my friends would be lost to the river.

I grabbed the rope and braced my weight against the same rock Weevil and I had used to climb out of the water, but with so much mud beneath my stockinged feet, I was mostly slipping around, almost falling back into the water myself. There wasn't much I could do to help them swim forward, but at least my hold was taking some pressure off the weight on the rope.

Finally, Della's head popped up from beneath the fence. I released the rope and reached out a hand to her, then pulled her onto the riverbank. Immediately afterward, Weevil and Jonas came through, similar to how he and I had done it. Della and I took their hands, and together, everyone made it to shore.

"What took you so long to come back?" Della asked.

Weevil and I shared a mischievous grin, which Jonas must've noticed because he only rolled his eyes. "Good grief. Now?"

While they continued catching their breaths, I asked, "Did any wardens see you?"

"I don't think so," Jonas said. "And they won't believe we ever made it upstream through that river. I don't think they'll look for us on this side of the fence."

"Of course they'll look," Weevil said. "Hopefully not tonight, though. Let's find a shelter to rest until morning."

We got up to begin searching, except for Della, who was smoothing the wrinkles from her wet, muddy dress. She said, "Well, Ani Mells, these ribbons are definitely ruined now, and it's all your fault." Before I could protest, she looked up at me and smiled. "Thank you for getting me this far."

"We have farther to go before we're home." I offered her a hand to stand up. "I'm glad you're with us."

Jonas suddenly patted his pockets, as if panicked, then shoved his hand in one and his face lit up. He withdrew a handful of thrushweed leaves, knelt beside Della, and offered them to her.

"Where did you get those?" I asked.

"They were in my cell in the infirmary. I asked the man in the neighboring cell about them. He said infirmary patients were given as many as they wanted until they felt healthy again."

This confirmed my suspicion that Colonists were healed of the Scourge once they went into the infirmary. However, I was still confused about why people were given the Scourge in the first place and what happened to the people after they were healed. Why heal people that nobody would ever see or hear from again?

Once Della had put a leaf in her mouth and begun chewing it, she made a face. "This tastes awful! River People like these? Have you never had real food before?"

I grinned. "If that's a hint you want to come for dinner in the river country one day, it won't work," I replied. "Once you get a taste for thrushweed, real food will never be the same again."

"It's not a hint," she said, though we all knew Jonas had a lot more thrushweed in his pocket to give her. She didn't have to like it, but he'd make sure she ate it.

There were no buildings on this side of the fence, and the terrain here was hillier than in the Colony, but otherwise, the two halves of the island felt roughly the same.

In the darkness, we slowly moved southward until Della noticed a rocky overhang with a shallow cave beneath it. Enough wind had blown around earlier that the ground was muddy, but little rain was falling there now. If we squeezed together, the four of us could fit inside the cave. I didn't mind that. Both Della and I had been shivering since getting out of the river, and other bodies near ours would keep everyone warmer.

Once we had wedged ourselves inside the cave, Weevil obviously wanted to talk, but Della said, "I still feel terrible. Can we figure everything out in the morning?" I didn't hear Weevil's answer, for by then, I had already fallen asleep on his shoulder.

CHAPTER
FORTY

The scene we awoke to was so beautiful, it was hard to believe a violent storm had passed through only hours ago. The skies were blue, birds were chirping overhead, and the trees and bushes were bright and glistening.

Everything was still dripping wet, and it bothered me to realize that wherever we went, we would leave behind a trail of prints in the mud. When I pointed that out, Jonas suggested we walk on rocks whenever possible, to at least slow down anyone who tried to follow our trail.

Weevil snorted, and I knew he was thinking that Jonas had lived in the towns too long. No tracker with a week of practice and the common sense of a fly would be fooled by that. But it was the best idea we had. Hopefully, wardens were stupider than the average fly. I was pretty sure at least a couple of them were.

"How are you feeling?" Weevil asked me.

"My legs are sore, and my neck is stiff from leaning on your shoulder all night. Otherwise I'm all right. You?"

He grinned. "My shoulder is sore from having someone's head on it all night, but I didn't mind."

Jonas was helping Della, who seemed to be feeling a little better and was already chewing on more thrushweed. She looked up at us and smiled. Maybe she was getting a taste for it, despite her protests. Some food would help her too, if we could find any.

"Where do we go now?" I asked. "Even if there are any boats still at the Colony, it's not safe to return there. I suppose we could build a boat ourselves, though we have no tools and it'll break apart when we're halfway across the sea."

Weevil's grin widened. "There's a reason my plan was to get past the fence. While in that tree last night, I think I saw something at the far end of the island. I could be wrong, but in one of the flashes of lightning, I saw what looked like the mast of a ship. For me to have seen it this far away, it must be fairly large."

My brows furrowed. "Why would the governor send a ship to this half of the island?"

Weevil shrugged. "I'm just telling you what I saw. A ship that size is bound to have a large crew, who probably won't be interested in taking us home. And if it didn't leave port before the worst of the storm, then it probably sank during the night."

"So," I said, "this isn't great news."

"But it's something," Della said.

She was right about that. It was, in fact, the only plan we had. Even a little hope was better than no hope at all.

So we set out walking southward, remaining cautious about whatever we might find once we reached the ship, but hopeful that it could prove to be an end to our troubles. Della was unable to walk for most of the time, but Weevil and Jonas worked together to carry her while I forged a little ahead, seeking out the best possible trails to follow.

As we walked, Della talked about her father's attempt to win the election against Governor Felling a year ago.

"He had great plans for Keldan," she said. "Ways to bring us together so that we can become strong again. He wants good things for everyone in our country." She turned to me. "Even River People, Ani. I'm so sorry for the names I called you before. My father taught me better than that."

"Our fathers worked together in an attempt to rescue us," I said. "When we find them, I think they'll be proud of us for coming together too."

Our conversation was cut short by the discovery of some food, which also provided a good opportunity to rest, something we all needed. The food wasn't much and certainly nothing tasty or filling, but the storm had unearthed some edible roots. If there was nothing better to eat, such as the crusty sole of one's shoe, for example, River People sometimes boiled these roots up and pretended they didn't taste like slimy dirt. But when I bit into one, I decided they were even worse raw. I offered mine to Weevil, who offered both of ours to Della, who said they weren't so bad and ate them down. The thrushweed must've numbed her sense of taste.

At our next stop to rest, we found several blueberries, which tasted perfect. The bush was cleared before any of us were ready to stop eating, but Della brightened up afterward and insisted on walking the rest of the way there.

"It's a relief not to carry her," Weevil whispered to me a few minutes later.

"Why?" I asked. "Are you afraid your muscles were getting too big from all that work?"

He grinned and brushed a hand down one arm. "I just didn't want these muscles to tear my shirt."

We laughed, and when Della asked why, Weevil quickly said, "Ani is jealous that I've been carrying you all day. She wishes it had been her."

That deserved an even louder laugh from me. And a sharp elbow to Weevil's side.

Hills gradually rose along the island's shores, particularly as we moved farther west. It bothered me to realize how well traveled our trail was. Had wardens carved out this path, beginning at the door Weevil found in the fence and leading to the ship? If so, why? And more important, when would they be on this trail again?

"Look!" Jonas said, pointing southward.

We had just rounded a bend in the trail, which gave us our first look at the southern end of Attic Island. We were higher in elevation than the shore but a wide beach opened up ahead. Until last night, it had probably been made of beautiful white sand, but now it was cluttered with fallen tree branches and whatever sea litter had washed ashore with the tide.

Most notably, however, a large vessel had washed onto the beach, which was probably all that had kept it from sinking in the storm. The ship had been braced by boards to keep it upright, but there was clear damage to the hull. A crew of maybe twenty men was already hard at work making repairs on it.

We couldn't risk being seen by these strangers before knowing a little more about who they were, so we shrank back into the cover of the foliage. Our tracks would show there, but at least we'd be out of sight. When we came to a clearing, Weevil suddenly grabbed my arm and yanked me down low, behind a fallen tree. Jonas and Della crouched beside us.

"What's wrong?" I asked.

"The flag," Weevil whispered. "Look again."

I rose up just enough to catch a glimpse of the ship's flag, shredded in the winds and wrapped around its post, but I knew the orange and gray colors well enough. It was the flag of Dulan.

"This isn't right," Della said. "Dulan and Keldan are enemy countries. They must've washed ashore in the storm."

"It's the ship I saw last night," Weevil said. "It was here before the storm began."

"Do you think they're planning an attack on Keldan?" Della asked.

"I heard Dulan wouldn't come anywhere near this island," Jonas said. "That they were too afraid of the Scourge."

"Unless Dulan knows the Scourge isn't real," I said. "Which would mean they are here in cooperation with the governor." My mind raced. "We know that Keldan citizens are given the Scourge, then forcibly taken to the Colony where they get so sick, it finally breaks their spirit, their will to fight. Once they are broken, wardens bring them into the infirmary and help them get better."

Weevil looked at me with widened eyes. "And once they get better, the wardens escort them out of the infirmary, and take them here. But why?"

"I think I know," I mumbled. "Before I left Keldan, Governor Felling told me I was a servant now. I think that was the exact truth. That's what the Scourge Colony is—a breeding place for people to be sold to Dulan as servants!"

"But why would the governor do that to her own citizens?" Jonas asked.

Della drew in a sharp breath. "What if she doesn't have a choice? Keldan was out of money—my father said our country was all but bankrupt. Then right before the elections a year ago, the governor suddenly had enough money for the country's needs. This must be how she got it!"

"And that's why she said that the Scourge was helping Keldan," I said. "To save us, she will destroy our people."

"She is still destroying us," Jonas said, pointing down the hillside.

Not far below, four wardens led by Warden Gossel and ending with Warden Brogg were escorting a group of nine people toward the ship. Nine people whom I had failed to rescue from the infirmary last night. Nine people who were about to discover a horrible reality. The Scourge was not a disease carrying a death sentence. The Scourge was servitude, carrying a life sentence.

While Jonas waited high on the hillside with Della, Weevil and I decided to sneak as low as possible to overhear the conversation between the Dulanian sailor and the wardens. It was a huge risk, but we had to find out as much as we could.

The sailor who greeted Warden Gossel was clearly upset. "My name is Bartek, and I'm in command here. We expected you last night."

"There was a storm last night," Gossel said without humor. "Perhaps you noticed it." Even from here, I could see a bulging bruise on his forehead. Maybe he had a bulging headache too, or at least, I hoped he did.

"We haven't seen you in a while, Warden Gossel, so you might have forgotten our agreement. If a storm is coming, you must deliver the slaves early so we can get off the shore." He pointed behind him. "Look at my ship now!"

"No one forced you to wait here," Gossel said. "You should have left."

"I will not return to Dulan with an empty ship," Bartek said. "Your governor was already paid for these slaves. She should have delivered them on time."

"My apologies, then," Gossel said, sounding more humble now. "We were delayed by more than a storm."

"You've never been delayed before. Why now?"

He cleared his throat. "We brought a couple of young people into the Colony from the river country. River People are not . . . cooperative. One of them, a girl, caused us particular trouble. We couldn't leave the Colony until she was under control."

Beside me, Weevil squeezed my arm and beamed with pride. I felt happy too, that I had caused enough trouble to get Warden Gossel into some trouble of his own.

"And is this . . . *child* who made life difficult for so many grown men finally under control?"

Gossel hesitated, then said, "She fell into the snake pit last night. We found her boots still there."

"So her boots fell victim to our snakes. How tragic. Where is the rest of her?"

"Probably drowned."

Maybe that sounded plausible to Bartek, but Gossel would've known that was a lie. That room didn't set fire to itself.

"You have the Colonists now," Gossel continued. "Take them and be gone. We'll have more ready for you next week."

307

Bartek looked over the group. "We were promised ten, but I only see nine slaves."

"The girl—she released some of the prisoners who were supposed to be here."

"And was this before or after the snakes got her?"

Gossel stiffened, but continued on. "We grabbed a few others this morning. It should make no difference to you who we bring, as long as they're ready to serve."

As long as they're broken. That's what Gossel meant.

"We were promised ten," Bartek said. "Or do you want me to report to my commander that Keldan does not honor its commitments?"

Warden Gossel scuffed his boot on the sandy beach and in a quieter voice said, "The warden at the back, the larger man. You can have him."

Brogg. He was staring at the sand beneath his boots right now, with no idea of what Gossel had just done. By then, I'd gotten a better look at who the wardens had brought with them. Marjorie was here, and Clement, and three of the men who had helped me on the treadmill. I doubted that was a coincidence.

"He'll do," the sailor said of Brogg. "We'll add him to our ship's crew, along with the others."

"Fine." Gossel waved his arm forward, and the wardens continued escorting the Colonists toward the ship. On a signal from Bartek, once they were close enough to the ship, more sailors pounced upon Warden Brogg, quickly disarming him and dragging him alongside the beached ship toward the rest of the Colonists. Brogg struggled at first and cried for help, but no one responded. After a few loud threats by the sailors, he merely gave up and began to comply with whatever orders they were giving him. Gossel turned away when it happened, as if it bothered him to betray one of his own men. Funny that it hadn't also bothered him to betray nine of his own citizens.

I had Weevil's hand in mine again and we sat there, frozen in place, while the wardens finished their business at the beach. Then Gossel turned and ordered his remaining men to walk back to the Colony.

"You gave up one of our own?" a warden grumbled as he passed Gossel. "Will you give me up next week?"

"Keep complaining, and I might!" Gossel replied. "What else can I do? It's those grubs who caused this. I warned the governor not to take River People, I told her this could happen, but she said that the punishment had to be honored."

Punishment.

I remembered then. On the day I was stuck in the vine-fruit tree, Gossel and Brogg had mentioned something about a punishment. In fact, now that I thought about it, Brogg had seemed angry that I'd overheard him. Perhaps that was the reason why he decided to take me with him. Otherwise, he might've passed me by. But whose punishment had he meant?

Gossel said, "When I get back to the Colony, I'll let Governor Felling know the terms of our agreement with

Dulan must change. We cannot sustain these numbers for much longer."

Another warden spoke. "The governor already left the island."

Gossel's tone sharpened. "Why wasn't I informed?"

A cough, then the other warden said, "There was no time, sir. As soon as the waters calmed, she wanted to return to Keldan. She wants everyone in the Colony turned over to Dulan, and she'll start with a fresh group, and stricter rules."

My eyes narrowed and beside me, Weevil grunted with anger. Gossel asked, "What rules?"

"I don't know. She only said it was something that would keep her cemented in power for life. She's giving a speech tonight in Windywood."

I knew that town well. They hated my singing more than most of the surrounding villages, so I earned a lot of money there.

Gossel added something under his breath at that point. Hoping to hear it, Weevil stepped forward, but his foot slipped in some mud and he flailed for his balance. I grabbed his arm and held him steady.

"What was that?" a warden asked. "Those footsteps we saw earlier. It must be the grubs."

We held our breath while Gossel took a step into the dense underbrush. Then from the ship, Bartek called, "If you Keldanians don't have anywhere better to go, maybe you should join our crew too."

Gossel jerked back so fast, I doubted he even realized he'd dropped his hat. "What if it was them?" he grumbled. "We have enough problems waiting for us at the Colony. Let the grubs cause trouble here for once. Let's go."

Weevil and I smiled at each other. I took that as a challenge, and I knew he was up for it too.

We waited in place for several minutes after the wardens had left. I didn't know what we should do next, and I doubted Weevil knew either. We couldn't let the ship leave for Dulan with Marjorie and Clement and our other fellow Colonists on board. Della was still too weak to be much help in fighting, and even if the rest of us did our best, we could never take on that entire crew.

"You two were gone so long, we got worried," Della said as Jonas helped her down the hillside to join us. "Is everything all right?"

The expressions on Weevil's and my faces told her otherwise.

When Weevil explained to them what we had overheard, Della's only response was, "I suppose you're going to try rescuing them."

We nodded.

"And I suppose it will be the most dangerous thing you've attempted since coming to this island, and that you'll forget about the fact that I still feel like I've been sent to that treadmill, and that you'll charge onto that ship before you even have a full plan in place."

Again, we nodded, and I'm sure Weevil's heart was beating just as fast as mine. This was sounding better and better.

"I can help," Jonas said, picking up the warden's fallen hat. In it, he seemed to stand taller than before. "I think I'm remembering what it is to be from the river country."

CHAPTER
FORTY-TWO

Jonas's leftover rope was cut in half, then used to tie Weevil's and my hands behind our backs. They weren't actually tied—a sharp tug against the ropes and we'd be free—but we looked like prisoners. The soft sand beneath my now bare feet completed the look of a future slave.

Della remained hidden in the underbrush. She wanted to come with us, but we all knew she was struggling with more pain than she was letting on. For both her sake and ours, she needed time to rest and recover.

With the warden's hat on his head, Jonas followed us from the trail onto the beach. He wasn't much older than us, but we hoped with the hat and clothes as dirty as the wardens had worn earlier, he would pass for a warden. My knife was in his hands, and he shouted orders at us as any warden might do.

"Walk faster, filthy grubs!" he shouted.

Weevil turned back to him. "You know, Jonas, coming from a filthy grub like you, that hurts my feelings."

I giggled, then tried to remain serious. "Stop it, Weevil. Try to look scared."

"I don't have to try," he said. "This is like jumping into a lake and hoping you don't get wet."

Bartek, the same sailor who had approached the wardens before, now hailed us from a distance and began walking forward. "What's this?" he asked. "We've got your full group."

"You've got only nine, and then took one of our wardens onto your crew." Jonas nodded at us. "These are the two young people we told you about before. I found them, and I want to exchange them for the warden you took. Two grubs for one warden. It's fair."

Bartek rubbed his stubby chin, looking us over. "They're younger than I expected. They couldn't have caused all that trouble."

I lowered my eyes and tried not to defend myself, to insist that, in fact, I hadn't yet reached my full potential for causing chaos and general mayhem. But Weevil had reminded me of one of the most important rules: Everyone who goes aboard that ship must be broken.

"They created plenty of trouble," Jonas said. "That is, until the storm last night, when I found them huddling beneath a rock, alone and scared."

"Just take us somewhere safe and with food," Weevil said. "We'll do anything you want."

I peeked over at him. He might've been serious about the food.

"All right," Bartek said, grabbing my arm. "I'll take these two. Let's go get your man."

As we walked to the ship, Bartek said to Weevil and me, "There are only two rules you both need to know before you come with us to Dulan. The first is that you must leave any thoughts of Keldan behind. You belong to us now, by treaty with Governor Felling. Serve us, and we will treat you well. Dulan is not a cruel place, unless we have to be. As long as you are loyal, you will be rewarded."

Then I was already breaking the first rule, for I would never consider Dulan my home. I had only one home, and it was amongst rivers and grassy banks and near Weevil and my family.

"The second rule is that disobedience will be punished. It took us a while to understand the Keldanian spirit. Some of you will sacrifice yourselves in the attempt to escape or to defy us. So Governor Felling suggested a way to be sure you would not disobey."

"What is it?" I asked.

He turned away to face the shore. "Once we reach the ship, I will show you."

That worried me, and Weevil too. He glanced over at me with a grim smile.

The ship was nearly finished with its repairs, and commanders were ordering their crew to dig out the beach to make it easier to haul the ship into the water. Brogg was already working with them and didn't seem to notice we had come. Even from here, I could see sweat glistening on his face. Ropes were being fixed to the bow to pull it. I assumed that would be our first assigned duty as Dulan's two newest slaves.

But until it was ready, Weevil and I were made to sit on the beach beside the other Colonists.

"You'll get your warden back once our ship reaches the water," Bartek said to Jonas.

Marjorie wasn't far from us. She looked our way with tears in her eyes and shook her head. At first I thought she was afraid for her own future, especially because she probably still felt sick. Or perhaps Marjorie had hoped we'd escaped during the night, and she didn't want to see us captured too. I tried to silently communicate a reply to her that we had deliberately come here, to rescue her and the others. No one from the river country would ever leave a friend behind, even at their own peril. Everyone seated around us now were friends. We would all escape together.

But for as hard as I tried to help her understand that through my tense expression and the flicks of my eyes, she only looked away and cried a little more. Then I glanced past her to where Clement Rust was staring at me. They must've grabbed him sometime after he was forced from the caves. He nodded back and gave a slight smile. He'd understood my silent message.

He leaned very slightly to whisper something to the man

next to him, who looked over at me. Then the message was passed to the woman at his side, who continued it on.

All we needed was an opportunity. I wanted it as late as possible, after the ship was repaired and back in the water, but before the crew had loaded us on board for the voyage to Dulan. If we fought too early, we risked not having enough people to launch the ship and save ourselves. If we fought too late, we'd become the property of Dulan.

After an hour of waiting, a sailor came around with some flasks of liquid he said we could share. All of us eyed them suspiciously. Finally, with a heavy sigh he said, "It won't harm you. This is a drink from Dulan. It'll give you strength to help us pull that ship into the water." Still, none of us took a drink until he grabbed one of the flasks back and drank it himself. Then we began passing them around with great enthusiasm. Everyone was thirsty, and the drink did boost my energy. In hindsight, that sailor would regret sharing anything that made me feel stronger.

When we'd finished, Bartek stood before us and said, "We're ready now. The crew will go behind the ship to push it toward the sea. You will each pair up and take a rope, and do all you can to pull it. This will be your first test as slaves of Dulan, and the way you perform will determine where you are assigned to work once we arrive. Work hard, and you might find yourself as a lady-in-waiting or manservant to the rulers of our country, a relatively comfortable position.

Appear idle, and we will find dirty, dangerous work that will cure your laziness." His eye fell on me. "Refuse to cooperate, and you will come to understand the most terrible of penalties."

Beside me, Weevil gasped and grabbed my arm. I thought it was a warning from him to not react, so I only shook him off and said for everyone to hear, "You said it didn't work to threaten a slave with his own life, but that Governor Felling did suggest a punishment that worked. What is it?"

"Ani, I see—" Weevil started.

"Hush, I'm arguing."

The sailor walked over to me. "Stand up, girl."

I obeyed.

"You're from the river country of Keldan—a grub?" When I nodded, he continued. "The River People have never gotten the Scourge before. But Governor Felling took you anyway. Did you ever wonder why she suddenly wanted River People?"

"She wanted five River People," I said. "In the end, she only took two of us."

"Three more will come, in time." He backed up, speaking again to all of us. "A few weeks ago, the crew of this very ship attempted an uprising, led by someone who thought he should not have to cooperate. The uprising failed, of course, so he had to be punished. Our agreement with your governor is that if you disobey any order, she will take one of your loved ones into the Colony. But if there is an uprising, and you cause others to disobey, she will take—"

"Five," I breathed. "She wanted five River People because it was a River Person who started that uprising. But everything started with me. I was the first of our people to go to the Colony."

"To go to the Colony perhaps," he said. "But you were not the first of the River People to be taken away." He gave a whistle and said, "Show yourself, grub!"

From around the back of the ship, a man came forward in rags and with chains around his wrists. He was thinner than when I'd last seen him but I knew him well, and he knew me too.

But most of all, he knew Weevil, who had already gotten to his feet beside me and held on to my arm for support.

The man in chains was Weevil's father.

CHAPTER
FORTY-THREE

Weevil's father clearly recognized us, but he only shook his head back in acknowledgment. Why? Was that a sign for us to say nothing of our connection? A message to end our planned revolt before we endangered more of our people? Or a sign of defeat, that in seeing his own son here, knowing why we had come, now he had at last been broken?

I didn't know what he meant by the simple shake of his head and wasn't entirely sure what to do next. Beside me, Weevil's hand wrapped tighter around my arm and began shaking.

Bartek said, "Now that you understand what it means to disobey, I suggest you all take ropes at once."

We went to the ropes, though I practically had to drag Weevil with me. "We've still got to fight," I whispered to him.

"My father's alive," Weevil mumbled.

"Yes, and he wanted to get free. He expects you to do the same."

"It was his uprising. We're here because of him."

I grabbed Weevil's arm and made him look at me. "Then we're here to save him, and everyone else. We still have to fight."

He nodded and said, "This can't fail, Ani. If it does, the governor will come for our families, and then more River People."

"I know." She was already looking for my father, and Della's father, though I suspected their fates would be much worse than a trip to the Colony.

With the ship already moving toward the water, the Dulanian sailors climbed rope ladders to take them onto the deck and from there shouted orders to their crew and to us. While Weevil pulled, Jonas and I went into the shadow of the ship, out of sight of the sailors. There, he hoisted me onto his shoulders, allowing me access to a porthole near the front of the ship. I had to pry it open with my knife, but once it was open, I slipped inside the ship's hull. Maybe they should've fed me better in the Colony. I might've gotten stuck if they had. Once I landed, I listened a moment to be sure that none of the other captives would betray what I'd done, and that no sailors were down here with me. But everything was quiet, and the ship continued forward. So far, so good.

Weevil climbed in next, though he needed my help to squeeze him through. Jonas was too big to fit through a porthole, as were most of the other captives. The rest of this plan was up to us.

"My father," Weevil whispered. "Do you think he recognized me?"

"Of course he did." I paused a moment to smile at him. "Couldn't you tell how glad he was to see you? He'll be even more proud once this is over. Now come on!"

Our plan at this point was a little vague. But in the short time it had taken Weevil to crawl in here, I'd had an idea. A pretty good idea, I thought, even if it was wildly insane. As far as I was concerned, those two always went together. When I whispered it to Weevil, he agreed with the wildly insane part.

"Whether it's a good idea or not," he said as a grin spread across his face, "there's only one way to find out!"

The hull of the ship had four cannons mounted into it, which in itself was surprising since Dulan was not at war with us and since Keldan had no similar ship to defend our country. Maybe that was the point. If they decided to attack, we would be defenseless.

It took some effort to maneuver the cannons. Neither Weevil nor I had ever handled cannons before, though my father had once explained them to me. I understood the basics. Turn the wheel at the back of the cannon until the angle is correct. Load the cannon with gunpowder. (I appreciated Dulan for having supplied us with a fine load of gunpowder in a barrel right next to the cannons. They were thoughtful people indeed.) Put a cannon ball in next, and use a long stick to pack the two close together. Finally, when ready to fire, light the fuse. It would carry the spark down inside the cannon, light the gunpowder, and explode the cannon ball out of the muzzle.

"Are you sure about this?" Weevil asked. "It seems far too dangerous."

"It is far too dangerous," I agreed. "And yes, I'm sure. We've got no more time to spare. The ship is almost to the water."

I waited until the sailors above called out that the front of the boat had reached water and that everyone should now move to the back of the ship to finish pushing it in.

Then I grabbed my knife and climbed the ladder up onto the deck of the ship.

Bartek noticed me right away. "How did you get up here, grub?" He saw the knife next. "You're in big trouble now."

"You're in bigger trouble," I countered. "You have no idea what weapons I have aimed at all of you, right this moment."

"What weapons?" Bartek asked. "That little knife? It won't save you from us."

He advanced on me, and I backed closer to the ladder. "I'm talking about the cannons below. Did you know they can be angled almost straight up? I admit that made them more difficult to load, but we managed that too."

Bartek swallowed hard. "We?"

"Everyone down below who is waiting for my orders to light those cannons. They will blow you back to Dulan with a fire on your backside."

Granted, when I said *everyone*, I meant Weevil. And when I said the cannons would blow them back to Dulan, the reality was much worse than a fire on their backsides. These sailors knew it too.

Bartek's eyes narrowed as he said, "There's no one below. Everyone else is too big to have gotten in."

"The wardens already told you about me, about what I did to the Colony in only a few days. That was an entire Colony, a former prison. Think of how much simpler it is to take over one small ship."

"If the cannons blow us up, you'll go with them."

I didn't move. "I've spent the last several days expecting to die or be killed at any moment. So I've made peace with whatever the cannons might do to me. Have you?"

His eyes narrowed. "What are your terms?"

"Simple. Abandon ship." I nodded to the bow of the boat. "The water might provide you with a softer landing, but you can jump onto rocks for all I care. Once everyone is down, the captive crew members and the Colonists will come on board."

"When Dulan hears of this, they'll come to war against Keldan."

"You're wrong," I said. "When Keldan hears of this, they'll come to war against you! The River People have been awoken now. Either Dulan will admit their wrongs and return our people, or you will have to fight us." I winked at him. "I'm not even the cleverest of the River People. Imagine what happens to Dulan when you meet the really smart ones."

Bartek folded his arms. "We're not leaving this ship, girl. You're bluffing."

I did not flinch. "I will count down from five. At zero, the first cannon fires. I hope it's not the one right beneath your feet."

He smiled. "Or yours."

My smile mirrored his. "Five. Four."

At four, an explosion burst from below, creating a large hole in the deck and sending pieces of wood everywhere. I nearly fell backward into the hold below, and saw Bartek had fallen too. One sailor had been standing very near the explosion, but he didn't look seriously hurt. Only sheer luck had saved him, though, and we all knew it.

From below, Weevil shouted up, "Sorry! I lit the fuse too early!"

Bartek looked down at him. "That's your team below? Another insane grub like you?"

"He's not insane, just terrible at counting." Then I continued from before. "Three. Two."

"I'm lighting the next fuse now!" Weevil yelled.

"All right!" Bartek said. "Abandon ship, or what's left of it now." He glared at me as his men jumped overboard. "You might think this feels like a victory, but where will you go? Dulan won't take you, and as damaged as this ship is, no other country is within reach. Keldanians are terrified of the Scourge. They'll welcome you home with pistols drawn, anything to keep from getting the same disease."

"The Scourge is not a disease," I said. "As of now, the Scourge is victory. We are the Scourge, and we're going home."

CHAPTER
FORTY-FOUR

The instant the sailors of Dulan exited the ship, I ran to Weevil and told him to stop lighting cannons and to join me on the deck. And I didn't need to tell the imprisoned crew members and Colonists to come up—they were already on their way.

Jonas had run back up the beach to meet Della, who was hurrying down to him. Although he held out his arms to carry her, she shook her head and continued walking on her own. I thought she must want to reclaim her freedom on her own two feet, and I was proud of her for it.

Marjorie was one of the first to arrive on the ship, and she nearly collapsed on the deck with either gratitude or exhaustion, or both. While I helped her find a place to sit, other Colonists continued arriving.

"I didn't know how you were going to do it," Clement said to me. "But I knew you would."

By the time Jonas got Della into the ship, she looked every bit as tired as Marjorie did, but her eyes were lit with excitement. "Please tell me there's food on this ship!" she said.

"I'm sure there is," I replied. "If you and Jonas want to find some, I think everyone on board needs to eat."

They nodded and went hand in hand to make a search.

Brogg came up next. I eyed him cautiously, trying to determine whose side he was on. He only removed his warden's hat and nodded at me and said, "If all River People are like you, then from now on, I want to be one of your people."

"We're all Keldanians here," I answered. "You are one of my people. Prove you're amongst the good ones."

He nodded at me. "I swear that I will."

Weevil was half bent over the deck's railing, watching for his father. I could practically see his heart beating from where I stood and though I wanted to join him, I didn't. This was his moment.

His father was the last to climb the ladder onto the ship, and by the time he reached the top, tears were streaming down both their faces. Weevil's father had always been a strong man, proud and confident. Now he fell to his knees and reached out for Weevil, who ran into his arms. From where I stood, I only saw Weevil's back, but his shoulders were shaking and I was sure he was crying too, but only for the best of reasons.

Weevil leaned back at one point and his father put his

hands on Weevil's face. They spoke a few words to each other, and then hugged again.

While watching them, I realized how much I missed my own father, and my mother too. First I had disappeared, and then my father. Did she know where he was? The River People would hide him and Sir Willoughby if they were asked to, but I doubted that my father would have dared put them at so much risk. By now, my mother probably wasn't even sure I was still alive. I couldn't imagine what she was going through.

I wanted so desperately to just go home.

Weevil must've felt me staring at him, for he finally turned away from his father and motioned for me to come over.

I brushed my sweaty palms against what remained of my skirts, walked over to them, and curtsied to his father. "You probably don't remember me, but—"

"Ani Mells. Could anyone else have done all this? You've grown into such a lovely young lady."

I brushed loose strands of hair away from my face. "I was in the storm last night. You can hardly see me through all this dirt."

"I can see you just fine," he said. "But I can never thank you enough."

"*You* brought me here, sir," I said. "The rebellion from three weeks ago—"

"I didn't intend to do it. I've worked here for more than a year under that threat from the governor. I hated working this ship, being a part of carrying my own people over to Dulan each week. But I would not rebel, and risk them coming after any River People. I knew the governor would probably avoid any confrontation with our people for as long as she could, so if I obeyed, you'd be fine. Then a few weeks ago, one of the Colonists smuggled a weapon on board the ship, a knife not too different from the one in your hand, Ani. She dropped it and was about to be caught. I knew what Dulan would do to her for having a weapon, so I grabbed it and said it was mine." He shrugged. "Last week, they told me they had taken two children from the river country, as punishment for what I'd done, though I had no idea it was either of you. You were to be tests for how other River People would do once they were taken."

Weevil chuckled. "I guess they got their answer!"

"They did, son."

Weevil nearly melted into his father's words, to have someone once again calling him "son."

"We need to get those chains off you," I said.

"I could pick the lock." Weevil glanced my way. "*If* I had unbroken needles."

"Snakes," I muttered back at him. "Big, nasty snakes."

His father nodded and got to his feet. "I know where the keys are kept. I'll help everyone out of their chains, and then we'll crew this ship to wherever you command." He tilted his head toward me. "Since you rescued us, I assume you're the one in charge."

I stepped back. "No, I only—"

"What do you want from us?" Clement asked. "We'll follow you anywhere, Ani."

Weevil was staring at me, as happy as I ever remember seeing him. So was his father, and the other crew members who had been prisoners here for at least as long. All wore smiles as wide as their whole faces. Everyone, I realized, was staring at me, ready for orders.

A small platform stood a few steps behind me. Carefully avoiding the hole Weevil had blown into the deck, I climbed up and looked over the group.

"Well?" Marjorie asked. "Are we going home?"

I took a deep breath. "Yes and no. For now, most of you will not be accepted at home. Much as your families miss you, they also believe you are victims of a disease that might spread to them. They will stand as far from you as possible, calling out their love but begging you to return to the Colony where you can die in peace. Even if you convince them you are no longer sick, a part of them will always doubt. So we are returning to Keldan, but not to go home. Before we go home, we must destroy the Scourge."

"You heard the lady," Weevil's father shouted to the other crew members. "Let's hoist sails and take this ship to Keldan. Where do we dock, Ani?"

"Near the town of Windywood," I said.

"That's close to river country," Weevil warned.

"It's also where Governor Felling intends to make a speech tonight." I smiled over at my friend. "We should be there to hear it."

CHAPTER
FORTY-FIVE

The freed crew members took over the work of sailing us toward Keldan, allowing the Colonists to rest and to eat as much as we wanted from the goods Jonas and Della had found. I didn't see Weevil for most of the ride. He was spending time with his father, as he should have. Instead, I wandered amongst the Colonists, getting to know each of them a little and assuring them I had a plan that would help them go home again.

"You won't share the plan with us?" Marjorie asked.

I shook my head. "Not yet." Mostly because what I had wasn't so much a plan as it was a determination to win—or die trying. Not the sort of thought I was ready to share with people who had spent far too long contemplating their likely deaths.

The crew suggested we dock off shore and a ways farther from the town. "Bringing a ship home with Dulan's flag will raise a lot of concern," one man said. "It's better if no one sees us."

"Then lower the flag and take us as close to shore as you can," I said. "We'll use the dinghy at the side of the ship and only bring a few people with us."

"The governor will have many wardens there to protect her as she speaks," Brogg said. "To fight them off, you'll need all of us."

"We're not fighting the wardens," I said. "There are other ways to win than fighting."

I wished Weevil could have heard me say that. He would've thought I'd matured.

The dinghy would only fit six of us. I asked Weevil to come with me, and his father. Jonas would also come, and Clement.

As I searched for the last person of our group, I noticed Brogg staring at me, clearly hoping to be chosen. "I was wrong," he said. "And you can force me to live with that for the rest of my life, or you can allow me to begin fixing it."

I folded my arms, still uncertain. "How can you fix it?"

"The wardens guarding the governor will know me. I can draw them away, letting you get close to her. Nobody else on this ship can do that. You must trust me, Ani."

He used my name. And as insignificant as that might seem, it made me think that perhaps I should give him a chance, so after a few moments of consideration, I nodded my permission at him.

"I need to come too," Della said.

I shook my head. "You're still too weak. You'll be safer here on the ship. Once everything is settled and safe, we'll send for you. The dinghy is full anyway."

"Governor Felling is from my class of people," Della said. "Unfortunately, there will be some in that crowd who will not listen to you. But they will hear me."

She made a good point. "All right," I said. So we would make room for seven of us.

With the extra weight, we rode low in the water, but those with the oars were strong and carried us swiftly to shore. From there, it was a two-mile hike into town. That would be a lot for Della, but she insisted she was strong enough for the journey. To her credit, she kept pace right along with the rest of our group.

As we walked, I explained what I wanted. Brogg would create distractions for the wardens closest to the governor. Clement, Jonas, and Weevil's father would see that the path was clear for me to get to the governor. Della and Weevil would come with me.

The town looked nearly abandoned at first, which made me nervous. "The wardens I overheard said Governor Felling would be speaking here tonight."

"That's where everyone is," Weevil said. "Maybe she's already here!"

"Then let's hurry," Della said.

We made our way toward the center of town, and while we were still a few streets away, we heard the applause of a large group. I breathed a sigh of relief. We were not too late, then. We hurried onward, and as we approached, I motioned for everyone to get to their respective places in the crowd.

As we entered the town square, Governor Felling was easily visible, with an elaborate orange dress, and her hair piled so high on her head, I wondered how she could balance beneath it all. She was on a wide wooden dais that clearly had been built just to accommodate her for this speech. Steps led up one side and also up the front, and it was draped with Keldanian flags. It infuriated me that she would offer herself as a symbol of a country she had betrayed with such cruelty.

"The Scourge is much worse than we previously thought," the governor was saying. "My dear friends, if we are to control its effects, we must be more vigilant than ever! You're afraid—I can see that in your faces—and you are right to be afraid, for I have just received information that conditions on Attic Island are worse than I had known."

"Were you on the island?" a woman shouted from the audience. "I heard your ship was seen traveling back to Keldan."

"I could not go to the island—obviously nobody can safely return from the Colony," the governor said. "But a message was returned to me from that ship. The Scourge victims weathered last night's storm as bravely as they have endured the disease itself. However, their peace and order was upset by the presence of some River People. They have nearly destroyed the entire Colony."

"My wife was in the Colony!" a man yelled. "What happened to her?"

"The wardens on the island got everyone to safety," the governor said. "But it shows the danger posed to Keldan by the River People. Therefore, I make the following proposal. First, I ask for expanded authority to test for the Scourge in your towns. It is not enough to ask people to voluntarily come in for testing or to test only those we suspect of being exposed. I wish to begin random testing so that we can weed this disease out of your town even earlier. Will you agree to this?"

"Yes!" the people shouted.

"*Random* testing," Della muttered beside me. "As if you were random, or me. Who in this crowd will randomly get the Scourge next?"

Still unaware of our presence, the governor continued. "Second, I am asking for any volunteers to test a new medicine for the Scourge. If you think you have been exposed, you can save the lives of your loved ones by offering up yourself as a test subject." She pointed into the audience at Thomas Cresh, the same physician who had given me the Scourge. I hadn't even realized we were standing so near each other, and I quickly edged farther away. "Doctor Cresh has led the research against the Scourge. He has just created a new medicine that may one day offer us a cure."

"It's a lie," Weevil hissed. "The medicine is only weakened spindlewill."

"I believe he did create something new," I whispered back. Not spindlewill, but a Scourge test filled with snake venom.

Hands shot into the air while Doctor Cresh beamed with pride. *The Scourge is not a disease!* I wanted to scream at them. *But that medicine will make you think you've got it.* My guess was that most families would get flasks full of harmless liquids that did nothing to protect them, but offered the family a feeling of false security. As long as they supported the governor, she would protect them. And then other families—those targeted families whom Della had mentioned—would be given flasks full of Doctor Cresh's new medicine. It would convince them they had the Scourge without the governor ever needing to administer a direct test. She was cutting out a step in her evil agreement with Dulan.

"Finally," the governor said, "we must remove those who threaten the safety of Keldan from within. We cannot fight both the Scourge and those who believe it is not real. There are two men who have been sneaking through our towns, taking shelter in your homes and barns and making wild-eyed claims about the Scourge. Perhaps you have heard them and even been convinced by them. But they were not telling you the whole truth, for both men had a personal stake in persuading you to believe their lies. Both men lost daughters to the Scourge a week ago. They hoped if you would follow them, you would join them on a quest to invade the Scourge Colony and bring their daughters home, and bring the disease back to your families in Keldan. Can we tolerate that?"

"No!" the people shouted.

I went weak in the knees. She meant my father and Sir Willoughby. Why would she have brought them into this conversation?

With a wave of her arms, two wardens came onto her platform, the first escorting my father and the other leading Della's. They were bound in chains, gagged, and showed evidence of having been beaten. I felt sick, but in an entirely different way than I did at the Colony. Still at my side, Della gasped and grabbed my arm.

Our fathers were sent to their knees, only to have their chains attached to bolts on the floor, preventing them from any escape. Normally, my father would've fought it, tearing up the floorboards if necessary to keep himself from being shackled in this way. But his head was down, as if he no longer cared about his fate. Sir Willoughby whispered something and my father looked over at him, then into the audience.

His eyes instantly locked on mine. After a moment of obvious surprise, a fire lit in his eyes again. He pulled against his chains, but they held firm. There was nothing he could do.

I started forward, but Weevil held me back. "Not yet," he said. "Not yet, Ani."

Once the wardens had left the stage, the governor continued. "These two men have betrayed our country's laws and our security. They would have endangered your lives, all for nothing. My friends, the Scourge spreads far more easily than we believed, and is far more deadly. To save you from the Scourge, do you accept my judgment upon these men, that of a sentence of death?"

"Yes!" the crowd shouted.

"Then bring forth the executioners," she said.

That was enough for me. I shook Weevil off and pushed my way through the crowd.

"This isn't the plan," he hissed.

"It is now," I said. "It is now."

CHAPTER
FORTY-SIX

I reached the stage before the executioners and even before the two nearest wardens could stop me. Weevil and Della followed in my wake and stood in front of the crowd, protecting me. "We are from the Colony!" Della shouted. "Get back, or I swear we will breathe on you!"

"I feel a sneeze coming on," Weevil warned. "A big, wet, slobbering sneeze!"

The crowd obeyed and stayed back. Brogg and the other men must've done their job well, or those wardens would've been coming toward us by now.

"Hello, Governor Felling," I said, smiling as sweetly as I could.

Her anger was so real I could feel it in the air between us. None of that was displayed on her face, though her teeth did seem too tightly clenched together. It was a wonder she could speak through them. "Ani Mells. They told me you drowned."

"River People belong to the water," I said. "We don't drown."

That wasn't exactly true, but it seemed to make the governor angrier and I liked that.

She looked around for the two wardens who had just been onstage, but they had disappeared. I wondered which of the men from the ship were responsible for that. Her eyes fell back upon me. "Maybe you don't drown, but you can be killed."

"By snakes?" I asked quietly. "By Dulanian vipers? Don't worry, Governor. I understand the Scourge now, and I'm here to help you warn these good people. For the sake of Keldan."

I felt my father's eyes on me, and Sir Willoughby's, but for now, I had to keep my focus on the governor and the audience around us.

Before the governor could speak or attempt to stop me, I turned to the audience. "Many of you know me. You've seen me here in the square, singing."

"Singing horribly," one man said.

I curtsied to them. "Yes, that's me. Back then, I had no idea how bad the Scourge was, how easily it could spread from one person to the next. I'd never even spoken to a Scourge victim before I got the disease, but the governor assured me I had it, didn't you, Governor?"

She nodded cautiously, confused as to why I would be agreeing with her. "Yes. This girl came from the river country. When she tested positive for the Scourge, I had to send her to the Colony."

Now Della climbed onto the stage with me. "Everyone with the disease must go there, correct, Governor Felling? You cannot show preference to anyone, no matter what their background, or the influence of their family."

"Of course not," Governor Felling replied. "That is the law."

"And not just those who've tested for the disease," Weevil said, coming to the stage. "Even if a person had just come into contact with someone carrying the disease, like me, they'd have to go to the Colony too, correct?"

"Y-y-yes," the governor stammered. "We cannot be too careful."

"We want to thank you for saving us," I said, wrapping my hands around the governor's waist. Della and Weevil followed, hugging her from each side. Weevil even leaned on his tiptoes to give her cheek a kiss. Disgusting.

Governor Felling squawked like an angry parrot and tried to get us off, and in the process of trying to peel our arms away from her, she scratched the old wound on my arm that Doctor Cresh had created when she first gave me the Scourge.

"She's drawn blood!" a woman on the front row yelled. "The governor will have the Scourge now!"

"I won't!" the governor yelled. "I don't!"

"You said it yourself," a man cried. "If you are around people with the Scourge, you will get it too!"

I stepped forward. "We ask you to follow the law—the governor's own law. We ask your permission to bring the governor back with us to the Scourge Colony, there to live out what little remains of her short, pathetic life."

"No!" the governor yelled.

But the crowd was no longer on her side. She had made them afraid of the Scourge, and if there was any chance she was sick, they were afraid of her too.

"Any wardens who try to stop us must also come to the Colony," Weevil yelled. "Protect your families from them!"

Led by those who had come with us from the ship, there were scuffles on the ground, bringing into control the few wardens that our men had not already taken down.

The crowd parted while Della, Weevil, and I took the governor's arms and began pulling her off the platform. She was trying to fight us off, but the three of us were managing her just fine.

"Take the doctor too!" a man from the crowd yelled. "If the governor has the Scourge, the doctor might also have it!"

"No, wait!" Hoping to avoid the crowd, Doctor Cresh ran onto the platform with us, his eyes darting about in full panic. "Governor Felling does not have the Scourge. I do not have the Scourge. Neither of us will ever get the Scourge."

"Are you sure?" I asked. "You were in the examination room and had to test me by cutting into my arm. You did this to me." I showed the audience where it had happened, with the wound now opened again. The crowd gasped in response.

"Don't say anything," the governor said, still struggling against Weevil and Della's hold on her. "We can fix this later, when we're alone."

"You won't be alone ever again," I said to Doctor Cresh. "We'll escort you all the way to the Colony. We want Keldan to be safe from you."

"The governor has medicine—" Cresh's uncertain tone wouldn't earn him much sympathy.

"Is it the same medicine we received at the Colony?" Della asked. "Or are there different medicines for the special people, like you?"

The crowd grumbled at that, becoming increasingly angrier. Doctor Cresh was forced to admit, "We know a way to heal the Scourge, to completely cure a person."

"So there is a cure?" I asked.

"Yes," Doctor Cresh said. "I mean, no. I mean, for me, and the governor . . ." He was giving up. He was breaking.

"It's not enough to cure the disease," Weevil said. "We don't want anyone to get it in the first place. How can you guarantee that the governor did not just get the disease from us?"

"Don't say anything else," the governor warned.

"They'll take us both to the Colony if I don't say something!" Doctor Cresh shook his head, and then he faced the people. "Three hundred years ago, the Scourge passed through Keldan. It was terrible and real. Then almost two years ago, the governor got word that Dulan was planning an invasion of our country. What could she do? We had no defenses, no money to build an army. Our defeat was certain."

"Stop talking, you fool!" the governor screeched. Then she brought her own appeal to the people. "I did it for you, for all of us. Dulan would've destroyed us, don't you understand? So to buy us some time, I told them we'd had an outbreak of the Scourge."

"I started researching ways to create symptoms similar to what the Scourge had once been," Doctor Cresh said. "There is a plant called spindlewill that, when ingested, will do this, but it's hard to find in Keldan. We were running out."

"We sent an exploration north," the governor said. "We hoped to discover more spindlewill, or something like it."

Beside me, Weevil lowered his eyes, no doubt thinking of his father again.

Silence fell across the audience, as if they couldn't quite absorb the shock of what they were hearing. Governor Felling seemed to take it as a sign that she had won. She glared back at me, then stepped forward, looking for her wardens, who by now were nowhere to be seen.

Then a woman from the audience yelled, "People have died from what you've done!" The crowd grumbled in response, sending loud jeers forward.

"But fewer people than if we had a war!" the governor countered. "Don't you see? I had to sacrifice a few to save everyone else."

That plea fell on deaf ears. Sacrificing a few had quickly turned into sacrificing far too many of our people.

With sweat beading on her brow, the governor went on. "Unfortunately, the exploration was captured by Dulanian soldiers. Our crew's captain confessed the nature of the exploration. Once Dulan knew the truth about the Scourge, I was sure an invasion was coming." Then oddly, she smiled, as if she believed whatever she had to say next would please the crowd. "Instead, Dulan came to me with an offer. They had a snake with venom that they believed could work even better than spindlewill, if we could find a way to deliver the venom. We made a bargain, one that has kept us at peace for a year, repaid our debts, and that will prolong the peace for many more years." Governor Felling pointed to me. "But we don't need to give them townsfolk, not anymore. We'll give them the grubs."

She looked around as if expecting the audience to charge at me and Weevil, or at least to applaud her words. But nobody moved, and the crowd remained perfectly silent. Their anger rose in the air like a dark cloud.

"The grubs were responsible for the first outbreak of Scourge," she said, her voice rising eerily higher in pitch. "They should pay now for this outbreak!"

"But there is no outbreak," Weevil said. "Only one person is responsible for the Scourge this time, and that is you."

The governor blinked hard and swallowed something. Possibly her tongue.

"From now on, River People and townsfolk are one people," Della said, stepping forward. "Keldan belongs to us all!"

The audience didn't cheer, exactly, but many of them nodded and began talking with one another. Something had clearly changed.

"I almost feel like singing," I whispered to Weevil.

"Don't," Weevil said. "Not when we've just made peace with them."

Realizing that she had lost, Governor Felling lowered her head. Doctor Cresh was already leaving the platform in the company of Brogg and Clement. It was over.

"We have to tell you our stories," Marjorie said to the crowd as she walked onto the platform. "And then we ask you to let us come home."

I didn't hear the stories, for someone had already released my father and Della's father as well, who each scooped us into their arms and carried us off the stage. Weevil went to find his father, and we retreated away from the town square, to our homes.

CHAPTER
FORTY-SEVEN

There would never be a way to know whose homecoming gave the most joy to their families.

I wasn't there when Weevil brought his father back to his family, but the next day, he described to me every detail of it. He had entered his home and merely told his family he had gotten lost for the past week.

"But," he'd added, "what is once lost can always be found again."

"What are you talking about?" Weevil's mother had asked.

"I left a surprise outside," he said.

His family flew to their door and flung it open, only to see their husband and father standing in the doorway, holding a handful of wildflowers he'd picked. I heard their joyful screams from my home.

My reunion with my mother was much quieter and filled with more tears. She had lost both me and my father that week, with no hope of ever seeing either of us again. We spent our first evening at home seated around the fire, sipping a warm tea as I told them the story of what had happened in the Colony.

I left out every detail I could, or at least, every detail that involved the risk of my life. I would eventually tell them everything, but not tonight. And likely not for another thirty years, maybe forty. My mother was better off not knowing too much about me too quickly. Based on the few questions he asked, my father probably guessed more of it than I wanted to admit.

I was told that Della's father threw her a large party that went on for nearly three days. We were invited to attend, but it was a long journey and one that neither Weevil nor I was in the mood to make. As far as we knew, we would never see her again.

We did see Sir Willoughby, though, who was soon named Governor Willoughby. He had acted swiftly to bring home all the Colonists from Attic Island and to expose the illegal treaty that Governor Felling had made with the rulers of Dulan. Public anger was such that for the first time, Keldan demanded war with Dulan. Dulan called for a response, but instead found its people ashamed and humiliated. Certainly, they would not fight to keep slaves they knew they never should have had. Within a few short weeks, many of those who had been forced into servitude were sent home, and more would follow. At least for the time being, our two countries would remain at peace.

By decree, the Scourge was over, though suspicion of those who had once been sick was slower to fade. Nobody meant harm upon former Colonists; they just had a hard time changing their understanding of how deep Governor Felling's betrayal of our people had been. In some ways, it was easier to believe that a deadly disease had spread across our land than to believe she would literally sell out her people in order to fill the treasury and maintain the peace.

Governor Felling, Doctor Cresh, and the wardens who had been involved were all given life sentences, this time in a prison here in Keldan. I didn't know exactly where it was and didn't much care. As far as I was concerned, they were no longer any part of my life.

The third act of Governor Willoughby's was to end all laws requiring my people to be sectioned off in the river country. From now on, it was legal for River People to live wherever we wanted. Most of us remained in the river country because it was still the finest home anyone might ever choose, but we gradually began to mix more and more with the townsfolk. The names "grubs" and "pinchworms" largely disappeared from use, only spoken by the coarsest of people, those without friends amongst either of our groups. The increasing trade between townsfolk and River People brought in more money to Keldan than Governor Felling's plot ever had. In the upcoming election, we'd have equal rights to vote.

For months after returning home, I found myself tracing the thin red line along my forearm, wondering what had happened to each of the Colonists I'd met, and whether all the slaves had returned from Dulan, and what their home-comings were like.

After a couple of years, the red line began to fade. I hoped it would never disappear entirely. It was too much a part of me.

Weevil said the line wasn't necessary, that the courage I'd discovered in the Colony was evident in my actions and in the strength of my voice. Maybe that was true, or maybe he was just saying those things because he loved me.

It took me that long to figure it out, and another couple of years to figure out I felt the same way too. When I was ready for him to propose marriage, I'd let him know.

Jonas must've proposed to Della too. One day, we got an announcement of their wedding and a request to visit them at their new home on Attic Island.

I was so surprised that I nearly dropped the announce-ment, but Weevil pointed out a note that was inside the letter.

It read, *Dearest Ani and Weevil, Weevil, at some point before you grow up, will you please change your name? It's a terrible name.*

I paused and laughed. "It's a perfect name."

"No," he said. "It's terrible, but it's still the only name I've got."

We continued reading, *We would've invited you to the wedding itself, Ani, but we were afraid you might want to sing for us.*

I took no offense at that. My singing was worse than ever. I'd nearly killed a bird last week when I tried to sing along with it.

Perhaps you are wondering why we chose to make a home on Attic Island. Well, the easy answer is that no one wanted it, so we were given as much land there as we wanted. The more complicated answer is that Attic Island has always begged for me to come back. It wants to prove that it is not a place for prisoners or for the dying, but it is a place for life. We are creating new buildings here. Homes for those who are truly sick, where they can come to a place that is quiet and peaceful and that can offer them hope to recover completely from their illnesses. Jonas and I will both train as physicians, and we will build our lives here and be happy. If either of you ever want to return to Attic Island, we will offer you comfortable places to live for as long as you want to stay. They can never equal the river country, I'm sure, but it would be the greatest joy to share in your company again. With love, Della

Weevil put an arm around me while I folded up the letter and reclined against him. "What do you think, Ani?"

I smiled back at him. "I think we ought to see the Colony one more time."

ACKNOWLEDGMENTS

The first spark for *The Scourge* began with the history of leprosy (Hansen's disease). Hardly the cheeriest beginning for a book for young readers, I know, but I was fascinated to learn that by the twentieth century, we understood this disease and how to treat it, yet in many places around the world, it still remained legal to take leprosy victims away from their families and place them in a leper colony, often for the rest of their lives. For most of human history, the stigma was worse than the disease itself.

And it began to occur to me how easily a stigma like that could be manipulated if the wrong people were in power.

From that strange inspiration, both Ani and Weevil began to emerge, each of them with strong, unique voices and an unshakeable friendship. My thanks to the Proclaimers for their song "I'm Gonna Be (500 Miles)" as the basis for that friendship—you'll see in the story where that pops up. Thanks also to Linkin Park for "Breaking the Habit." It could be Ani's theme song.

My greatest love and appreciation will always go to my husband, Jeff, who supports me every step of the way, even when I get author crazy. (Okay, *especially* when I get author crazy.) Love also to my children, who are greater than I ever could have hoped for.

Deep appreciation goes to Lisa Sandell, whose talent, intelligence, and passion for her work combine to make her an exceptional editor and the dearest of friends. It is an honor to work with her and a privilege to publish with the great Scholastic family. I am so grateful to everyone there. Thanks also to my agent, Ammi-Joan Paquette, whose unwavering support, advice, and enthusiasm buoys me, propels me, and keeps me forging ahead.

Final thanks to you, my readers. Each year, so many amazing books are released. Thank you for choosing one of mine. I hope this story brings you as much pleasure in reading it as it gave me to write it.

Whatever comes, I hope to find each of you on that road with me. I wouldn't have it any other way.

ABOUT THE AUTHOR

Jennifer A. Nielsen is the acclaimed author of the *New York Times* and *USA Today* bestselling Ascendance Trilogy: *The False Prince, The Runaway King,* and *The Shadow Throne.* She also wrote the Mark of the Thief trilogy: *Mark of the Thief, Rise of the Wolf,* and the forthcoming *Wrath of the Storm;* the historical thriller *A Night Divided;* and the sixth book of the Infinity Ring series, *Behind Enemy Lines.* She collects old books, loves good theater, and thinks that a quiet afternoon in the mountains makes for a nearly perfect moment.

Jennifer lives in northern Utah with her husband, their three children, and a perpetually muddy dog. You can visit her at www.jennielsen.com.